Praise for *Devil's Harbor*

"You're there, amidst the action, feeling, hearing, even smelling the tension. This is one of those labyrinths of mystery readers crave."   —Steve Berry

"[A] thrill-a-moment first novel . . . The ending is an unexpected nail-biter that crackles with tension. Readers will look forward to seeing more of Nick."

—*Publishers Weekly*

"Buy it! Recommend it! The writing is exuberant yet controlled, the plot is twisty and devious yet easily tracked, the characters are freshly imagined . . . the revelations are startling."   —*Booklist* (starred review)

"Hooked me from page one! Dark, knowing, and suspenseful, with a twisty undertow of impending tragedy. This timely and provocative thriller—with its complex hero, cinematic setting, and heartbreaking consequences—makes debut author Alex Gilly a must-read."

—Hank Phillippi Ryan, *USA Today*
bestselling author of *The First to Lie*

"One of those rare thrillers with a bark to match its bite, a vibrant, high-energy thrill ride with a subject both timely and topical. Echoing Don Winslow, T. Jefferson Parker, and James Hall at their level best, Gilly proves to be as polished a writer as he is a storyteller, and *Devil's Harbor* is a can't-miss great read."   —Jon Land, bestselling and
award-winning author of *Strong from the Heart*

DEATH RATTLE

ALEX GILLY

FORGE®

A TOM DOHERTY ASSOCIATES BOOK
NEW YORK

DEATH RATTLE

A Forge Book
Published by Tom Doherty Associates
120 Broadway
New York, NY 10271

www.tor-forge.com

Forge® is a registered trademark of Macmillan Publishing Group, LLC.

ISBN 978-1-250-79073-6

Our books may be purchased in bulk for promotional, educational, or business use. Please contact your local bookseller or the Macmillan Corporate and Premium Sales Department at 1-800-221-7945, extension 5442, or by email at MacmillanSpecialMarkets@macmillan.com.

First Edition: July 2020
First Mass Market Edition: May 2021

Printed in the United States of America

0 9 8 7 6 5 4 3 2 1

For Oskar and Gabriel

DEATH RATTLE

PROLOGUE

WITH the swell and the way the wind was gusting, Marine Interdiction Agent Vernon Gomez was struggling to keep the spotlight locked on the panga. One second the little open boat was inside the circle of light, the next it had slid back into the surrounding murk. Agent Nick Finn stood under the Interceptor's canopy, glancing from the panga to the rain clutter on the radar screen, thinking, a night like this, it was a miracle they'd found it at all.

The panga, as usual, was packed to the gunwales. Gomez's spotlight clung to it long enough for Finn to glimpse a woman clutching a child and two men bailing water. He also had time to see that some genius had hacksawed away the forward flotation compartment to make room for more passengers. He took one look at how low the boat was in the water and picked up the radio mic.

"Long Beach, this is Interceptor One, over."

A voice crackled back. Finn spoke up against the rain pelting the hardtop. He said, "I'm looking at a suspected illegal entry vessel, twenty-foot-long open boat, taking on water. Looks like her engine's out. I need a chopper and a utility out here to take everybody off."

"Interceptor One, what's your position?" said the voice.

Finn gave their position, some ten miles southwest of

Newport Beach. Finn was vessel commander, so this was his operation. He turned to tell the newbie, Marine Interdiction Agent Antonio Figueroa, to do a head count of the people aboard the panga. But Figueroa was bent over the rail, throwing up. So Finn turned instead to Marine Interdiction Agent Amanda Chinchilla. "Ask them how many people they've got aboard," he said.

Chinchilla's voice boomed through the bullhorn. The squall lulled, and Finn heard a man at the rear of the sinking boat shout back, "*Veintidós!*"

Even Finn, no linguist, could understand that. He relayed the information back to Long Beach before Chinchilla had a chance to translate. He asked how long till his backup got there. "Stand by," said the voice on the radio. Finn looked at Chinchilla and Gomez. By their solemn faces, he figured they were thinking the same thing he was. What he was thinking was, the panga was going to sink long before the chopper arrived. Finn decided on a course of action, then let five seconds pass, counting them off in his head.

No better idea presented itself.

He hung up the mic.

"Here's what we'll do," he said. "I'll bring us round their weather side. Gomez, you keep them lit up. Chinchilla, you tell them we want the children first, then the women. Let's go."

Gomez and Chinchilla nodded and moved to their posts. No one paid any attention to Figueroa, still throwing up. Finn maneuvered the Interceptor between the panga and the swell. The squall picked up again and blasted rain across his face. Cold water had somehow slunk under his jacket and now found new courses to follow each time he moved. He felt it trickling toward his socks.

Sheltered behind the much larger vessel, the panga righted a little. But it was still dangerously low in the water—by the glare of Gomez's spotlight, Finn could see maybe a foot and a half of freeboard above the waterline.

Another thing that worried him: the confusion on the radar screen. They were in the middle of the southern fairway into Long Beach, one of the busiest shipping channels in the world, and he couldn't see a thing. A couple of years back, a three-hundred-foot cargo ship had crushed a twenty-five-foot fishing boat right here in the channel, and the cargo crew hadn't even noticed. Finn fiddled with the clutter control. Nothing. He'd switched on every light the Interceptor had, figuring if he couldn't see, at least he could make himself as visible as possible. If he'd had a Christmas tree in the bow, he'd have lit that, too.

His socks squished when he stepped over to Figueroa, still bent over the leeward rail. He grabbed the newbie by the back of the collar, hauled him over to the windward side, and pointed out at the wet darkness.

"I don't care if you puke all over yourself. You're on lookout duty, you hear? You see anything at all out there, you shout it out. Anything at all, even if you're not sure it's an actual thing, you yell out. Got it?"

Figueroa groaned and moved his head in a way that might've been a nod, but which might not have been.

Finn shook him, hard.

"Show me you understand what you gotta do."

"Look out. Got it," came the weak reply.

Finn let go of the young man's collar and went back to supervise the rescue operation.

◆◆◆◆◆

Chinchilla stepped over to him. "They say they got four children!" she said, shouting against the sound of the rain.

"Bring them up!" he said at the same volume.

She went back to the rail and started shouting in Spanish at the guy standing by the dead outboard at the panga's stern, the guy whom Finn surmised was in charge of the whole catastrophe. Finn remained at his station with one hand on the wheel and the other on the throttle, ready to respond if Gomez, who had a clearer view of the sinking boat, hand-signaled to him to back off. The Interceptor was forty feet long, twice the size of the panga. A gust in the wind or freak wave could easily thrust them over the top of it.

He glanced over to the other rail. Figueroa was still upright, throwing up into the wind. He turned back to see Chinchilla bend over the side, haul up a small child, and set her down on the forward deck. Within two minutes, she'd hauled three children aboard. Then something went wrong; Finn heard yelling before a grown man appeared over the side. Finn recognized him as the guy from the back of the boat.

He waved the guy over to him. The man stumbled across the shifting deck and through the rain and wind toward the cockpit. Finn grabbed him by the collar.

"I said women and children first," he said, calling the guy one of the Mexican cusswords that his wife, Mona, had taught him. He resisted the urge to throw the fellow over the side, but not the one to fling him down on the deck. He looked up. Chinchilla was shouting. Something was going on in the panga. Finn stepped over the *pendejo* and went to the rail. A young woman wearing an oversized white T-shirt and spandex leggings was trying to push a child up the ladder. The child had clasped her tiny hands to the ladder's lowest rungs and wasn't letting go. The other people in the panga were crowding around the ladder, yelling at her, unbalancing the open boat. Chinchilla was shouting at them to step back, but they weren't listening. Their refusal to heed orders was the first sign of a panic that Finn knew could prove fatal. He jammed his knees under the Interceptor's rail, leaned down as far as he could, got a hold on the girl's forearms, and said, "I got you, sweetheart. You can let go," in English. Two terrified eyes met his. Her tiny hands remained clenched around the rungs. Then the young woman below said something to the kid in Spanish, her voice firm and reassuring, not panicky. The child said something that sounded like a prayer—Finn heard the word *Dios*—shut her eyes and let go of the ladder. Finn hauled her up over the side. He settled her against the rail with the other children, then bent over the side again, extending his arms to the young woman this time. Her long black hair was plastered to her face. She reached up and took hold of Finn's forearms.

A wave shouldered its way between the two boats, separating them. Finn felt the woman's arms yank out of his hands. She splashed into the strip of roiling water.

"Man overboard!" he screamed. He pointed and kept pointing at the spot where he'd seen the young woman go in. He felt the Interceptor backing away—Gomez making sure they didn't run over the person in the water. Chinchilla had the spotlight now. She swept it back and forth over the foam.

No sign of the woman.

Finn knew, like every mariner, the first rule of man overboard is, keep it to *one* man overboard. You throw the man a life ring, a life vest, a line, anything; you *never* dive in after him.

Finn ignored the rule. He had trained as a rescue swimmer with the navy's Maritime Expeditionary Security Force. He unclipped his utility belt.

The moment he hit the water, his clothes became instantly heavy. He also got a shock from the cold: it was March, and the water temperature hadn't broken sixty degrees. He kicked hard to get his head above the surface, and when he did, he heard the shriek of the wind, like an endless piece of paper being torn. Voices in Spanish and

English screamed from both boats. The DHS seal on the Interceptor's side—an eagle with an olive branch in one set of talons, arrows in the other—looked huge from the water's surface. Waves surged over his head. He swallowed mouthfuls of seawater. Chinchilla was still sweeping the light over the spot where the young woman had gone under; he swam toward it and dived.

Beneath the surface, the spotlight's muted shine penetrated three or four feet, and in this dimly lit sphere the sea's dark shades shifted in sudden streaks like wet paint beneath an artist's scraper; below that, it was entirely black.

At the very edge of the reach of light, he glimpsed a flash of white.

He took two big strokes and swept a hand in front of his face as though pushing aside a curtain; it brushed against something solid. He reached around the woman's torso with one arm and with his free hand pressed the inflator trigger on his emergency vest. He burst through to the surface and into the howling wind.

An emergency-yellow flotation sling attached to a line hit the water next to Finn. He wrangled the woman into it, clipped her in, then tugged on the line. He watched her get lifted out of the water, hauled up, he imagined, by Chinchilla's barbell-tooled arms. Someone on deck kept shining the spotlight down on him. By its light, he noticed dozens of twenty-dollar bills floating on the surface all around him. He swam for the ladder on the side of the Interceptor, grabbed the lowest rung, waited for the hull to roll toward him, kicked hard, and pulled himself out of the sea.

•••••

Gomez helped him over the side and kept holding him. Finn shrugged him off and made it clear he was all right.

But his teeth were chattering, and he wrapped himself in the space blanket that Gomez handed him. He felt something sticking to his cheek. He peeled it off: a twenty-dollar bill.

He turned his attention to the girl supine on deck. Chinchilla was kneeling beside her, her ear to the young woman's mouth, listening for breath. After a moment, she pinched the woman's nose, covered her mouth with her own, and blew hard, her cheeks puffing; the marine interdiction agent pulled away, and the young woman puked; Chinchilla stuck two fingers into the woman's mouth, scooped out vomit, then bellowed another lungful of air into her; the woman coughed, puked some more, opened her eyes. Her white T-shirt was hitched up above her belly button, revealing a money belt. Finn noticed that its zipper had split open.

Then he looked up and saw Figueroa with his back to the wind, staring at Chinchilla reviving the woman.

"Figueroa! Goddammit, keep your eyes *outward*!" he yelled.

The young man wheeled around. Finn grabbed the spotlight and scanned the nearby water until he found the panga. It had drifted away twenty feet and was even lower in the water now. Two guys were frantically bailing with buckets; everyone else was scooping with their hands. Finn calculated that there were still sixteen people aboard. Only the children, the young woman that he had rescued, and the captain were safely aboard the Interceptor. Without taking his eyes off the panga, Finn held up his open hand and yelled, "Gomez! Watch my signal! Another ten feet forward and to starboard . . . Hold!"

On the command *Hold!* he clenched his fist. The Interceptor drifted alongside the panga, closing the gap. Chinchilla joined Finn at the rail. Finn said, "Tell them if they crowd the ladder, they'll capsize."

Chinchilla turned to the people below and fired off a series of commands. He was relieved to see that there was no rush for the ladder. The migrants came up one by one, moving with orderly haste, shuffling around to rebalance the panga whenever a person stepped off. As each person came over, Finn handed them each a space blanket, then directed them where to sit on the foredeck, distributing the weight. He noticed the young woman he'd pulled out of the water curled up under a silver sheet, next to the child she'd helped out of the panga. They were both looking at him gratefully. He unclenched his jaw a little. The operation was almost over.

Right then came a scream from the dark side of the boat. Everyone turned to the windward rail. Looming out of the night, high as a mountain, was the bow of a container ship.

Finn's heart broke its chains and rushed his throat.

◆◆◆◆◆

Viewed close up and from sea level, even in the dark, the bow of the cargo occupied most of the sky, and Finn had to tilt his head back so far to see its top that the back of his skull pressed against the top of his inflated life preserver.

The freighter blasted its foghorn. The bone-shuddering volume left everyone aboard the Interceptor shell-shocked. Finn shone his spotlight on its red bulbrus bow shouldering aside the sea, displacing a huge wave, coming at them like a locomotive. He knew that this close, a ship that big hadn't enough room to veer, let alone stop, and that it would crush them the way a battle tank crushes a lizard. If the people aboard the panga and the Interceptor wished to remain alive, the ship's horn was saying, they needed to get out of the way.

Now.

He turned away from the monster and tamped down his own terror. The Interceptor had been designed to go fast; if he moved now, they'd clear the freighter's path. But moving now meant abandoning the remaining people in the panga. He counted four still in it, plus one on his way up the ladder. He figured he needed ninety more seconds to get everyone aboard. He turned back to the freighter.

"What's it going to be, boss?" said Chinchilla, her voice quicker than usual.

Finn met her gaze.

"Carry on," he said.

She nodded, went back to helping people come over the rail. Finn handed them emergency blankets and pointed where to sit. They had enough time, he told himself. It would be close, but they had enough time.

"Are you crazy?" said a voice behind him. Finn wheeled around. Figueroa. His eyes as wide as eyes can go.

"We'll all die!" he screamed. He waved his hand at the freighter. "We have to get out of the way!"

"Sit down, Figueroa," said Finn.

But the young man didn't listen. He shoved Gomez from the wheel. "I don't want to die!" he screamed. "We have to g—"

He slumped to the ground, midsentence. Gomez calmly reholstered his Taser and returned to his position.

Finn shone the spotlight back on the panga and saw that in the commotion, the two boats had separated. The two men still aboard, the ones who hadn't stopped bailing since the Interceptor had found them, looked back at him. They'd stopped bailing now. What was the point?

"Ten feet forward, Gomez," said Finn, making his voice calm. Searchlights from high above swept back and forth over the people huddled on the Interceptor's foredeck. If it'd been day, the freighter would've blocked out the sun. The Interceptor came back up alongside the panga. The first of the last two guys scrambled onto the ladder and started climbing. The giant ship was blaring her horn nonstop now, so loud that Finn nearly didn't hear Gomez shout, "We gotta go, boss!"

The Interceptor began to rise on the freighter's bow wave, going up fast like they'd stepped onto an escalator. The last migrant now had his arms on the ladder—the moment his feet were off the panga, Finn shouted, "Go! Go!"

He hauled the guy aboard, then turned and saw the whale-sized red bulb just meters away and rushing at them.

He thought, *Too late. I've killed us all.*

•••••

Everybody in the Interceptor stared back. Only Finn, Chinchilla, and Gomez were focused forward, straining with everything they had, wishing for the Interceptor's propeller blades to take hold of the wind-whipped water.

It came down to five meters. The freighter's bow was no more than five meters from the Interceptor's stern by the time the speedboat's four propellers at last gripped the water and slingshotted her forward, sending her surfing down the ship's bow wave. The noise of the outboards, the wind, the bow wave, and the ship's horn were earsplitting, but through it all Finn still heard the cracking sound of the ship pulverizing the panga.

Gomez had opened the Interceptor's throttles all the way. The Interceptor rushed ahead of the ship, launching off waves. When they had gained maybe fifty meters, Gomez started arcing the boat east, out of the freighter's path.

A minute passed, and now they were in the great ship's lee. Gomez pulled the throttles back into neutral; the Interceptor came off the plane and drifted to a stop. The rain had stopped, and the clouds were dispersing. No one said a word. Finn breathed what felt like the first breath of the rest of his life. The migrants stood at the rail, silver foil wrapped around their shoulders, and stared at the cargo ship parading past, a fast-moving sheer wall of steel darkly visible in what light the night sky had to offer, the ship going on and on, like it would never end. Chinchilla, Finn, and Gomez stood under the hardtop by the console. Figueroa was coming to on deck.

From the direction of Long Beach behind them came the thrum of a helicopter approaching.

ONE

THERE are two towns named Paradise in California: one in the north, in the wooded foothills of the Sierra Nevada, and one in the south, in the treeless desert near the border with Mexico. Mona Jimenez drove around the parking lot of the migrant detention center outside the southern Paradise, looking for a patch of shade to park in. According to her dash, it was an unseasonable ninety-five degrees outside—it was only the first of April. She'd heard someone on the radio say that on average, March had been hotter than the previous July, which would've worked as an April Fools' joke if she hadn't just spent the past four and a half hours driving over baking mountains and through parched desert, mirages shimmering on the blacktop up ahead, air-conditioning blasting. Now the air-conditioning was making an irritating rattling sound, and Mona was worried. She didn't need it failing—home was Redondo Beach, four and a half hours in the other direction, and she didn't think she could take ninety-five degrees for four and a half hours.

But the Paradise Detention Center had been designed for one function only, and that function didn't extend to providing shade trees in its parking lot for the overheating cars of migrants' rights attorneys from the coast. In fact, a cynic might argue that the Border Security Corporation of America—the private company that ran the center on behalf of the federal government—had chosen to build its newest facility in the bleached-bone nowhere between Yuma and El Centro precisely to *discourage* migrants' rights attorneys from visiting, and at that moment, Mona was feeling cynical. The BSCA legal liaison with whom she'd spoken by phone had warned her to watch her step in the parking lot.

"For what?" she'd said.

"Rattlesnakes."

There wasn't a patch of shade to be found anywhere, so Mona parked in the baking sun as near as possible to the detention center itself. She switched off the engine, killing the air-conditioning with it. Then she pressed her forehead against the side-window glass and carefully scanned the ground. She'd never actually seen a rattlesnake in real life, only on TV, and she preferred to keep it that way.

A moment passed. No snake rattled.

Mona sighed, flipped down the sun visor, and checked her face in the vanity mirror. *Doesn't mean they're not out there,* she thought, refreshing her lipstick. *Could be just waiting for me to get out. Could be watching from some rattlesnake hidey-hole.* Did they even live in holes? How would they dig, without limbs? She checked the ground one more time before opening the door.

Stepping from the air-conditioned car into the bakery-oven heat cut her breath.

"Fuck," she said, instantly breaking a sweat and re-gretting the pantsuit she'd put on in the near-dark that morning, dressing quietly so as not to wake her husband, Customs and Border Patrol Marine Interdiction Agent Nick Finn, who'd been working night shifts; she'd chosen the suit because it looked sharp and showed she meant business. She knew from experience that private prisons were operated by men prone to calling women they'd just met *sweetheart,* and she wanted to preempt that. But the suit was cut from a fabric too heavy for this heat, and she exhaled with relief when she was buzzed into the air-conditioned building. By the time she'd gotten through all the usual formalities (metal detector, pat down, brief-case inspection, surrendering her cell phone, reading the conditions of entry, signing the visitors' log), she'd almost stopped sweating. So she was disappointed when a guard led her not to a nice cool air-conditioned visiting room but to a fenced-off visitors' section of the outdoor recreation area, which consisted of a row of picnic tables on a concrete slab laid under a canvas sunshade rigged between pylons. The canvas blocked out the sun's direct burn, but the air beneath it was still almost unbreathably hot.

Mona took off her jacket, sat down at a table, took out a pen and yellow legal pad, and asked where all the detainees were.

"In the canteen. It's lunchtime."

She waited for him to bring out her client. While she waited, she looked round the empty yard; beyond the picnic tables was a long stretch of dirt interspersed with brittle bushes. A few benches with concrete legs had been installed along the perimeter fence, which had razor wire spiraled atop it.

They needn't have bothered with the fence, she thought; if anyone escaped, the rattlesnakes would get them.

•••••

Mona heard the *beep* of a scan card and then the *clack* of a heavy lock, and then a guard led out a black-haired young woman wearing an orange jumpsuit and plastic Adidas sliders. Mona already knew this much about her: her name was Carmen Vega, she was twenty years old, and she had been plucked from a sinking panga while attempting to enter the country illegally. She had had a large amount of cash on her, much of which was lost during the rescue. She was in detention because it wasn't her first attempt—attempted reentry after removal was a felony, and the new administration had mandated that every case be prosecuted, no matter the circumstances. The new policy, which the administration had dubbed Operation No Return, had been a boon for the for-profit prison business. Carmen had been sent here to Paradise because the government's own facility in San Bernardino was full. All this Mona had learned from her husband, Nick Finn.

Mona stood and introduced herself. "I'm the lawyer from Juntos," she said in Spanish. Mona worked for a not-for-profit called Together for a Safe Border. Everyone called it simply Juntos. The two women shook hands, Mona noticing how bright Carmen's black eyes were, like stones in a shallow stream. They sat down. "First, let me ask, how are you doing in here?" said Mona.

"Fine." The girl shifted her gaze to the still-virgin page on Mona's yellow legal pad.

Mona put down her pen. "How's the food?" she said.

"It's fine."

One thing Mona knew, prison food was *never* fine. "Listen, Carmen," she said, "I'm not from border patrol. Juntos has nothing to do with the government. We're on your side. You understand?"

Carmen's gaze lingered.

Mona could tell she was being sized up. "For me to be able to help you, I need to know you're telling me the truth. Everything you say to me is confidential. Understand? *Everything*."

Carmen nodded. "The food here is disgusting."

Mona smiled. It was a small truth, a first step. "What about the guards?"

Carmen looked over her shoulder at the dough-bellied man in uniform by the door. "The guards are disgusting, too."

Mona softened her eyes, waited for more. When nothing came, she said: "Carmen, has anyone forced you to do anything you don't want to do?"

Carmen shook her head. "Not like that. They violate us with their eyes. And they don't respect us. They make us eat with plastic cutlery, for our own protection, they say. The knives are useless. We end up eating with our hands like animals."

Mona wrote it all down. Carmen was warming to her subject.

"The toilets overflowed last night. They didn't fix it until this morning."

Mona reflexively scrunched up her nose. Paradise Detention Center was less than a year old. She'd read somewhere that the BSCA had received $15 million in taxpayer-funded subsidies.

Yet the toilets overflowed.

"I bet you can't wait to get out," she said.

"I don't want to go back to Mexico. I'd rather stay here."

Mona nodded. She could detect Carmen's Chilango accent. "You told the agent at Long Beach you're from Tijuana, but you don't talk like a northerner," she said.

The girl shrugged. "I grew up in Ciudad Neza," she said, meaning Ciudad Nezahualcóyotl, a well-known slum east of the capital. Mona asked how long she'd lived in Tijuana.

"Five years."

Mona calculated she must've left home at fifteen. "Did you finish high school?" she asked.

Carmen shook her head.

"Too boring."

"Why did you go north to Tijuana?"

The girl hesitated before saying, "To find work in a *maquiladora*."

"Which one?"

Carmen gave the name of a company Mona had never heard of. Mona wrote it down. "What do they make?"

"Electric components. For automobiles."

"How much did they pay you?" Mona asked casually.

"Thirty pesos an hour," said Carmen.

About a buck eighty. Pure fiction, thought Mona. She knew the real figure the border factories paid the women they employed. And Finn had told her about the money belt and all the cash floating on the water. Far more than Carmen would've made working in a factory. She wrote down Carmen's number anyway. Out of the corner of her eye, she noticed Carmen shifting in her seat.

"Are you married?" said Mona casually.

"No."

"A boyfriend?"

"No."

Mona gave Carmen a friendly smile. "I'm surprised. You're very pretty. You remind me of someone . . ."

Carmen didn't ask who. Her guard stayed up.

Mona softened her eyes. "Let's talk about how you got here. It must've been terrifying when the boat started to sink."

"The man said it would be safe."

"Which man?"

"The man in Tijuana."

She paused, and her expression changed.

"Thank God for the lifesavers," she said. "The captain saved my life."

Captain. Mona suppressed a smile. Four days earlier, her husband, Nick, had pulled Carmen out of the water. Mona thought she might try calling him *Capitán* when she got home, see how he liked that.

"What made you get into that panga, Carmen?"

"To escape poverty and misery."

It was a stock answer the coyotes trained their clients to give. Mona had heard it a hundred times.

"But you had a good life in Tijuana. A good wage, no husband or boyfriend weighing on you—"

"I don't want to work in a *maquiladora* for the rest of my life."

"What *do* you want to do?"

Carmen sat up a little taller. "I want to be an actress on television."

Mona's expression didn't change. Everybody has dreams.

"I can imagine you on-screen. You're pretty enough."

This time, the compliment outflanked Carmen's guard. She started twirling a lock of hair. Mona tapped her pen on the pad. "I remember now who you remind me of: Do you watch *Aprendí a Llorar*?"

Carmen looked coy. *Aprendí a Llorar* was a hit Colombian TV show about a teenager named Dolores Romero who loses her parents when their private jet crashes into a mountain. Dolores inherits their fortune but can't touch it until she turns eighteen. Her uncle becomes her legal guardian and tries to poison her. She survives and runs away, but the toxin leaves her horribly disfigured. Penniless, she gets a job with a traveling circus, selling tickets from a darkened booth. She falls in love with a handsome young knife thrower but doesn't dare show him her hideous face.

"You look just like Dolores at the start of *Aprendí a Llorar*!" said Mona.

"That's just a stupid telenovela," said Carmen. Mona shrugged. Telenovelas were her guilty pleasure. It's how she switched off after work. That's why she knew that the lovelorn but disfigured Dolores strikes up a friendship with a sideshow snake charmer, who works out what kind of toxin the uncle used and concocts an antidote. Dolores blooms into a ravishing beauty and becomes a target for the knife thrower, spinning on his wheel. A television producer sees their double act, signs them up, and makes them famous. The uncle recognizes Dolores on TV, tracks her down, and tries to murder her again, but the knife thrower saves her just in time, killing the uncle in a flurry of blades. Millions tuned in to watch the finale, in which Dolores returns to her family's hacienda and marries her knife thrower on her eighteenth birthday.

"How much did you have in your money belt?" said Mona.

"Five thousand dollars."

Mona raised an eyebrow. "You saved up $5,000 just from working at the *maquiladora*?"

Carmen shrugged. "I work hard."

"How much did you pay the man on the beach?"

"One thousand."

"Did you pay the same the first time you tried to cross?"

No answer.

Mona looked candidly at Carmen. "I want to make sure you understand how serious the situation is," she said. "The first time a person gets caught trying to cross the border, it's a misdemeanor. *La migra* sends you back and tells you not to try again, like they did"—Mona consulted her notes—"on August 26 last year, at San Ysidro. But the new laws mean if you get caught a second time, they can send you to prison for two years."

Mona paused. Then she leaned forward and said, "But it's not just that. You almost died in that boat. You want me to tell the judge you risked your life just to go to *Hollywood*?"

Mona watched Carmen closely. She really was very

pretty, her black eyes gleaming beneath long lashes and attended-to brows. Mona was almost certain the girl had never seen the inside of a *maquiladora*. She was a pretty young woman in a coarsened world. Mona could see she was thinking hard.

"What do you want me to say?" said Carmen.

Mona put down her pen and took Carmen's hands in hers. "You don't have the hands of someone who works in a factory, Carmen."

The guard said, "Hey. No contact."

Mona let go of Carmen's hands. "I want you to trust me."

"I had a boyfriend," said Carmen.

"He gave you the money?"

Carmen stiffened. Her voice got sharper. "I took it."

Mona could tell she'd touched a nerve. "Where is he? In Tijuana?"

"Sometimes. I don't know. He moves around." Carmen rubbed the back of her hand.

"Why did you leave him?" said Mona.

No reply.

"Did he hurt you?"

Carmen put her arms across her chest. "He was . . . he was finished with me."

"What do you mean, 'finished' with you?"

"I mean it was finished between us. You understand?"

Mona shook her head.

Carmen's black eyes flashed. "If he finds me," she said in a whisper, "he'll put me in with the snakes."

A moment passed. Mona realized she was holding her breath.

"That's what he did to the last girl he was finished with," said Carmen. "Put her in the box with the snakes. When they found her body, her flesh had turned black."

"He threatened to kill you?"

Carmen nodded.

Mona made a note. "Carmen, this is important," said Mona, her voice low. "Did your boyfriend ever hurt you?"

Before Mona could stop her, Carmen unzipped the front of her jumpsuit, pulled up her T-shirt, and showed Mona her breasts. Where her flesh should have been smooth and beautiful, it was burned, pitted, the color of rancid milk. Mona broke out in goose bumps, as though the rec yard had suddenly turned freezing cold. She couldn't help but avert her eyes.

"In Hollywood, there are the best plastic surgeons in the world," said Carmen, her black eyes glowing. "That's why I took the *hijo de puta*'s money. He did this to me. He made me ugly. He's going to pay to make me beautiful again."

❖❖❖❖❖

It was dark by the time Mona got back to Redondo Beach. The whole drive home, she'd replayed the scene in the rec yard over and over in her mind's eye. She hoped Carmen hadn't noticed her recoil when she had revealed her wound. Mona had never seen the effect of battery acid on human flesh before. Now it was etched so deeply into her memory that she doubted she would ever forget it.

She got out of the car and stretched the cricks out of her neck and back. Her lower back ached from the hours behind the wheel. She was grateful for the nearness of the sea and the distance from the desert.

Inside, Finn was at the stove. The rich aroma of roasting chicken filled the room. Mona put down her bag, put her arms around him, and pressed her cheek against his back. He smelled of garlic and grease. He had the TV on, watching a Lakers game. He turned around and kissed her.

"Hungry?" he said.

"Starving. But I want to take a shower before we eat. It was a thousand degrees out there." She nodded toward the oven. "Have I got time?"

Finn pulled open the oven door and examined the bird. Mona could hear its juices sizzling in the pan.

"You've got time," he said, taking it out of the oven. "You have to let it rest."

Mona smiled. He always said that.

Ten minutes later, wearing comfortable jeans and a blouse, she was sitting at the table. Finn had brought the candles out. He'd turned off the TV, dimmed the lights, and tuned the radio to a smooth-grooves station. She watched him carve the bird, each piece coming away cleanly on his carving fork. He'd put a wineglass and a bottle of white wine next to her plate. Finn was drinking his usual iced tea. It'd been three years since his last drink.

"How was your day?" she asked.

"Simple. Went for a run down at the beach. Went to a meeting, had lunch with some of the guys after. Then I went to the grocery."

It was his day off, and he looked relaxed. There'd been a time in their marriage when Mona hadn't known what to expect on his days off, and she'd almost left him because of it; but he'd worked to fix himself, stayed off the drink and started going to Alcoholics Anonymous, and now when she came home, she never had to think twice before opening the door.

"How'd it go with the girl?" said Finn.

The smile slid from Mona's face.

"She grew up in a rough part of Mexico City. Left home young, at fifteen, and headed up to Tijuana, to work in a factory—or so she says. In TJ, she got mixed up with an enforcer for the Caballeros cartel by the name of Salvador Soto. She tried to get away from him, so he threw battery acid over her. She's burned from the neck down."

Mona picked up her wineglass and poured half of its contents down her throat. She didn't add that Carmen had been tortured after U.S. border agents had returned her to Mexico. In the anger that had consumed her in the car, Mona had felt a need to blame someone, and the people she felt were most obviously responsible were the border agents at San Ysidro who had sent Carmen back to her horrific fate. But Nick was a border agent, and she knew he would hold the cartel thug responsible, not his colleagues at San Ysidro. He'd be right, of course; the border agents were just doing their jobs, enforcing the law. But right at that moment, Mona didn't need him to be right.

After her shower, Mona had seen Finn's dress uniform hanging in the closet, and for a moment had felt a rancor against him. Her work colleagues were always surprised when they learned what her husband did for a living, and when her job confronted her with the cruelty in the heart of people, as it had that day in the detention center, she was sometimes troubled by the notion that she had married the enemy. She reminded herself that it was Finn who had saved Carmen, and it was Finn who had asked her to help her.

"Know what a 'herper' is?" she said finally.

Finn shook his head.

"It's someone who keeps snakes as pets. Carmen says that this psychopath, Soto, is a herper. Just *loves* snakes. Especially the venomous ones. He collects them from Australia, Thailand, all over. She says he has aquariums filled with cobras and rattlesnakes. She says he gets them out to impress his narco buddies, scare them a little. And she says when he wants to kill someone and make a point of it, he puts them in a box with the snakes. He threatened to do it to her."

Mona took another sip of wine and made a conscious decision to relax and enjoy the remainder of the evening.

Like any institution, the CBP had its good guys and bad guys. One thing she knew for sure, her husband was one of the good ones. "Anyway. Guess what she called you?" She smiled. "Her *salvavida*. Do you know what that means?"

When he shook his head, she said, "Lifesaver."

He chuckled. "*Salvavida*. That's my Spanish word for the day."

"I thought you'd like that. She also called you *capitán*."

His dimple appeared. "So you'll take the case?" he said.

"Of course. Your wish is my command, Captain Lifesaver," said Mona. She took another sip of wine. It left a tingle on her tongue. She was starting to relax.

Mischief flashed across Finn's eyes. "Well. I just hope she realizes how lucky she is, getting the best legal counsel in California," he said. Casually adding, "Best-looking, too."

About then, Mona had an urge to walk over to her husband and straddle his lap. Instead, she stripped meat off a drumstick with her teeth and gave him a look that said, *You're next.*

TWO

SHORTLY after nine the next morning, a Tuesday, Mona was at her desk at the Juntos office in Boyle Heights when Joaquin Vargas walked in.

Joaquin wore an open-collared dress shirt, dark pleated trousers, smart shoes. He'd recently started dyeing his hair, according to Natalie, the legal aide who also worked the reception desk part-time. "I think he does it himself," she'd whispered.

"How was your trip?" said Joaquin.

"Long and hot," she said. She pictured rattlesnakes but didn't mention them.

Joaquin smiled. "And the girl Finn rescued?"

"They've got her on illegal reentry. Arraignment's on Monday."

Joaquin settled into the seat across from Mona's desk. "Talk me through it," he said.

Mona thought for a moment. "She grew up in a slum in the capital, but she's been living in Tijuana for the past five years. She's smart and tough. She's also terrified. She got involved with a guy who turned out to be a psychopath. An enforcer with the Caballeros. She ran away, got stopped at San Ysidro and sent back. To punish her, he poured battery acid on her."

Joaquin's features clustered into a knot of revulsion.

"The boyfriend's name is Salvador Soto," continued Mona. "He's pretty high up in the organization, according to Carmen. She says he can reach Oriel whenever he wants."

Joaquin raised both eyebrows, impressed. Oriel, the head of the Caballeros de Cristos cartel, was the most wanted man on earth.

"You know *Forbes* put him on their rich list?" he said. Mona said no, she didn't.

"He's worth, like, two billion," said Joaquin.

"They give a figure? *Forbes* did an audit on Oriel?"

Joaquin scratched the back of his head. "Good point. Who the hell knows how they came up with the number." He went quiet for a moment. Then he said, "From what you've told me, I don't see much of a case."

One great thing about working for a not-for-profit, the hierarchy was flat. Though Joaquin was nominally her boss, he never actually pulled rank or vetoed any of her initiatives. But he liked winning, and if a case appeared hopeless to him, he always argued against taking it. She'd often heard him say that he'd worked too long in the not-for-profit sector to charge at windmills, and she'd had many robust discussions with him about various cases she had taken on. Now she leaned back in her chair and waited for him to say his piece. When he leaned forward, she noticed his gray roots.

"Illegal reentry's a felony, not a misdemeanor," he began, "which means federal court, not immigration, which means you won't be fighting just to keep her in the country; you'll be fighting to keep her out of jail. Right there, you've tripled your workload. On top of all that, she has criminal associations. The court won't like that."

"She's a torture victim. If she goes back, Soto will kill her."

"You'll have to prove that. You'll have to prove they were in a relationship. How are you going to do that?"

Mona spun her computer monitor around.

"She gave me her Facebook password," she said. She pointed at a photo on Carmen's page. It showed Carmen in a bikini, standing on a beach next to an unsmiling, fully dressed man with a black mustache. Carmen had an arm around his shoulder. Her other hand was on her hip. She was arching her back, thrusting her breasts forward, posing. The photo had been taken before Carmen's boyfriend had poured acid on her.

"You going to show *this* to the court?" said Joaquin. "She looks like a hooker."

Not a word Mona used, but she let it go.

Vargas looked up. "*Is* she?"

Mona shrugged. "Does it matter?"

"It will to the judge. He'll cry moral turpitude." Joaquin looked dubiously at the photo again. "She's smiling. She looks happy."

Mona shook her head. "She's not smiling because she's happy. She's smiling because there's a camera. In the picture, she's seventeen."

He sighed. "I don't know, Mona."

"She says he's killed dozens of people. He's crazy, she says. He would lock her in the closet and leave her there for hours. And that was *before* the acid. He threatened to kill her."

"Have you got any evidence? Anything at all?"

Mona picked up her phone and keyed a code into the screen.

"She gave me the PIN to her message service. Listen."

She held up her phone toward Joaquin. A man's voice played from the phone: "*Voy a matarte, puta. Lentamente, para que sufras. La víbora te va a besar.*"

He made a hissing sound.

"'The snake's going to kiss you'? What does that mean?" said Joaquin.

"He's threatening to put her in a box filled with snakes. That's what he'll do to her if she goes back. She says he's done it to others before."

"Look, I feel for her. I really do," said Joaquin. "But I just don't think you have a case, Mona. That's the cold hard truth." He tapped his fingers on the arm of the chair. "Nothing I'm saying is making the slightest difference, is it?"

Mona smiled.

"No," she said.

♦♦♦♦♦

Mona didn't see Joaquin again until the end of the day, when he said a quick goodbye and disappeared into the elevator with Natalie, leaving Mona alone in the office. She swiveled around to the window and watched the last of the light slip down the glass faces of the skyscrapers downtown. Her thoughts turned to her parents, to how, like Carmen, they'd also crossed the border, drawn to the work and the opportunity for a better life this nation had provided them. Mona was born in the United States and knew no other country. But she also honored her parents' experience; what it had cost them to leave their homeland, and the efforts they had made once they had reached their adoptive one. She knew she'd gotten into college thanks to the solid foundation her parents had laid for her. They'd worked hard and taught her and her brother to do the same.

The sun dropped below the horizon, and the sky turned bruise purple. She thought about her older brother, Diego. She remembered how angry she'd been when he'd gotten out of the navy and promptly joined the border patrol's air and marine unit at Long Beach, which her college-student self had insisted on calling *la migra* out of a sense of solidarity. Diego justified his action by saying there weren't many jobs for ex-navy personnel that allowed him to stay close to home. "It's either that or the coast guard," he'd said. "And I'm done with the military."

Then, a year later, it was Diego who had introduced her to Nick. Not that she'd been looking to meet anyone; she had recently graduated law school and had just been recruited full-time to Juntos. When Diego had badgered her into coming to a family barbecue at the Long Beach Air and Marine Station, she'd done so reluctantly and had gone determined to make sure the irony of her presence was lost on no one. "Just so there's no misunderstanding, I'm here to support Diego. I'd rather die than date a border agent," she'd said to Finn when Diego introduced them. Finn had simply smiled his dimpled smile and asked if she was hungry. Then he'd gone off to fetch her a plate of bar-becued beef and pinto beans. Mona ended up dating him anyway. And then it was Diego who died.

Three years had passed since Diego had been killed in the line of duty, but the grief still sometimes flooded through her in waves so powerful, they left her out of breath. She waited for the feeling to subside. Outside, the city's lights twinkled like stars on the surface of the sea. Her pulse settled. She swiveled back around to her desk, switched on the desk lamp, and got back to work.

The hours passed. She reviewed the relevant laws and made notes of those that might be helpful. She reviewed summaries of pertinent cases. When she caught herself rereading the same line three times without registering it, she looked out the window again. The moon was high. The clock on her computer told her it was two in the morn-ing. Enough. She grabbed her handbag, switched off the lights, and took the elevator down to the underground parking garage.

Mona walked past a gleaming, pearl-white Porsche

Macan. It belonged to the guy who ran a tech start-up on the top floor. Mona felt a twinge of envy. The guy looked like he was twenty-five, tops. She'd once sat at her desk and calculated that if, instead of going into the not-for-profit sector, she'd joined one of the big firms that had tried to recruit her out of law school, just the late-night billable hours she clocked as a matter of course would've paid off a Porsche outright. Instead, she made monthly payments on the Toyota. She was thirty-two.

She pressed the Unlock button on the fob. The RAV honked like a startled goose and switched on its head-lights, illuminating the concrete wall of the parking bay. At least her car was a better color than the Macan, she thought. The RAV4 was a tawny red that the dealer had told her was called, tautologically, *hot lava,* whereas the Porsche was a cold, almost blue shade of white. It occurred to Mona that it was the kind of color a sociopath might choose, and in her tired and cranky state of mind, the thought was pleasing to her. She found the tech entrepreneur objectionable. She'd shared the elevator with him a couple of times, a tall, scruffy boy who wore cargo shorts to work, for heaven's sake. In the elevator, he'd carefully avoided making eye contact, as if meeting her gaze would cause him to explode like a volcano.

Mona sighed, got into her RAV, and turned the key. The car started right up, reliable as ever. Well, Finn *had* told her that it was a mechanically sound automobile, and Mona *had* pretended that it was his advice, and not the color, that made her decide to buy it.

THREE

WHILE Mona was working late, Finn was at a bar. Six days had passed since the rescue operation, and he was concerned that the close call with the freighter had rattled everyone's confidence. He was conscious that he had pushed the envelope out there. So he had organized for his crew to get together outside of work. He wanted to give everyone a chance to decompress. Plus, he had a problem he had to deal with.

They met at Catalina's, a sports bar behind the Long Beach Convention and Entertainment Center. Finn, who no longer drank, but who'd started following the Rams since they'd returned to LA, appreciated the signed jerseys and photos of Rams legends past and present: Vince Ferregamo, Jack Youngblood, Isaac Bruce, Deacon Jones. The number 80 Isaac Bruce jersey in particular brought up strong feelings in Finn. He sat at a long wooden table beneath it. On the wall opposite was a bank of flat-screen TVs. Chinchilla sat to his right, Gomez and Figueroa opposite him. He turned to Chinchilla.

"You tell Ella about the panga?"

Ella was Chinchilla's wife.

Chinchilla gave a shrug. "I painted a general picture. I didn't get specific."

"Which bits in particular did you leave out?"

"Details like the space between us and the freighter."

Across the table, Gomez gave a mock look of astonishment. "There was space between us?"

"Enough to slide a sheet of paper through," said Chinchilla.

She gave a nervous laugh, and Finn noticed a vein pop in her neck. She patted his arm.

"Don't worry, Finn. You made the right call."

Gomez agreed. "It was on us to do everything we could to save them," he said.

Finn appreciated them saying that. The decision he'd made that night had saved twenty-two lives, but could easily have gone the other way. There'd been so little in it. One thing he was certain of, defeat can always be snatched from the jaws of victory.

In 1994, the year Finn had started fourth grade, his mother had started dating a new guy. The guy had shown up one day with a Rams jersey for Finn, one with Isaac Bruce's number on it, and Finn had quickly adopted the team as his own. He'd sat on the carpet in front of the TV, wearing the jersey and mimicking his mom's boyfriend's shouts of joy and frustration, an unfamiliar feeling of belonging rushing through him. Then the Rams had quit LA and moved to St. Louis, and not long after that, the boyfriend had left, too, to eventually become just another of the many men his mom had dated, men who had appeared, then disappeared from Finn's life. He had never worn the number 80 jersey again.

Finn glanced at Figueroa. He looked uncomfortable. They'd only sat down a couple of minutes ago, but his beer was already empty. Finn wondered whether he should say anything about the seasickness, how it happened to everyone, but thought against it. There was something about Figueroa that displeased him. An arrogance, a sense of entitlement, a blowhard attitude. Then he told himself Figueroa was still young, and the young often seemed that way to their elders. Finn wasn't so old he'd forgotten what it was like to be young. Plus, Finn wasn't immune to sea-sickness. He knew how debilitating it could be.

"You like the Rams, Figueroa?" he said.

The young man nodded. "Yeah."

Finn smiled. They talked football for a while. Gomez went to get another round; Chinchilla went to lend a hand. When they were gone, Finn asked, "Where were you before you joined Air and Marine, Figueroa?"

"I was at San Ysidro for a year, working the booths."

Finn nodded. "It's a rite of passage." Then, in a quiet voice, he said, "Listen, about what happened on the water. I'm not going to report you for insubordination. But I want you off my boat."

The young man looked into his empty glass. Finn couldn't tell whether he was relieved or angry.

"You want my advice, you should consider whether Air and Marine is the right fit for you," said Finn. "There are plenty of land-based jobs at the CBP."

Now Figueroa looked up at Finn, his eyes filled with hate.

"I don't want your advice," he spat.

Just then, Gomez and Chinchilla returned, each carrying two drinks. Finn thanked Gomez for the lemonade. Gomez was in a chatty mood.

"Does anyone else feel like there are more pangas out there than before?" he said. "That was our fifth intercept this month."

"All this talk about a wall, it's pushing them out to sea," said Chinchilla.

"We're getting a lot of good intel from AMOC. That's made a difference," said Finn.

AMOC was the newly expanded Air and Marine Operations Center that had just opened out at the air base in Riverside. It gave the CBP the capability to monitor air and marine traffic far out into the Pacific Ocean.

Figueroa stood. He looked like he was seething. He muttered good night.

When he was gone, Chinchilla said, "I don't think I can do another patrol with that guy, Finn."

"You won't have to. He's off the boat," said Finn.

"Bummer. I never got a chance to apologize for Tasering him," said Gomez.

"You didn't write him up? For stepping up to you out there?" said Chinchilla.

Finn shook his head. He leaned back and sipped lemonade through a straw.

"I told him to consider other career options that don't involve going to sea," he said. "Whether he does or not is not my problem."

◆◆◆◆◆

The following evening, Finn walked into the briefing room at the station, where he found the crews of the three boats on patrol that evening had already assembled—twelve people in all. He was surprised to see Figueroa there. Had he managed to find himself another boat already? The young man avoided making eye contact with him. Finn sat down, nodded at Chinchilla and Gomez, then turned his attention to the man standing at the front of the room.

Station director Keith Klein was in his late fifties and kept in shape. He was of medium height, clean shaven, and what hair he still had he kept cropped short. He wore a short-sleeved, button-down khaki shirt with a star on the collar, indicating his rank. Finn liked working for Klein. He appreciated his boss's plainspoken approach. Klein had been a navy pilot before joining the CBP, and Finn felt for him the kinship that veterans who served in the same service often feel for one another. Finn knew that Klein was coming up on mandatory retirement and that he wasn't happy about it. He returned Klein's nod, then took a seat.

"All right, everybody's here. First up, I want to congratulate the crew of Interceptor One for the outcome of your mission last week. Your professionalism and selflessness in horrific conditions saved twenty-two lives. You did good."

The assembly broke out into spontaneous applause. When it had died down, Klein continued. "Okay, tonight's missions: Interceptor One, you take the same sector. It seems to be happy hunting grounds for you, so may as well keep you there. Interceptor Two, you take the southern sector. Interceptor Three, you go north. Plus, you've got a new crew member, Agent Antonio Figueroa, so please make him feel welcome."

Chinchilla looked at Finn, eyebrows raised.

"Any questions?" said Klein.

When no one raised a hand, Klein launched into his stump speech.

"You are members of the largest civilian air and marine force in the world. We have boats, we have planes, we have satellites, and we have drones. But most of all, we have our people. You. Our opponents are the cartels who want to smuggle drugs and people into our country. They have go-fasts, pangas; they have their own planes and submarines. Our job is to stop them. Ladies and gentlemen, go make our borders safe."

Everybody stood and made for the exit.

As the room emptied, Finn went over to Klein. "Got a minute?"

Klein nodded.

"You put Figueroa on another boat?" said Finn.

"Well, you didn't want him on yours."

"He's not a mariner, boss."

Klein threw up his hands. "Oh, I know that. You couldn't teach that kid to be ballast. But that's what they send me, Finn. I can only take what they send me."

"If he falls overboard, don't say I didn't warn you."

"If he falls overboard, he'd be doing me a favor."

"One more thing. We're only intercepting people-smugglers. We haven't seen a narco for months."

Klein raised an eyebrow. "Well, get out there and find 'em, then. It's not like drugs have run dry in this country."

Finn realized he wasn't making himself clear. "What I mean is, there's something not right about the intel coming out of Riverside. Seems like they're only seeing pangas. Every time we get a heads-up from them, it turns out to be a panga. How come they're not picking up any narcos?"

Klein gazed at Finn like he was considering his reply.

"Okay, I'll tell you what I'll do," said Klein. "I've got a heads-of-station meeting next week. The AMOC director will be there. I'll put it on the agenda, see if he can explain it. All right?"

"All right."

"All right. But, Finn, chances are, it's just a statistical cluster. Like fishing. One day, you're catching more yellowtail and sea bass than you can fit in your cooler. Next day, same spot, you're catching nothing but eels. Doesn't mean you stop fishing."

Finn nodded.

"Thanks, Chief," he said.

He headed for the door.

*****

At midnight, Finn cut the engines. After four hours' patrol, it was nice to have a moment's respite from the constant roar of the outboards. Conditions were benign, the water glassy, the stars bright. Finn, Chinchilla, and Gomez sat on the gunwales and listened to the lapping against the hull.

The serenity didn't last more than a minute. The VHF crackled to life.

"Interceptor One, Interceptor One, do you read."

Finn grabbed the mic. Chinchilla and Gomez crowded round the radio.

"Long Beach, this is Interceptor One, I read you clearly, over," said Finn.

"Interceptor One, Riverside has a visual of a vessel traveling dark, position 33°18′50″ north, 118°03′27″ west, bearing zero-six-zero, speed ten knots. Heat signature indicates multiple people aboard."

The speed and number of people aboard told Finn that this was almost certainly another people-smuggler. Gomez checked the electronic chart.

"At thirty knots, we're on them in twenty minutes," he said.

Finn examined the chart himself. He used the roller ball to measure the distance between the panga and the shore. Then he pointed at Crystal Cove State Park between Laguna and Newport.

"They're heading toward Crystal Cove," he said. "Traveling at ten knots, they won't land for another two hours." He pointed out to sea. "Meanwhile, this sector is left wide open."

He looked up at his two crew members. "If we bear south, then east, we can at least cover the rest of the sector and still have time to come up between the panga and the beach at Crystal Cove. What do you think?"

"It's risky," said Chinchilla. "What if they speed up and get to the beach before us?"

"Riverside will watch them. If they accelerate, we'll alter course."

He paused, to allow Chinchilla to voice any other concerns she might have. When she didn't, he said, "Strap in."

•••••

The thirty-nine-foot Midnight Express that Finn commanded weighed more than sixteen thousand pounds, was powered by four three-hundred-horsepower Mercury outboards, and had a top speed of sixty knots. It also had seats mounted on shock absorbers, which, of its many features, was the one Finn most appreciated. He loved driving fast boats, but he knew what a thirty-nine-foot hull slamming against the sea could do to your knees.

He clipped himself into the three-point harness in the seat in front of the wheel. Gomez strapped into the seat next to him, Chinchilla into one of the two seats behind. She was wearing night-vision goggles. Gomez's job was to scan the screen for anything suspicious picked up by their own radar. Chinchilla's was to scan the horizon for body heat.

Finn checked that his shipmates were strapped in, then pressed down the throttles. Even strapped into the shock-mitigating seat, Finn's body felt the impact each time the hull launched itself off the top of a wave, hung suspended for a moment in the air, then slammed down on the water, all the while maintaining a forward speed of fifty knots. His body felt weightless every time the boat's hull left the water, then crushed when it hit the surface. It was absolutely exhilarating.

They drove like that for a quarter hour, not seeing anything. Then Finn felt a tap on his shoulder. He pulled back the throttles. The boat slowed, the hull sank into the water, and the engines' roar diminished to a low rumble.

"Bodies five hundred yards off the starboard bow," said Chinchilla.

Finn put on his own night-vision goggles. They were still at a distance that was at the limit of the goggles' range, but it was a clear night, and he could distinguish two human figures standing in the cockpit of a speedboat. A speedboat traveling with its lights out.

Finn put down the goggles.

"Take the starboard gun," he said.

Chinchilla unstrapped herself from the seat and positioned herself at the rifle mounted on the starboard gunwale. Finn pushed the throttles forward until they hit twenty knots and headed straight at the speedboat. He switched on the lights and the siren.

Finn didn't need to ask why the speedboat was traveling with its lights out. Its reaction to the Interceptor told him all he needed to know. The go-fast took off. Finn accelerated to keep up. They were close enough now to see what they were dealing with. A sleek, forty-foot boat with four outboards.

Chinchilla, who was still wearing her night-vision goggles, shouted, "There are three guys aboard, not two!"

Finn put the Interceptor in their wake. He was running her at 80 percent throttle and was easily keeping up with her. The Interceptor was about fifty feet behind its target. He knew that he could jump up alongside the go-fast whenever he wanted. He didn't want to get too close until he knew what they were up against.

A minute later, whoever was driving the go-fast must've realized that he wasn't going to outrun the Interceptor. He wasn't going to reach his destination. So he turned south, toward the border. Finn tapped the throttle forward and set a course to cut them off. Very quickly, he closed the distance to twenty feet. Fifteen. Ten.

Then the fun began.

The go-fast turned abruptly toward them. The two boats passed each other so close, the spray from the go-fast's outboards splashed onto the Interceptor's canopy.

"Hold on!" shouted Finn. He threw the Interceptor into a tight turn. She leaned right, over almost to the portside gunwale, so far over that Gomez, who had unwisely unclipped himself from his seat, crashed into the rail. Finn straightened the wheel and opened the throttle all the way. He glanced over at Gomez, who had scrambled back to his seat.

"Tell them to stop," he said.

Gomez got on the mic and started saying over and over through the loudspeaker, *"Alto! Para el barco!"*

The boat kept running. Now Finn was running alongside on the starboard side and slightly back. He could make out the silhouette of the driver against the moonlit water. Suddenly, he saw a splash of white water. Then another.

"They're throwing cargo overboard!" shouted Chinchilla.

Gomez kept shouting, *"Alto! Alto!"*

The boat kept running. The two men who weren't driving kept throwing large packages overboard. Finn was trying to keep count. So far he'd counted eight. And they were still going.

Finn killed the siren and called out to Chinchilla, "Fire a warning shot."

Chinchilla opened fire.

The *rat-tat-tat* of her automatic weapon filled the air.

Still the boat didn't stop.

She fired another volley. The boat kept going.

Finn said, "All right. Take out her outboards."

Chinchilla nodded, adjusted the rifle on its mount, and opened fire for the third time. Finn saw the casings of the go-fast's outboards splinter. The speed fell off the go-fast, and Finn had to pull right back on the throttles to avoid running into the back of her. Chinchilla kept her gun trained on the men in the boat. No one was throwing bales overboard now. With their outboards shot out, they weren't going anywhere. All three heeded Gomez's shouts to put their hands in the air.

Finn brought the Interceptor alongside the go-fast. Gomez got his sidearm out and jumped into the Interceptor's bow. When they were close enough, Gomez jumped across to the go-fast. He shouted at the smugglers. They lay facedown on the deck and put their hands behind their heads. Finn called in their intercept. Long Beach replied that they would dispatch a helicopter and call in another Interceptor to help recover the bales that the smugglers had jettisoned.

Finn hung up the mic, then tied the Interceptor to the go-fast and jumped across. While Gomez and Chinchilla provided cover, Finn started cuffing the three guys. One of them, lying with his face pressed against the deck of the go-fast, said, when Finn slapped the cuffs on his wrists, *"No debe estar por aquí."*

•••••

With all they had to do following the intercept—recover all the bales, process the three traffickers, wait for a coast guard cutter with a crane to come and pick up the disabled go-fast—Finn and his crew went into overtime, and it was well and truly day by the time they headed back to base. Passing through the Long Beach breakwater, Finn realized how tired he was. He was looking forward to getting home, getting warm, and getting dry. He knew Mona was leaving early that morning for a court appearance in Paradise, and he had hoped to see her before she left, but now the best he could do was send her a text saying good luck.

They pulled in alongside the pier. Chinchilla and

Gomez made the boat fast. Finn made a note of the fuel level in his log, then killed the ignition. The four outboards fell silent.

While Chinchilla hosed down the deck, Gomez scrubbed with a hard-bristled broom. Finn stood on the deck and finished writing up the patrol in his log. When he was finished, he put the log back in its waterproof pouch.

The three weary mariners walked up the pier. The sun was over the horizon in the east. They entered the station and made their way to the locker rooms—Finn and Gomez to the male locker room, Chinchilla to the female one.

Finn and Gomez were still getting changed when Klein appeared. Finn wasn't surprised to see him; Klein often came in early if there'd been a major interdiction operation out on the water. But he *was* surprised by the grim look on Klein's face.

"Listen, there's no easy way to say it, so I'll get straight to the point," said Klein. "There has been a complaint filed against you. Both of you."

"What?" said Gomez. "By who?"

Finn laughed without meaning to. "Figueroa, right?"

Klein looked at him apologetically. "I can't tell you. I'm supposed to protect his anonymity," he said.

"What a load of bullshit," said Gomez. "Can't you shut it down?"

"He went over my head. The inspector general's investigating, which means I have no choice but to take you both off active duty until they've finished."

Finn's spirits sank. If there was any government department that could be counted on for endless bureaucratic process, it was the Office of Inspector General.

"Come on, Keith. You're the director. Surely you can make this go away," he said.

Klein shook his head. "There's nothing I can do. You're just going to have to wait it out."

"How long?" said Gomez.

Klein shrugged.

"So now what?" said Finn.

"Got any leave due?" Klein asked.

"A couple of weeks," said Finn.

"It's gonna take longer than that."

"You telling us to take unpaid leave?" said Gomez.

"No. I just don't know what to do with you. You're my best crew. You're no good to me on land."

Klein leaned against the wall and tapped his foot.

"There's one thing I could do. I'm supposed to send people to Riverside, to familiarize themselves with the new systems there. They say they want to get us ready for the future. I could start with you two."

Finn reflected. The Air and Marine Operations Center at March Air Reserve Base in Riverside was a ninety-minute drive away. He didn't relish the prospect of spending three hours a day behind the wheel. On the other hand, what else was he going to do? He looked at Gomez and raised a querying eyebrow. Gomez gave a resigned shrug.

"All right, fine," said Finn.

Gomez shook his head. "You should've cited Figueroa," he said to Finn.

"Cited him for what?" said Klein.

"Forget about it," said Finn.

Klein nodded. "This new administration, they're recruiting like crazy, but nobody wants to work for CBP anymore. We're scraping the bottom of the barrel."

Finn reflected for a moment. Then he said, "Should we be worried, Chief?"

Klein shook his head. "It's just procedure. The OIG will send someone to interview you both, as well as Chinchilla. Your stories will match. You'll all say you acted appropriately. I'll write a glowing assessment, saying you're my best crew. And that'll be that. Oh, and one more thing."

"What?"

"You should call the union."

"You just said there was nothing to worry about!" said Gomez.

Klein had one foot out the door.

"Just in case," he said.

FOUR

THE U.S. district courthouse in Paradise, California, was a dreary cinder block box surrounded by baking asphalt. Someone had tried to gild the lily by planting greenery out front, but the desert shrubs only emphasized the building's desolate air. Mona parked in its shadow, next to a row of BSCA prisoner-transport buses liveried with the company's logo of a swooping eagle. She replied to Finn's text with a series of emojis: a boxing glove to represent the fight, a set of scales to represent justice, and a heart to represent her feelings for him. Then she climbed the steps into the courthouse.

In contrast to the parking lot, the courtroom was teeming with people. Rows of shackled, jumpsuited prisoners sat crammed along the benches in the public gallery; more stood lined up along the back wall. Even the jury box was packed with defendants. Mona scanned the room but couldn't see Carmen anywhere. A tired-looking clerk with an armful of files elbowed past.

"I'm looking for my client, Carmen Vega?" said Mona.

"Keep looking," said the clerk, barely slowing to answer. "We've got 111 cases on the docket today."

Mona squeezed her way past the bar to the defense

table, where an attorney sat holding a phone to her ear, despite the big notice on the wall saying NO CELL PHONES. Mona pointed at the seat next to her and mouthed, "Is that free?"

The attorney cradled the phone between chin and shoulder and removed her box file from the chair. "I was saving it for my colleague, but looks like he's a no-show, again," she said. She hung up the phone and slid it into her handbag.

Mona sat and put down her own box file on the table. The attorney introduced herself.

"Kristin Chase, public defender's office. First time in Paradise?"

Mona nodded. She looked around at the crowd. "Is it always this busy?" she said.

"Operation No Return," said the attorney, referring to the new law that made every reentry an automatic felony. "Keeps the place ticking over, as you can see. To speed things up, the judge hears a dozen cases at a time."

Mona raised an eyebrow. "I'm guessing he's not a due-process kind of guy," she said.

The attorney sighed. "Judge Ross wouldn't know due process if it came flying down the fairway at his country club and nailed him between the eyes. He's a lock-'em-up kind of a guy. Every single person here'll be back in lockup by the end of the day. It's so predictable, my colleague hardly bothers showing up anymore. He doesn't see the point," she said, checking her phone again.

"Are they all like this?" said Mona.

"All? The county's got only two judges, one bad and the other worse."

"Which one's Ross?"

"The worse one. No one wants to live in Paradise anymore. The town's been dying since all the water dried up.

Used to be crop fields all around. Now all the young people are moving to wherever you've just floated in from.
LA, I'm guessing?"

Mona nodded. When the woman asked which firm she
was with, Mona said, "I work for Juntos. Most of the time,
I'm in immigration court."

The attorney pulled a squirt bottle of hand sanitizer
from her purse. "A lot of these people haven't been medi-
cally screened," she said, squeezing goo onto her hands.
Mona caught a whiff of antiseptic. The attorney went
on, "I've read about Juntos. Great outfit. But immigration
court, that's the civil system. You're in the criminal justice system here. And believe me, it's not a sanitary place.
You'll want some of this," she said, offering the squirt
bottle to Mona.

"I can't see my client anywhere," said Mona, declining
the sanitizer. That stuff dried her skin.

"Sometimes they keep the overflow in the conference room until their cases come up," said the attorney.
"What's the charge? Illegal reentry?"

"Illegal reentry," said Mona, getting up. She remembered seeing the door to the conference room out in the
corridor, and she wanted to talk to Carmen before proceedings started, if only to reassure her. But then came a hush,
like a crowd on a platform when the train is running late:
everyone peering in the same direction, on edge. A moment later, the judge walked in. Everybody rose.

The attorney whispered to Mona, "I'd wish you luck if
I thought it would help."

"Wish it anyway," said Mona.

The attorney smiled. The judge didn't. He shot Mona a
look of displeasure. Judge Ross was a small, jockey-sized
man who wore his gray hair trimmed short, army-style,
revealing a diamond-shaped birthmark high on his neck.
He wore thick-rimmed spectacles that would've been

trendy on a younger person. When he sat in his high-backed chair, he seemed taller, and Mona guessed that behind his bench, he'd had a raiser installed beneath him.

The room stayed quiet while he spent a moment getting himself organized. Then he nodded to the clerk, who called the first case on the docket: a group of eleven defendants. They turned out to be the group already sitting in the jury box. The attorney sitting next to Mona was defending them.

The judge read out the charge: illegal reentry after removal. He said that the new federal laws provided for them to be arraigned together. The court's time was precious, he said. He told them they were facing two years in jail, after which they would be deported. The judge spoke in English. An interpreter translated into Spanish. A court reporter tapped it all into his machine. Then the judge called each member of the group to stand and asked them one by one, "How do you plead?"

Every answer was the same: "*Culpable.*"

The judge's mood visibly improved.

"Eleven guilty pleas means there's no need for this court to set a trial date," he said. "I am happy to hear statements from the prosecutor and the counsel for the defense right away, and then, if no one objects, this court can proceed directly to sentencing." Mona noticed that the judge had looked at the public defender when he had said, with a slight emphasis, *if no one objects.*

Over at the other table, the prosecutor stood. Mona got the impression he was just going through well-rehearsed motions; he didn't seem to have put much effort into preparing his case. He recounted how Border Patrol had found the eleven, thirsty and lost, in the desert outside El Centro. Their coyote had abandoned them. Six were Mexican, the rest were what Border Patrol dubbed OTMs—Other Than Mexican. He didn't even bother giving their actual nationalities. They all had removal orders against their names, he said. It was a clear-cut case. He sat down, and the attorney next to Mona stood.

Her strategy, Mona was dismayed to hear, was simply to plead for leniency in sentencing. She reminded the judge that she was one of only two public defenders in Paradise—the other wasn't answering his phone. She hadn't had the chance to meet any of the defendants until that morning. Because the conference room was occupied, she'd been obliged to meet them in the corridor, a public place that made a farce of lawyer-client privilege; she'd spent at most two minutes with each defendant, enough time to note down their names and backgrounds, and to tell them that, without more time to work out a defense, their best option was to plead guilty to minimize their sentences. None of these people had criminal records, she said. They were just regular folk looking to improve their lot in life. The system was letting them down. Some of them were fleeing war or civil strife. Mona tried not to shake her head in contempt; the attorney was like a dog with the fight whipped out of her.

The judge sentenced all eleven to fourteen months in jail.

"This court will refrain from applying the full sentence to the defendants because they pleaded guilty, thus saving the court a lot of time and the taxpayer a good deal of money," he said before bringing down his gavel.

Mona checked her watch. From arraignment to sentencing had taken fifteen minutes.

"Fourteen months is good," said Kristin Chase in a low voice. "It means he's in a good mood. He usually goes for eighteen, even *with* the guilty plea."

"This is an outrage."

The woman looked at Mona curiously. "This isn't Santa Monica. There's no crowd of activists waving placards outside. Judge Ross is probably the most popular figure in Paradise." She paused, packed away her documents, then went on, "I've tried to do something, believe me. I wrote to our congressman. I've written letters to the Judicial Council. I wrote to the *LA Times* and *The San Diego Union-Tribune*. You know what that's gotten me? I'm the most hated person in town. If people here had their way, I'd be the first person cast out of Paradise since the devil. This is *his* town," she said, nodding toward the door to the judge. She watched sadly as the bailiffs led out the eleven. "The town's dying, and people here are looking for someone to blame. Judge Ross just gives them what they want," she said. "He'll be reelected by a landslide."

◆◆◆◆◆

During the recess, Mona managed to corner the bailiff long enough to discover that Carmen's case was the first on the docket after the break; she told him she *absolutely* needed to see her client beforehand. The officer left the room saying he would fetch Carmen, but didn't reappear until twenty minutes later—just moments before the judge returned. Carmen arrived wearing shackles around her ankles and a frightened look in her dark eyes. Mona insisted the bailiff remove the shackles.

"You okay?" she said in Spanish.

Carmen forced a smile. That was all the conversation they had time for. The judge settled back into his high-backed chair and signaled for proceedings to resume. The prosecutor started reading the charge against Carmen as if he were calling a race at the track. The interpreter kept missing details.

Mona stood. "Your Honor, with your leave, we ask that opposing counsel slow down. The interpreter cannot keep up, and my client isn't fluent in English."

The judge let his gaze linger on Mona for a moment

longer than was courteous, then gave a nod. The prosecutor resumed, slower now. Mona felt the muscles in her jaw slacken.

The prosecutor began with a summary of what had happened out on the water in the small hours of March 28. He pointed out that the panga had been intercepted within U.S. territorial waters, that it had not been seaworthy, and in fact was sinking when the Interceptor found it. He emphasized that there had been four children aboard. He painted a picture of recklessly selfish people with no regard for the law or the lives of others. He made no mention of how Carmen had helped save a child's life. He said nothing of the troubles they were trying to escape. Nothing about battery acid. Nothing about torture.

"When immigration agents at Long Beach processed these people, Your Honor," he said, drawing out *these people,* "they discovered that this wasn't the defendant's first attempt to enter the country illegally: On August 26 of last year, agents at the San Ysidro port of entry discovered Ms. Vega concealed in the trunk of a car. On that occasion, according to her A-file, the acting deputy assistant district director of San Ysidro issued an expedited removal order on Ms. Vega. Furthermore—and again, these documents are all in the defendant's A-file, Your Honor—Ms. Vega swore an affidavit on that occasion admitting to the misdemeanor charge of illegal entry and acknowledging that she was banned from reentering the United States for five years. So given her previous attempt, Your Honor, under Operation No Return, ICE officials at Long Beach had no choice but to charge Ms. Vega under 8 USC 1326—reentry after removal."

The prosecutor made a show of gathering his thoughts before continuing, "Your Honor, it is the government's position that the charge against Ms. Vega admits no doubt or dispute. But there's more to it than a simple reentry charge. It's one thing to hide in the trunk of an automobile; it's quite another to put your own life, and those of others—including *children*—at risk. And yet that is exactly what the defendant did, in circumstances that can only be described as aggravating. We encourage the court to send a strong message to deter others from getting into unsafe vessels and risking not only their own lives but those of the brave men and women of our border force who have to rescue them. A strong message of deterrence is the *humanitarian* thing to do, Your Honor."

The prosecutor glanced in Mona's direction before sitting down. She wasn't 100 percent sure, but she thought she saw a nod of assent from the bench. The judge shifted his gaze back onto her. She stood. Before she had a chance to speak, the judge said, "I don't know you, Counsel. You're not from the Paradise public defender's office."

"No, Your Honor," replied Mona. "I'm from the not-for-profit Together for a Safer Border. I'm representing Carmen Vega pro bono—"

The judge waved some papers at her. "I know all that, Miss Jimenez. It's all in this bio you provided, along with your motion to dismiss. What I mean is, we don't know each other."

"I'm not sure I understand, Your Honor."

"Let me try to make it clear for you, Counsel. I don't know you, and clearly you don't know me. If you knew me, you'd know I don't like a clogged docket. You'd know that I have never dismissed a border case and that I'm not about to start. If you knew me, you'd have known this motion of yours is a complete waste of time. And I don't like wasting time, Counsel."

"I just know the law, Your Honor—"

"I haven't finished, Miss Jimenez."

Mona said nothing. Specifically, she didn't throw at the judge the cussword loitering under her breath. He waved the sheaf of papers again.

"Now, because I don't like to waste time, I'm going to nip this in the bud. I started reading your motion in my chambers, Counsel. I got as far as the first page. You actually expect me to dismiss this case because you claim the defendant was illegally *deported*?"

"Your Honor, when the acting deputy assistant district director at San Ysidro signed the removal order on Ms. Vega on August 26, neither he nor any of the Border Patrol agents who took her into their custody that day informed her that she was eligible for relief from deportation. This substantially prejudiced my client, Your Honor, since it violated her right to due process—"

"Due process! She was hiding in the trunk of a car!"

"Your Honor, as the court well knows, every person who passes through our legal system is entitled to due process."

The judge sniffed. "Do you know how many immigration cases were heard just in the Southern District last year, Counsel?"

"Yes, Your Honor." She gave him the exact figure.

His eyes narrowed behind his spectacles.

"That's more than were heard for drug offenses, Your Honor," continued Mona.

"I don't need a lesson, Counsel."

"Very well, Your Honor."

"My point is, there's a national crisis, and *we* are the front line. Hell, just look around my own courtroom, Ms. Jimenez. I've got ninety-nine more cases to get through just *today*. I don't have time for frivolous motions."

"With respect, Your Honor, a violation of due process isn't frivolous. As a point of law, the indictment against my client cannot stand. Since Ms. Vega was illegally removed on August 28 last year, she cannot now be indicted for reentry after removal."

"Nonsense. The agents were well within the law when they removed Ms. Vega. She was attempting to enter illegally."

"Your Honor, I don't dispute that Ms. Vega entered the country illegally; I dispute that she was *removed* from it legally. The acting deputy assistant district director at San Ysidro overtly misadvised Ms. Vega that she had no possibility of relief from deportation, whereas in fact, Ms. Vega was fleeing persecution and therefore had an inalienable right to apply for asylum. As a result of the deputy assistant district director's egregious haste, Your Honor, Ms. Vega was returned to Mexico, where she was subjected to horrific violence. The government improperly denied my client judicial review, and she almost died because of it. Moreover, Your Honor, as a point of law, since Ms. Vega was illegally removed, she cannot now be indicted for reentry after removal. If I may cite the Supreme Court's opinion in the case of *United States v. Mendoza-Lopez:* 'If USC 1326 envisions that a court may impose a criminal penalty for reentry after *any* deportation, regardless of how violative of the rights of the alien the deportation proceedings may have been, the statute does *not* comport with constitutional due process.'"

Mona became aware that in her outrage, she'd allowed the tempo of her speech to accelerate, and now the interpreter was struggling to keep up with *her*. She took a deep breath and looked apologetically in the poor woman's direction. She'd broken a golden rule of court work: *never get angry except on purpose.* She looked down and took a deep, calming breath. When she looked up again, the judge had a condescending smile plastered across his small, round face.

"Let me see if I've got this straight, Counsel," he said.

"You're arguing that if the border agents at San Ysidro had informed the defendant of her right to asylum when they caught her in the trunk of a car on August 26, she would've applied, and that by *not* informing her, they violated her constitutional rights, and therefore her removal was unconstitutional."

"If it please the court, that's *exactly* what I'm saying, Your Honor." *And so is the Supreme Court, you idiot,* she thought but did not say.

His smirk widened. "So your argument rests on whether the defendant's application for asylum would've been successful," he said. "Because if it wasn't successful—and I'm just following your own logic here, Ms. Jimenez—then the defendant would've exhausted all administrative remedies to her removal and the original order would've been legitimate. Is that right?"

"Your Honor, the outcome of Ms. Vega's asylum application is speculative and therefore irrelevant in law, although I believe she has a strong case. The point is that she was not offered that recourse."

"I get to decide what's relevant or not in my courtroom, Counsel."

"Very well, Your Honor." Mona literally bit her tongue.

"On what basis would the defendant have applied for asylum?" said the judge.

"Your Honor, as the court well knows, that is outside the scope of this court—"

"Once again, that's for me to decide," said the judge, his voice rising.

Mona thought, *What is this place? Where in hell am I? Does the law not apply here?* "My client's fear of persecution is genuine, Your Honor."

"You haven't answered my question, Counsel," said the judge.

"Your Honor, Ms. Vega intends to apply for asylum on the basis of belonging to a persecuted group."

"And which group is that?"

"Women in Mexico who experience domestic abuse, Your Honor."

The judge laughed out loud. "*That's* her claim? She's persecuted because she's a woman? Why not let in *all* Mexican women, Counsel?"

Mona thought of all the women murdered in Ciudad Juárez. If they'd been a few hundred meters north, in El Paso, they'd be alive today.

"While we're at it, why not let in all women everywhere in the world?" continued the judge. "Do you think we ought to give asylum to *all* the women in the world, Counsel?"

"Only those who request protection from systemic gender violence, Your Honor."

The court was dead quiet now. Everyone paying close attention. Mona could taste blood on her tongue.

"Asylum law requires that the social group claiming prosecution be visible, Counsel," said the judge. "Otherwise, it's not a group. Now, how in the world are you going to convince this court that women in Mexico who experience domestic abuse are visible as a distinct group? Do they meet at a clubhouse? Do they wear distinctive clothing?"

"For some groups, being visible is just too dangerous, Your Honor."

Before she could expand on that, the judge interrupted her with his own train of thought. "And what I want to know is, if Ms. Vega felt so threatened by her spouse, why didn't she just leave him? She didn't need to sneak into the United States in the trunk of a car just to get away from him. She could've just moved to another town within Mexico."

"Ms. Vega's abuser has a reach much greater than most,

Your Honor. He's a high-ranking member of the Caballeros de Cristos cartel. He could get to her pretty much anywhere in Mexico. Internal relocation is not a reasonable option for Ms. Vega."

"Then why didn't she just go to the police?"

Mona almost laughed. "Your Honor, the present state of security in Mexico prevents Ms. Vega from having any confidence that the police could or would provide her with adequate protection. Her only reasonable recourse was to leave the country entirely."

The judge gave an exasperated wave of the hand and leaned back in his chair. "I'm losing patience, Ms. Jimenez. Women are not a group, the defendant's asylum request is not plausible, and I'm dismissing your motion. You've wasted enough of my time already. This is an arraignment, and your client must enter a plea. But before she does," he said, tipping himself forward, that supercilious smile returning to his face, "I want to make sure she understands her rights. I would hate anyone to accuse *me* of denying Ms. Vega due process."

"Your Honor—"

"No, that's enough, Counsel. Sit down." The judge told Carmen to stand. He asked her to confirm her name, nationality, and age. Then he said, "Carmen Vega, do you understand that you are facing two years' incarceration in a federal institution? And that at the end of any sentence you may serve, you will be returned to the custody of ICE, who will remove you from the United States?"

There was a delay while the interpreter did her job.

"*Sí*," said Carmen.

"And do you understand that after your removal, you will be banned from returning to the United States for a further ten years, or face felony charges carrying penalties of up to ten years in jail?"

Carmen said she did.

"Then I hope, for your sake, that your lawyer bore all that in mind when she advised you on what to say today," said the judge. "Carmen Vega, to the charge of illegal re-entry after removal, how do you plead?"

Carmen glanced anxiously at Mona. Mona gave her a reassuring nod. Carmen took a breath, straightened her back, and said, "*Inocente.*"

Unnecessarily, the interpreter interpreted. There followed a long silence.

"The court has noted that the defendant has pleaded not guilty to the charge of illegal reentry after removal, 8 USC 1326," said the judge in a flat tone. "The court will now set a tentative schedule for trial." Another long silence while he looked at something on his desk, Mona figured a calendar. Finally, he set a date sixty days hence, saying that was the earliest slot available. Mona knew that sixty days was the maximum delay allowed between arraignment and trial. Judge Ross didn't need to wait sixty days, she thought. He was doing it to punish her. She stood up.

"Your Honor, given the extraordinarily long delay until trial, we move that the court review Ms. Vega's bail status," she said.

"Motion denied. I don't grant bail to illegal entries, Ms. Jimenez. They just disappear into the population. The defendant can stay at Paradise Detention Center with the rest of them. Be grateful, Counsel; at least there, she'll be safe."

"Then I move that the court set an earlier date."

The judge gave a theatrical sigh. "I wish I could accommodate you, Ms. Jimenez. However, as you can see, mine is a busy court. Sixty days is the earliest I can do."

Judge Ross brought down his gavel, stood, and disappeared through the door to his chambers. Mona turned to Carmen. The bailiff was already putting the shackles back on her ankles.

FIVE

THE following Monday, Finn got up early, drove over to Torrance, picked up Gomez, then drove sixty miles east on the Riverside Freeway to March Air Reserve Base.

"You call the union?" said Gomez.

"No. You?"

Gomez shook his head.

"I was going to, but then I figured, I'm still getting paid. Why not take it easy for a while out at Riverside? Learn something new. Let things run their course."

"You're not wrong."

"Also, I *did* Taser him. There's no denying that."

"You did. Any regrets?" said Finn.

"Hell no."

They talked shit about Figueroa for a while, then fell into an easy silence.

At March Air Reserve Base, they went through one security checkpoint at the perimeter, then a second one at the AMOC campus located within the base. An agent met them at the security gate. Young and friendly, she introduced herself as Leela. Finn only learned her last name—Santos—from her name tag. From the badge on her arm, he learned that she was a detection enforcement officer. She wore thick-rimmed spectacles and two diamond studs in each ear. He and Gomez followed her into a plain, warehouse-type structure that, Leela informed them, was known as Building 605C.

"605C. Pretty bland name for a place that watches half the world," said Gomez.

"This isn't a place that wants to draw attention to itself," said Leela.

"How long have you been at AMOC?" said Finn.

"A year."

"What were you doing before?"

"Before I joined CBP, you mean? I worked in retail while I was at college."

"You went straight to AMOC out of college?"

"Yup."

"What did you study at college?"

"Computer science."

Finn nodded. Before he'd joined the CBP, he'd served in the navy's Maritime Expeditionary Security Force in Iraq during the insurgency, guarding oil terminals from sabotage. Klein was right. Times *were* changing.

They came to a set of doors that required Leela to use her swipe card. Finn heard the door's locking mechanism click, and he followed her and Gomez into a vast, dimly lit room.

"Welcome to the AMOC nerve center," said Leela.

At the far end was a screen maybe eight feet high and thirty feet wide, onto which were projected four separate radar displays. The one in the center covered the entire continental United States. Finn recognized the outline of Florida on the right side of the screen, covered with thousands of moving green crosses. Below the wall screen were several rows of cubicles, along which were arranged dozens of monitors. There were about seventy or eighty people in the room, their faces softly lit by the monitors' glow. It occurred to Finn that he hadn't been in a command and control center like this since Iraq.

"So I was thinking I'd start by showing you what I do, then show you the different operations," said Leela. She led them to her station, which comprised a triptych of monitors in a cubicle. Finn sat down on one side of her, Gomez on the other. Leela typed in a password, and all three screens lit up. She dragged the cursor over a projection of the coast of Southern California.

"So we get data from a bunch of different sources," she said. "Air traffic control radars, satellites, radar balloons, aircraft like P-3 Orions, and UAVs. My job is to monitor it all and flag anything suspicious. This here, for example, is a satellite feed."

Finn looked to the screen she was pointing at. He saw dozens of little green crosses moving across a digital map of the sea off Long Beach.

"It's usually busier than that," said Gomez.

"That's only what the satellite's showing us. If I add all the shipping data, it looks like this." Leela clicked a checkbox on the menu on the right of the screen, and dozens more crosses appeared—vessel identifiers broadcast from transponders aboard cargo ships. Finn saw that most of the new crosses were crowded into the fairway leading into the Long Beach container terminal.

"And then I can overlay air traffic over all that," said Leela, checking another box. Instantly, hundreds of red crosses appeared, clustered into the corridors leading into the various airports around LA. Now there was so much happening on the screen that it was almost impossible to read. He pointed at the jumble of dots and crosses.

"You can pick something suspicious out of all that?" he said.

"Sometimes. I look for signature behaviors. Like, for instance, if a plane veers outside its flight path, or a ship stops far out from the coast. But most of our useful maritime data comes from visuals. I usually check them before I flag anything for interception. Especially if the vessel is too small to pick up on radar or satellite."

"Visuals from planes, you mean?"

"Sometimes. Although we're using UAVs more and more. Like this."

Leela typed, and an aerial view of the sea appeared on one of the monitors. Finn could see sailboats from above.

"This is live," said Leela. She pointed at the sailboats. "We can't see anything that small from satellites. That's why the UAVs are so useful. Unlike regular aircraft, they can stay in the air for twenty-four hours."

Finn pondered. Every intercept they'd made over the past three months had been that small. He looked around the room. "What's its altitude?"

"Overland, the FAA says it has to stay above nineteen thousand feet. Overwater? Whatever we want. We usually cruise at five thousand feet."

"Who's flying it?" he said.

"The UAV operators. They work in crews like in real aircraft. One to fly the UAV, one to operate the cameras and sensors."

"Where are they?"

"They've got their own room, just down the corridor. We call it the *drone den*."

"Can we see it?" said Finn.

He detected a moment's hesitation before Leela said, "Sure."

⁕⁕⁕⁕⁕

Leela led them to a door with a sign on it that read UAV GROUND CONTROL. AUTHORIZED PERSONNEL ONLY. NO

FOOD OR DRINK. Her swipe card didn't work here. She had to knock.

The door swung open, and a tall young man stuck his head out, saw Leela, and smirked.

"Leela," said the young man, drawing out the vowels—*Lee-laa*—and touching his tongue to his lip on the middle *L* in a way that struck Finn as discourteous, at best. Leela gave the dude an icy look. She turned to Finn and Gomez.

"This is Agent Nader. He operates the UAV's sensors," she said.

Nader glanced from Leela to Finn and Gomez. He scanned the badges on their uniforms. "You the guys from the Long Beach station?"

Finn nodded.

Nader held open the door. "Welcome to the den, gentlemen," he said. "Please, step inside. You, too, Lee-laa."

Finn, Gomez, and Leela entered the room. Nader shut the door behind them. It was a small, musty-smelling space crowded with equipment: screens and dials, keyboards and joysticks. In front of the controls were two large, padded, tilting chairs, not unlike La-Z-Boys. The space struck Finn as part flight simulator and part computer-game lounge. One of the two chairs contained a young man wearing a headset, holding a joystick, and drinking a can of Rip It energy drink, which he presently perched precariously on the control panel in front of him in order to give a wave to the visitors. Nader introduced him as Harrison Sperling.

"Harrison flies the aircraft. I'm the eyes," said Nader, sitting down in the empty chair. Finn, Gomez, and Leela stood at the back.

The two largest screens in front of the operators showed the same bird's-eye view of yachts crisscrossing a square of sea that Leela had shown them in the command center.

The yachts' sails cast long, triangular shadows on the water. Finn saw the numbers on the screen giving the UAV's navigation data: airspeed, ground speed, altitude, heading. The drone was at five thousand feet, as Leela had told him. The resolution was extraordinary. As the drone traveled, a peninsula appeared at the top of the screen. Finn instantly recognized the round structure of Catalina Casino.

"Pretty cool, huh? You ever seen anything like this before?" said Nader.

"We had drones in Iraq."

Finn figured neither operator was old enough to have served in Iraq.

"Not like this one," said Nader, who seemed annoyed by Finn's response. "The MQ-9 Predator drone. Costs $16 million. The cameras alone cost two and a half million bucks. They're amazing. Watch this."

He hit some dials, and the screen started zooming in on one of the yachts in Avalon Bay. Finn kept expecting the resolution to diminish, but it stayed sharp. Soon he could count the number of people in the cockpit. He could see that the man at the wheel was wearing a blue hat. Nader kept zooming. A woman wearing a bikini was sitting with her legs up in the yacht's cockpit. Nader zoomed in on her breasts.

"It's a blue-sky day." Nader smirked. "Great visibility. Even from five thousand feet."

"You're not authorized to monitor U.S. citizens," said Leela.

"You think she's a citizen? I can't tell from this angle," said Nader.

Finn thought about what Klein had said, about scraping the bottom of the recruitment barrel. If this was the best that the CBP could attract to fly aircraft worth millions, the agency was in trouble.

"Explain to me why you're flying over Catalina," said

Finn. "I've patrolled that sector for ten years. Traffickers don't go to the islands. They head for the mainland."

"I like the view," said Nader.

The pilot, Sperling, was more circumspect.

"Mostly, we preset the trajectory," he said. "Then we let the plane fly itself. That lets us focus on looking for any signature behaviors—overcrowded vessels, evasive actions, traveling dark, that kind of thing—that we can signal to you guys out on the water."

"How do you determine the trajectory?" said Finn.

"It depends on a number of factors," said Sperling. "We know traffickers like to be over the horizon when they cross the sea border, out of sight of land. We know they like to time it so that they start coming into shore under the cover of darkness—that's another consideration. Add into that all the FAA's regulations and airspace controls—we can't put the drones in the way of airport approaches, for instance, and we need to stay above and below certain altitudes—as well as weather forecasts, and you start to get the idea. We can't cover everything, so we try to cover a different sector each sortie. Anything to increase our chances of finding people doing things they shouldn't be. We come up with a flight plan, then we discuss it with the operations director during the briefing. He has final say."

SIX

MONA was so busy with other work, she didn't manage to get out to Paradise again until almost three weeks after Carmen's arraignment. Mona didn't need to go, but she felt close to Carmen. She wanted to show her a friendly face.

She set off early, with a mug of coffee and a pack of doughnut holes. She had the radio playing. A few miles outside Paradise, the hourly news bulletin came on. The big story that day was that the president had nominated Michael Marvin, the CEO of the Border Security Corporation of America, to head the Department of Homeland Security. The news bulletin carried a sound bite of the president: "Michael's a businessman, like me. He's someone who knows how to get things done. We need someone in charge of Homeland Security who knows how to deal with these people."

Mona switched off the radio. *These people.* It was getting hot, so she turned on the AC. The vent started rattling. She reminded herself to get it checked out. The car was long overdue for a service.

Finally, she pulled into the detention center lot. Although she hadn't seen a snake, she still checked the ground before opening the car door. Once she was sure it was all clear, she grabbed her briefcase and a Nordstrom

bag from the passenger seat and made her way to the entrance.

Thanks to Operation No Return, the private-prison
business was booming. Yet more people had arrived at
PDC since Mona's last visit, and to accommodate them,
the center had erected a hangar-sized tent in the yard.
When Mona asked the guard if the tent was heated—in
the desert, the temperature dropped to thirty degrees at
night—he shrugged. "We give them blankets," he said.

She sat down and waited at the table where she'd first
interviewed Carmen.

When Carmen appeared, Mona barely recognized her.
She'd put on more weight than Mona thought possible in
three weeks. Her skin was blotchy, her hair dirty and un-
kempt, her eyes devoid of the river-stone gleam that had
struck Mona the first time they'd met. After just a month
in detention, her features had coarsened; her nose and
ears seemed larger, and her eyes farther apart, as though
she'd aged a decade. She reminded Mona of a drug addict nearing bottom—the dead look in the eyes, the bad
skin. Incarceration ought to come with a health warning,
she thought. Not only was prison food disgusting, it was
unhealthy; Mona had pulled up next to a man unloading
catering supplies from a truck. She'd seen him forklift off
a fifty-five-gallon drum of cooking oil and had pictured
the giant fry cookers inside the detention center kitch-
ens, all the lumps of cheap, preprepared foods sputtering
through them. No wonder Carmen looked the way she
did. *I should've brought her some fruit,* Mona thought.

"I haven't been feeling well," said Carmen, as though
reading Mona's thoughts. "The toilets overflowed again.
Everybody's getting sick."

"Did you ask to see the doctor?" said Mona.

Carmen hesitated. "Yes. He gave me some medicine."
Then, changing the subject, she pointed at the tent and

said, "Did you see that? Fifty more people arrived. They told me 150 more are coming. But they didn't build any new toilets. Two hundred more people using toilets that are already overflowing? *No es posible*."

It was depressing to hear the emptiness in Carmen's voice. Mona tried to sound cheery.

"I brought you a present," she said. She placed the Nordstrom bag on the picnic table, hoping its contents wouldn't be too small. "It's to wear in court. The first impression you make on the jury is vital. I thought this might be appropriate."

Carmen opened the package and unfolded the dress it contained. It was a conservative long-sleeve number that fell below the knee. Mona had told the sales assistant she wanted something she could wear in church.

"Americans like women who don't threaten them," she told Carmen. "Hopefully, you'll feel comfortable in it, too."

There was also a navy cardigan in the package, which Mona said was to guard against the courtroom air-conditioning, as well as a pair of sensible flats.

"Do you need some shampoo or conditioner?" said Mona in what she hoped was a neutral tone. "I can give you more credit at the commissary."

Carmen smiled. "*Está bien,*" she said. "I got a job washing dishes in the canteen. It earns a few cents. They pay it into my commissary account."

But there was still nothing in her voice. No hope, no sense of nervous anticipation about her trial. Like she'd been vacated.

"Carmen, I am *very* confident about your case. Remember how I told you *la migra* made a terrible mistake in San Ysidro? Well, the judge made an even worse one when he denied you bail. Once I show the jury what they did, the law says that they're going to have to let you go. And they can't force you to go back. You understand?

You'll be able to stay in America until your application for asylum is processed."

Carmen smiled distractedly. "He knows I'm here."

Mona furrowed her brow. "Who?"

"Soto. He has found me."

Mona shook her head. "No. That's impossible."

Carmen hugged herself. "Do you know why snakes stick out their tongues?" she said. "To smell. They use their tongues."

She's depressed, thought Mona. *I need to get a psychiatrist in here to assess her mental health, maybe get her on some medication.*

"Last night I had a dream," said Carmen. "He came to me and flicked out his tongue. He said, '*I can* smell *you,* puta. *I know where you are.*'"

Mona glanced at the guard. He was the same one she'd met the first time. He was looking the other way. Mona took the girl's hands in hers. They were trembling.

"Carmen, listen to me," she said. "It's the stress of being in here. It makes you dream crazy things. It's natural; it happens to everyone. Try not to think about it."

Carmen shook her head. She was adamant. "No. I'm not crazy. He's *here.* I can feel him."

Carmen bit her lower lip, trying to stop the tears. For a brief moment, Mona felt an unkind impulse to tell Carmen to pull herself together. Mona could control the administrative stuff, and she was a brilliant legal scholar, but there was little she could do when people behaved irrationally, and that annoyed her. She tried to hide it by nodding sympathetically and pressing the girl's hands while she cried.

"I miss my parents," said Carmen. "I miss my sister."

It was the first time she'd ever said she missed them.

"Do you want to call them?" said Mona.

"No. Absolutely not," said Carmen. She wiped away the

tears with the back of her hand and made an attempt to pull herself together. "I'm fine. You're right; it's just a bad feeling. I'm better now."

Mona gave her a warm smile. "Tell me about home," she said.

She smiled. "My mother is probably cooking. My father is probably watching football on TV. My sister, Clara, is probably at school. The same middle school I went to, near the stadium. We could hear the crowd roar whenever our team scored. I knew before I got home whether we'd won or not and what kind of mood my father would be in."

"What team does he support?"

"Los Cementeros, of course."

Mona knew she was talking about Cruz Azul, a storied Mexico City soccer team founded by a cement company.

Carmen looked at the label of the dress Mona had brought. "*Oyé, mujer,* what size do you think I am? I'll have to go on a diet," she said with a put-on frown. That's when Mona noticed her nails. She'd chewed them back to the flesh. Mona fished a bottle of neutral nail polish out of her handbag. "Here," she said. "We have the same skin tone. It'll look good on you."

"Beige. Perfect for court," said Carmen with a little smile.

"Exactly. In court, you'll be like Dolores Romero before she finds . . ." Mona was about to say, "The snake charmer who gives Dolores the antidote." But Mona knew there was no remedy for the scars Soto had left on Carmen. Not even in Hollywood. "Before she finds love," she said simply.

SEVEN

WHILE Mona was driving out to the desert to see Carmen, Finn was sitting in Klein's office. He had arranged a meeting to discuss the complaint filed against him.

"I've called everyone," said Klein. "No one can give me any answers."

"I'm dying out there in Riverside, Keith," said Finn. "Staring at a screen all day."

"What can I tell you? It's a great big bureaucratic swamp. Has been since 2002. Nothing happens."

"Just give me a number and a name. Someone I can talk to."

"You want to call up yourself, hassle the inspector general about their investigation of *you*? Bad idea," said Klein. "Listen, I'm in charge of this station, and I want you back on the water more than anyone. Believe me, I've tried everything. I called Bill Olds, the head of Air and Marine, a guy I've known twenty years, ever since I joined what was then still just Border Patrol. You know what Bill says to me? 'Sorry, Keith, I can't help you. Try Delford Payne.' I say, 'Delford Payne, who's that?' He says, 'The new assistant secretary for complaints and whistleblowers at the OIG.'"

Klein threw up his hands to signal exasperation.

"So of course I call this guy, the assistant secretary for complaints and whistleblowers, as soon as I get off the phone from Bill. And *he* says, 'The investigation is progressing normally.'

"I say, 'Excuse me, but I was born on the Fourth of July. This year, I turn fifty-seven. You know what that means? Mandatory retirement. Before I retire, my one patriotic wish is to see Marine Interdiction Agent Nick Finn back out on the water, intercepting bad guys. Am I gonna get my wish?' He says, 'I cannot comment on an ongoing investigation.'"

Klein shook his head dismissively.

"Asshole," he said.

"What about the secretary of Homeland Security?" said Finn.

"The *acting* secretary, you mean? Steve Fishman? He won't do a damn thing. Doesn't want to rock the boat. He's just there to keep the seat warm until Michael Marvin's confirmed. Maybe when Marvin's in, he'll fix this. He seems like the type of guy who gets things done. But until then . . ."

Klein threw his hands in the air again.

"It's a goddamned mess, Finn. Nobody knows anything. Everybody's covering their butts. My best Interceptor captain's sitting on the dock, twiddling his thumbs, and nobody's responsible. Meanwhile, they're pushing this surge in recruitment, but no one wants to work for the CBP anymore, so they're hiring anybody who shows up at the booth. Guys like Figueroa. In all honesty, I'm looking forward to retirement, Finn. I don't recognize the CBP today. It's not what I joined."

Finn felt for Klein. Morale was down across the whole agency. Nobody was happy, including him.

Klein leaned back in his chair. "You know what I'm gonna do when I retire, Finn? I'm gonna go to my condo, and I'm gonna catch some fish."

Finn smiled. "Where's the condo?"

"Loreto. On the Sea of Cortez."

"Plenty of fish still in the Sea of Cortez," said Finn.

Klein gave Finn an apologetic look. "I hope you get back on the water before I do, Finn. But there's nothing more I can do. You have to be patient."

Finn got up.

"Where're you going?" said Klein.

"Riverside. Where else?"

"Are you learning anything useful out there, at least?" said Klein. "Have you seen the future?"

Finn pondered this.

"Yes. She's twenty-four years old and has a degree in computer science."

Klein shook his head.

"Jesus H. Christ," he said.

◆◆◆◆◆

Building 605C had its own canteen. Today was Chinese day. At lunch, Finn loaded up on kung pao chicken and an immoderate pile of fried rice. He noticed Leela put only vegetables on her tray and a small amount of steamed rice. Gomez was off that day.

Finn and Leela stood at the end of the food counter holding their trays, scanning the room for an empty table. Finn saw a group of young men, Nader and Sperling among them, sitting together, laughing loudly. Leela headed in the opposite direction, away from them. Finn followed. They found a quiet table in the far corner.

Finn, still despondent from his meeting with Klein that morning, started eating mindlessly. After a minute, he became aware first of the look of aversion on Leela's face, then of the fact that he had already shoveled half the plate of rice into his mouth.

"Sorry," he said, his mouth half full.

"Don't apologize. I eat when I'm stressed, too."

Finn swallowed what was in his mouth and put down his fork.

"I spoke to my station director this morning," he said. "I'm no closer to getting back on the water."

Leela nodded. "I'm sorry to hear it," she said.

An awkward silence ensued. Finn made an effort to put aside his gloomy mood.

"My wife's happy, at least. She gets anxious that something'll happen to me out there," he said.

"What does your wife do?" said Leela.

"She's a lawyer. She represents undocumented migrants," said Finn.

Leela opened her mouth to ask the question that Finn guessed was on her mind.

"We're happily married," he said preemptively.

"No. Of course. I didn't mean . . ."

"It's fine," said Finn. "People want to know how we do it, a CBP agent married to a migrants-rights activist. It's pretty simple. We don't discuss our differences in front of other people. If there's something we need to discuss, we talk when we're alone."

Leela looked impressed. "That's so basic. I mean, I get it. But it's so basic."

"Yeah. We figured it out early." In fact, they'd figured it out when they'd first started dating after Diego had introduced them. But Diego's death still grieved him, and he wanted to avoid the "How did you two meet?" question he sensed was coming. He changed the subject.

"What about you?" he said. "How did you get from computer science to working for Customs and Border Protection?"

"The CBP had a booth at careers day at my college. They were offering bonuses to anyone with a computer science degree who signed up for two years. I figured two years wasn't long, and the bonus helped pay down my college debt. How about you?"

"I joined up right after I got out of the navy."

"Right. You were in Iraq. What was that like?"

"Not that different from what I do here. I was in the Maritime Expeditionary Security Force. We guarded oil terminals in Basra from insurgents. We patrolled the bay, basically."

Leela picked up an orange from her tray and started peeling it.

"Seems like a lot of the old guys who work here are veterans. The guy who parks his motorcycle next to mine in the lot has got a 'Proudly Served' plate on it."

Finn didn't usually feel old, but spending time with Leela shifted his frame of reference.

"How do you know he's an old guy?" he said.

"Rides a Harley," said Leela.

Finn smiled.

"What are the young people riding these days?" he said.

"Right now I'm on a Kawasaki Ninja 650, but I'm saving for a bigger bike."

Finn nodded.

"The CBP's a good place for us old guys," he said. "Lets us do something useful in civilian life. That's all you can ask for. What about you? What are you planning to do after your two years?"

"I'll probably go to the private sector."

"In computers?"

"IT, yeah. With AMOC on my résumé, I could probably get something good in data security. I've become really interested in data security since working here."

"I don't know much about computers."

"No, you don't," agreed Leela.

"Data security, that means passwords?"

"It means protecting data. I'll give you an example. You know everything we see on the cameras from the drones, that's all recorded, right?"

Finn shook his head. "I did not know that."

"It's all stored on our servers, and we're supposed to destroy it after five years. Imagine if someone got ahold of that."

Finn thought of Nader zooming in on the yacht.

"Do they store just the video or all the data?" said Finn.

"They store everything. All the surveillance recordings and all the flight data."

Finn stared at Leela. "How hard would it be to get into our system?" he said.

Leela lowered her voice. "Honestly? A high school hacker could do it."

⁙

After lunch, Finn sat next to Leela at her station. Leela started typing.

"How come you're so interested in the flight paths?" she said.

Finn thought for a moment. He liked and trusted Leela, but he wasn't ready to share his hunch with her.

"The Interceptors patrol predetermined sectors," he said. "But we don't know where the drones are flying. I figure if we coordinated our missions, we'd be more efficient. We'd cover more area."

Leela nodded. "Makes sense," she said. She pointed at the middle of her three screens. "All right, here we go. Here are the logs of every flight out of Riverside for the past six months. They'll give us distances, altitudes, flight time, fuel loads . . ."

"Can you show us the flight paths on a map?" said Finn.

"Sure."

Leela maneuvered the cursor around the screen and clicked a few buttons. A map appeared. Finn saw a red line leaving Riverside, bearing southwest, over the sea to south of San Clemente Island, then back east toward San Diego before finally heading north, back to Riverside. On the screen, it looked like a slice of pizza, with Riverside at the pointy end, San Clemente at one end of the crust and San Diego at the other. He noted that the drone descended to an altitude of five thousand feet overwater, which allowed it to survey a five-mile-wide corridor of the sea beneath it.

"Can you overlay all the flights? To compare them?" asked Finn.

Leela opened the next file. This one covered another pizza slice, but a few miles south of the first one. She opened another, and then another, until she had opened them all. When she had finished, almost all the sea off the coast of Southern California was covered with drone flight paths.

Almost.

Finn saw a narrow, sixty-five-mile-long unpatrolled corridor from the maritime border with Mexico north of the Coronados to Dana Point.

"They're sending pangas to distract us," he murmured.

"What?" said Leela.

"We've picked up just one drug boat so far this year," said Finn. "And that was only because I ignored the intel. I made the intercept here."

He pointed at a spot off Dana Point, inside the corridor.

"They're sending pangas into the drones' flight paths. They know we're going to find them. Then they sneak go-fasts through here."

Finn thought back to the night he had intercepted the

go-fast. He remembered what one of the narcos he'd cuffed had said: *"No debe estar por aquí."*

Finn looked around the operations center.

"The cartel knows where the drones are flying," he said.

•••••

"Who else knows about this?" said Klein.

"Just Detection Enforcement Officer Santos," said Finn.

"The computer science kid?"

Finn nodded. He was in Klein's office again, eight hours after he'd been there the first time.

Klein picked up the phone on his desk and pressed some keys.

"This is Operations Director Keith Klein at the Long Beach Air and Marine Station," said Klein into the phone. "I'd like to speak with the commissioner of Customs and Border Protection, please . . . Yes, as soon as he can. Be sure to tell him it's urgent."

Klein hung up. He checked his watch. "He's giving a briefing at the White House. He's going to call me back."

He leaned back in his chair and looked at the ceiling pensively. "Jesus H. Christ," he said. He tilted forward again and turned to Finn. "The computer science kid. Can *she* find the hacker?"

"She's working on it. But it might *not* be a hacker."

"What do you mean?"

"It could be someone on the inside, feeding the cartel information."

Klein stared at Finn. "Jesus H. Christ," he said again. "You're right."

"Someone who has access to the UAV flight briefings. Who knows the flight plans."

Klein scrunched up his face. "You mean a *pilot*?"

"Or a systems operator."

Klein thought for a moment. "All right. I'll speak to the commissioner. We'll set up a probe and do background checks, see if anyone's been looking at things they're not supposed to, or spending more than we're paying them. But, Finn, if there *is* a mole, we don't want to spook him. All right? Everyone carries on as normal. Tell the computer science kid."

Finn gestured at the map of Southern California hanging on Klein's wall. "What about the corridor?"

"We'll have to put an Interceptor there, plug the hole," said Klein. "I'll call you as soon as I've spoken to the commissioner."

EIGHT

MONA left the detention center feeling completely spent. The moral effort she had made to boost Carmen, along with the exhausting tedium of the long drive she'd made to get there, had drained her of all her energy.

She decided to take a room at a motel she'd passed on the way into town. She would head home early in the morning. She knew she wouldn't be able to expense the room, but the alternative—driving back to Redondo in the dark—felt like more than she was capable of.

The motel was called the Eden Inn. She took the cheapest room, lay down on the bed, and looked at the ceiling. It was a hideous ceiling, with peeling paint and a damp patch in one corner. She considered taking a walk outside to take in the beautiful colors in the evening sky, but her weary mind could not shake the idea that the desert was crawling with snakes, and she did not have the energy to defy what she knew was an irrational fear. So instead she took an unsatisfying shower—the stall was cramped, the water pressure barely existent—then wrapped herself in the threadbare towel. Realizing she hadn't eaten, Mona opened the bar fridge and discovered a bowl of apples with a laminated card reading, "Complimentary fruit from the Garden of Eden."

Mona bit into an apple and called Finn.

"You sound tired," he said.

"I couldn't face the road, so I checked into a motel. I'll be home tomorrow."

"Good idea. Where are you?"

"The Eden Inn outside Paradise."

"Sounds nice."

She took another bite. "It isn't," she said. "I miss you."

"I miss you, too."

"Anything happening with the complaint?"

"I went to see Klein. He hasn't heard anything. He said to wait."

"I'm sorry. But at least I don't have to worry about something happening to you out on the water."

"Yeah. Listen, today at Riverside, I found something shocking."

"What?"

"I think maybe the cartel knows where our drones are flying. That's why their drug boats are getting past us."

"How do you know?"

"We haven't seen a go-fast for months. None of the crews have. I had a hunch something's not right. So I looked at the flight path data. Every flight, the drone covers 90 percent of the sector. There's always a corridor left open."

"You think the cartel knows this?"

"I think they're seeing the flight paths before the drones fly. Either someone's giving it to them or they've hacked the system. Leela says the system security there is really bad."

"Who's Leela?"

"She's a detection enforcement officer at AMOC. She's been showing me around."

Another irrational fear rose up in Mona. She ignored it.

"Do you trust her?" she said.

"Yes," said Finn without hesitating.

"Have you told anyone else?"

"Klein. He's taking it to the commissioner."

"Do you trust him?"

"The commissioner of Customs and Border Protection?"

"No. Klein."

"He was at our wedding."

"Of course. Sorry."

"You sound as tired as I feel," Finn said.

"So what's happening next?"

"Klein will tell the commissioner. My guess is, the commissioner will take it to the secretary of Homeland Security."

For the third time that evening, a feeling of unfounded dread took hold in Mona. "Michael Marvin?"

"No. He's not confirmed yet. The acting secretary. Steve Fishman. He may take it to the White House."

"Nick?"

"Yes?"

"Promise me you'll be careful."

•••••

Mona fell asleep. She dreamed strange dreams: standing in the desert, looking up at a beautiful cloudless sky, then a moment later standing in a torrential downpour facing Carmen, who was wearing a bikini, steam rising from her burning skin, but Carmen still smiling, a persistent buzzing sound coming out of her mouth. Mona woke with a start. She realized the buzzing was coming from her cell phone vibrating on the bedside table. She reached for it. The call was coming from a number with no caller ID. Butterflies took flight in her stomach.

"Ms. Jimenez?" said a man's voice she didn't recognize.

"Yes?"

"My name is Lou Pischedda. I'm the warden at Paradise Detention Center. One of our detainees, Carmen Vega, designated you as her contact."

"Carmen? Is she all right?" said Mona.

"I'm afraid not, Ms. Jimenez. There's been an incident. Ms. Vega is dead."

✦✦✦✦✦

"She was still breathing when I got there," the doctor said.

They were in the warden's office at Paradise Detention Center. Mona was sitting in one of two visitors' chairs in front of the warden's desk. The doctor was sitting in the other. He had a lanyard round his neck with a security pass on the end, the pass resting on the bulge of his belly. His shirt was too tight, the fabric straining away from the buttons when he twisted toward her. His name was Dr. Woods.

"We did everything we could," the doctor went on.

"The well-being of our detainees is paramount to us," added the warden. "We've never had anything like this happen before."

Mona's briefcase was on the edge of the warden's desk, next to his nameplate: LOU PISCHEDDA. He handed Mona a document.

"The incident report," he said.

"Who wrote it?"

"I did."

Mona started reading. Shortly before six the previous evening—about an hour after Mona had left—the guards did their usual head count when the detainees came in from the yard for dinner. The count came up one short. They found Carmen slumped on a bench near the perimeter fence. The bench was not visible from the door leading into the canteen, on account of the tent that had been erected in the middle of the yard. At 6:05 P.M., they called the nurse.

Mona looked up. "The guards who found her. Are they trained first responders?"

"Excuse me?" said Pischedda.

"They found her unconscious and called for assistance. Why didn't they try to revive her themselves?"

"They followed our protocol. When it's an emergency of a medical nature, our people are trained to call one of our medical professionals."

"That's your protocol in an emergency? Stand around and wait for a nurse to show up?"

The warden's leather seat squeaked.

Mona turned to Dr. Woods. "It says here, you gave her a shot of epinephrine. Why?"

"She presented a weak pulse. Her tongue was swollen. I determined she had had an anaphylactic episode."

"You didn't realize it was a snakebite?"

"Anaphylaxis is one of the symptoms of opioid overdose."

Mona bristled. "You thought she was on *drugs*?"

The warden intervened. "It's around, unfortunately. They find a way—"

"No. Carmen did not use drugs."

"Well, let's see what the coroner finds," said the warden, his show of sympathy failing to mask the condescension in his tone.

Mona turned back to the doctor. "It says here, you called 911 at 7:20 P.M. It doesn't say when you gave her the epinephrine," said Mona.

"Shortly before I made the call."

"How shortly?"

Dr. Woods looked at the warden, not Mona, when he said, "I examined the patient. I determined she was in anaphylactic shock. Accordingly, I gave her a shot of epinephrine. When I saw that the epinephrine was having no effect, I called 911."

"Are you even *able* to identify the symptoms of a snakebite, Dr. Woods?"

"If I may, Ms. Jimenez," said the warden. "I don't think we can draw any conclusions until the coroner's office have finished their report. But I've heard of cases like this. It's more common than people think."

Mona looked at the early light streaming through the high window above the warden's head. It was 6:15 A.M. She turned her attention back to the warden. Lou Pischedda was bald on top. He was wearing a suit and tie. He looked concerned. Or he was trying to look concerned. One or the other.

"Cases like this?" she said.

"When someone gets bitten and doesn't realize it, on a riverbank, or in the long grass. It happens so fast, people don't even realize they've stepped on a snake. They think it's just a bug, a hornet, or something like that." He moved his hands a lot when he talked.

"I thought they rattled," said Mona. "I thought you could hear them."

Pischedda shook his head. "Not all the time. Sometimes they're quiet."

"So let me get this straight: You think Carmen got bitten by a snake, didn't realize it, sat down on the bench, and died without anyone noticing?"

"Well, no. She was still alive when we found her. She died in the ambulance."

Mona searched the report. "At 7:36 P.M. Sixteen minutes after Dr. Woods called 911."

Neither man had anything to add to that.

"What did you do for those sixteen minutes, Dr. Woods?"

"I monitored the patient."

Mona stared at him the way a farmer stares down a gun barrel at a fox that's been taking her chickens. "You monitored her?"

"I made sure her airway remained clear. I gave her oxygen."

The warden intervened again. "Ms. Jimenez, I really think it's best if we wait for the coroner's report," he said. "To avoid any confusion."

"I'm not confused," said Mona. Then she said, "There's an expression in Spanish: *La serpiente se oculta en la hierba.*"

"I'm sorry?"

"I've been in the yard. There's no long grass. It's just dirt and concrete. If there were a snake on the ground, Carmen would've seen it. There's nowhere for a snake to hide."

The warden got up. "I don't think we can help you any further, Ms. Jimenez. As I said to you on the phone, this is an extremely rare and unusual incident. And of course tragic, too. Thank you for coming all the way out here."

Pischedda gestured toward the door.

"We'll be in touch," he said.

●●●●●

Outside, the cold lingered. Mona got into her RAV, turned on the ignition, and started the heater. The vent started rattling. She dialed Finn.

"Carmen's dead," she said. "She was bitten by a rattle-snake."

She started crying.

"I'm at the detention center. The doctor here didn't re-alize she'd been bitten. He didn't give her antivenin. He wants me to believe that Carmen nodded off. That she was a dope addict."

"I'm so sorry," said Finn.

"None of it makes any sense," sobbed Mona.

"Come home," said Finn.

Mona composed herself.

"No," she said. "She's at the hospital. I need to see her. I'm heading over there now."

•••••

At Paradise Hospital, Mona asked for whoever had signed Carmen's death certificate. While she waited, she looked at her reflection in the glass of a painting on the wall behind the reception counter, and wiped away the smudged makeup below her eyes. A balding man in scrubs appeared. He introduced himself as Dr. Aguirre.

"I'm trying to understand what happened to my client Carmen Vega," she said. "I was hoping to have something to tell her family."

"For a full report, you'll need to wait for the coroner," he said. "But I can tell you right now, your client was bitten by a snake. A big one. Three times on the right arm."

"How do you know it was big?"

"I'll show you."

The doctor led Mona to an office. He sat down at the desk and tapped something into the keyboard. Then he swiveled the monitor around so Mona could see.

Mona found herself looking at a tightly framed photo of human flesh. She saw two dark red dots. The flesh around them was swollen and black.

"This is a photo of one of the places where she was bitten, on the underside of her right arm, just below the elbow," said Dr. Aguirre. "You see these two red marks? Those are the fang marks. You can tell the size of a snake by the distance between its fangs. There's almost an inch between these two marks. A snake with fangs an inch apart is a big snake."

Mona looked away from the screen.

"It's rare, isn't it? What happened to Carmen?" she said.

Dr. Aguirre reflected.

"It's pretty rare to see bites from a snake this big," said Dr. Aguirre. "And it's especially rare to get bitten three times like Carmen did. That's why I took the photo. To show my residents. But it's not all that rare to get bitten. I've been working ER here for ten years, and we get a dozen or so snakebites every year, sometimes during spring, but mostly during summer. We rarely get fatalities, though. The last one I remember was back in 2010, a hiker crossing a stream up in the mountains who got bitten on the ankle. We get more people who die from dog bites than we do from snakes."

"Dr. Woods, the staff physician out at the detention center? He said he didn't realize that Carmen had been bitten by a snake."

"So I understand," said Dr. Aguirre. His face took on a set expression. Mona sensed that Dr. Aguirre didn't hold a high opinion of Dr. Woods. She guessed that a feeling of professional solidarity prevented him from articulating it.

It wasn't a feeling she shared.

"Dr. Aguirre, do you believe Carmen could've been saved? If Dr. Woods had proceeded differently, I mean?"

The ER doctor chose his words carefully. "Look, there's only one thing that works reliably against envenomation, and that's administering antivenin as soon as possible. If someone gets bitten by a snake, the best thing to do is keep them calm, try to get them to sit up so that their heart is higher than the limb where they were bitten, and get them some antivenin. Usually, that means getting them to the nearest hospital that stocks it."

"Do you stock it?"

"Of course. This is rattlesnake country."

"Do you know if they stock it at PDC?"

"What did Dr. Woods say?"

"He didn't."

Despite his best efforts, Mona spotted the cloud of disapproval pass over Dr. Aguirre's face.

"Antivenin is expensive stuff. My understanding is, they do things on a shoestring out there," he said.

"How expensive?"

"About $2,500 a vial. For a bite from a snake the size that likely bit Carmen, I would've used at least ten to fifteen vials."

A cold rage gripped Mona's heart. Did Carmen die because the BSCA was cutting costs?

"Dr. Aguirre, can you talk me through what it feels like to get bitten by a rattlesnake?"

"Certainly. Almost immediately, you'd feel a burning pain around the bite. The area around the bite would start swelling. You'd start feeling nauseous and light-headed to the point of throwing up. Your vision might go blurry. You might have trouble breathing. Most people panic, which makes it worse. Eventually, you'd start hemorrhaging internally. In a worst-case scenario, your heart would fail. That's what happened to Carmen."

"Dr. Woods believes Carmen may have been high on drugs—"

"If she was, it'll show up in the toxicology report."

"—and that as a result, she may not have realized it when the snake bit her."

Dr. Aguirre sniffed.

"That is not an opinion I share," he said.

"Do you have any idea how quickly Carmen died after getting bitten?" she asked.

He shook his head. "It depends on the dose. The bigger the dose, the quicker the effect. We'll have to wait for the toxicology report to find out how big a dose of venom she received, but based on the inter-fang distance, it's likely to be huge."

"Dr. Woods gave Carmen a shot of epinephrine. Would that have helped?"

Dr. Aguirre scoffed. "For someone suffering anaphylaxis, yes. For a snakebite? Nothing."

A moment passed.

"I'm very sorry for your loss, Ms. Jimenez," said Dr. Aguirre. "Your client was unbelievably unlucky. Very, very few people who get bitten by a snake die from it. If you get antivenin within two hours of being bitten, you've got a 99 percent chance of surviving."

Her voice cracking, Mona said, "Can I see her, Dr. Aguirre?"

Dr. Aguirre shook his head gently. "I'm sorry. Not unless you're family or have written authorization from them."

Mona thanked him and headed to her car.

All the way back to Redondo Beach, his words kept running through her mind: *Very, very few people who get bitten by a snake die from it.*

NINE

MONA got home and went to bed. She slept for twenty hours straight but was still tired when she woke up. Her joints were stiff as rods. The muscles in her neck were all knotted up. She had a headache.

But she made herself get up. She took a steaming-hot shower, then wiped the condensation off the mirror and took stock of what she saw.

She looked terrible—bags under her eyes, pasty-faced.

She got dressed, then returned to the bathroom and started carefully putting on makeup. Today was a day for a generous amount of concealer.

Finn came into the bathroom and looked at her in the mirror over her shoulder.

"You going out?" he said.

"I'm going to the office."

"Really?"

"I'll go crazy if I don't," she said.

Finn nodded. "I'll make breakfast," he said.

Mona came out to a huge fry-up in the kitchen: eggs, beans, bacon, a freshly brewed pot of coffee.

"This is hangover food," she said.

"You'll feel better after you eat."

Mona downed two Advil with her coffee, gave Finn a long hug, then drove to work. On the way in, she listened to the news bulletin on the radio. Some members of Congress had criticized the president's nomination for secretary of Homeland Security. They were saying his background in the for-profit prison industry created a conflict of interest. Mona lost the signal when she drove into the underground parking garage. She parked next to the white Macan.

The elevator door opened to reveal Joaquin in the Juntos reception area, standing over Natalie's desk. They broke off their conversation as soon as they saw Mona.

"I'm so sorry," said Joaquin.

Natalie got up and hugged her. "You okay?"

"Yes. I mean, no. I don't know. I think I'm still in shock," Mona said. She'd left home feeling better after Finn's breakfast, but hearing Michael Marvin's name on the radio had set off the jitters again.

"Take some time off. Go somewhere. I can cover your caseload," said Joaquin.

Mona shook her head firmly. "No. I've got work to do. I owe it to Carmen."

"It's over, Mona," said Joaquin gently. "There's no more case. I'm sorry."

"There's still a case."

"What do you mean?"

"We can sue the BSCA for wrongful death."

An awkward silence ensued. Finally, Joaquin said, "You know, Mona, sometimes things are exactly as they appear."

"If we were in court, I'd object on the grounds that you're being obscure," said Mona.

"The hospital said Carmen was bitten by a snake. So, maybe that's what happened. She was bitten by a snake."

"She *was* bitten by a snake."

"So what grounds do you have for a wrongful death suit?"

"If a diabetic inmate dies because the prison didn't provide her insulin, the prison is liable. Carmen was bitten by a rattlesnake, yet no one gave her antivenin. She died on the way to the hospital. That's neglect, Joaquin."

More silence.

"A wrongful death claim can only be brought by the victim's estate," said Joaquin.

"I know."

"Have you contacted her family?"

"No."

"So you have no one to represent."

"I'll find them."

"How?"

It was a good question. She didn't have much to go on. Carmen had told Mona that she'd grown up in Ciudad Nezahualcóyotl but that she'd left for Tijuana and that she'd had no contact with her parents or younger sister since leaving. So all Mona knew about Carmen's family was that they either lived or had lived in Ciudad Neza.

"I'll go to her hometown. Someone will know her."

"Where's she from?"

"Ciudad Nezahualcóyotl."

Joachim's face tightened. "A million people live in Ciudad Neza. You'll never find them."

"I can try."

"And even if you do find them, what then? The BSCA is the biggest private-prison operator in the world. The CEO is going to be the next secretary of Homeland Security. We're not the ACLU, Mona. We don't have the resources to fight them."

"It's the right thing to do, Joaquin."

"You're going to make me go prematurely gray," he said.

Natalie, who was standing next to him, looked up at his head.

"You already are. I can see it in your roots," she said.

Joaquin ignored her.

"Okay, let's just say by some miracle you find her parents and they agree to sue," he said to Mona. "Break it down for me. What would be your strategy?"

Mona had spent four and a half hours driving back from the detention center thinking about exactly that. To win the wrongful death claim against the BSCA, she would need to jump through a series of legal hoops: first, she would have to prove that the BSCA had a duty of care to Carmen; second, she would have to prove that the corporation was in breach of that duty; and finally, she would have to prove that Carmen died because of it.

"The BSCA built its detention center in known rattlesnake country. That's indisputable. There are signs all along the highway out there warning people not to stray from their cars. A reasonable person would assume that the BSCA's duty of care would include protecting the inmates in their facility from the rattlesnakes. Yet they put in place no measures to keep the snakes out. They don't stock antivenin in their medical center. And their training program for their guards is woefully inadequate: Why did it take so long for Carmen to receive medical attention? If they had intervened in a timely manner, she might not have died, Joaquin."

"You realize they'll throw everything at you, right? Armies of lawyers getting paid hundreds an hour picking over every word you submit. They're a Goliath."

"Good. That makes me David. David won."

Joaquin's shoulders slumped.

"Listen, I can't stop you," he said. "I can imagine how you feel. But Carmen is dead. There are hundreds— thousands—of *living* people in detention who need your help right now. The right thing to do is help *them*. Nothing you do will bring Carmen back."

"If I don't fight for her, Joaquin, no one will."

⁕⁕⁕⁕⁕

Going against her long-standing habit, Mona closed her office door. She felt like she was going to burst into tears, and she didn't want to do that in front of Joaquin and Natalie. She sat down at her desk. With the door closed, the tears came. Maybe her grief and anger had made her lose sight of her mission. There were migrants in detention who needed her help right now. Carmen's death was a tragic accident, a bitter irony, one more wretched border story. But nothing Mona could do would bring her back.

To distract herself, Mona started doodling on the internet. She checked her social media accounts. She visited an online shopping site and bought some shoes she didn't need. She checked her social media accounts again, which were now filled with banner ads for the shoes she'd just bought. An acquaintance had a new job. A college friend had broadcast to everyone she knew that she was feeling sad, without explaining why. A colleague who worked for the ACLU had posted a link to a story from the *LA Times* with the hashtag #resist. Mona clicked through to the story. The headline read:

President Nominates Head of Private-Prison Firm for Secretary of Homeland Security

The *Times* had run a photo of Marvin wearing a puffer jacket with a fur-lined hood. The caption read "Michael

Marvin arriving at the World Economic Forum in Davos, Switzerland, in 2018."

He was a jowly white man with wavy hair, a fake tan, and, through a wide smile, obviously whitened teeth.

Mona stared at the picture. The man in charge of the prison where Carmen had died of neglect was one Senate hearing away from being in charge of the entire southern border.

At that moment, looking at that photo, Mona knew exactly what her mission was.

She had some translation work to do.

TEN

WHILE Mona was working in the office, Finn went out to the Long Beach station for the second time in three days. Klein had left him a message, saying he had good news.

"So, I spoke to Salazar," said Klein. "He's taking this straight to the FBI."

David Salazar was the commissioner of Customs and Border Protection. He answered to Steve Fishman, the acting secretary of Homeland Security. Fishman answered to the president.

Finn was taken aback. The FBI was part of the Department of Justice, whereas the CBP was part of Homeland Security. In Finn's experience, government departments jealously guarded their own, even the criminals.

"Salazar's going to the FBI?"

"He says if he goes to Fishman, he'll want to keep it in-house. He'll just give it to the Office of Inspector General, and the Office of Inspector General is, as you and I both damned well know, an unsatisfactory outfit. The FBI knows about cybercrimes. They're geared up for it."

"If Fishman finds out that Salazar went to Justice without going through him first, he'll fire him," said Finn.

"He's not going to find out. We're going to keep this thing quiet, the FBI are going to investigate, and by the time they've figured it all out, Fishman will be gone and we'll have Marvin. Marvin will be glad we got it done. He won't care how."

"I don't know, Keith."

"Listen, this is how it works in Washington. I don't like it any more than you do, but I want to catch this hacker, or mole, whoever he is, and I want to do it before they force me to retire, all right? I want to leave a clean house. The FBI knows what they're doing. They'll find him, and they'll find him quickly. Speaking of which, they want to speak to your computer science kid. What's her name?"

"Detection Enforcement Officer Leela Santos."

While Klein wrote it down, Finn scratched his chin.

"So now what?" he said.

Klein capped his pen. "Salazar says hang tight, wait for the FBI to contact you. Meanwhile, I'm putting you back on the water. Gomez, too."

Finn was surprised.

"You don't look pleased," said Klein.

"I thought you said that once it had gone to the inspector general, it's out of your hands."

Klein leaned back in his office swivel chair. "What's the date today, Finn?"

"April 24."

"April 24. In ten weeks, they'll give me a gold watch and tell me, 'Thank you for your service.' Until then, this is still *my* station, and I will not have my best marine interdiction agent sitting on the dock. If anybody's got anything to say about that, they can talk to me. Hell, they're kicking me out anyway, aren't they? What more can they do? Go fishing, Finn. It's what you do best."

ELEVEN

TWO days later, a Friday, Finn and Mona were on an early-morning flight to Mexico City. Finn had switched shifts with a colleague so he could go with her, and now, sitting in the plane looking out the small window, he was struck by how similar Mexico City looked to LA, with its sprawl and nearby mountains. He could see no sign of its notorious smog, and indeed, a half hour later, he and Mona stood in clear, bright, high-altitude sunshine in the queue for a cab outside the terminal. It was Finn's first time in the Mexican capital, and the airport alone elicited in him a discordant sense of both arriving somewhere new and discovering it to be familiar, as though, after years of staring at the moon through a telescope until he could recognize its every sea and crater, he was for the first time seeing its dark side. Mona—who, Finn knew, had spent a semester in Mexico City during college—seemed lost in another world entirely.

They climbed into a cab and asked the driver to take them to Ciudad Nezahualcóyotl. The guy shook his head. No way, he said. The driver of the car behind him refused as well. So did the next one. Finally, they gave up and went back into the terminal, where Mona asked someone where they could catch a bus.

On the bus, Mona explained where they were going.

"Carmen told me she grew up in Ciudad Neza and that she could hear the crowd roaring from the stadium whenever the home team, the Cementeros, scored a goal. So I looked up the stadium. Then I did a search for middle schools within shouting distance of it. There's only one. That's our starting point."

Finn shook his head in wonder. "You're a genius, you know that?"

Mona gave him a sad smile, then leaned her forehead against the window.

The bus dropped them outside the school gate. Finn looked around. The school's perimeter wall was entirely tagged in graffiti. The high metal gate was locked. Across the street was a row of double-story, flat-roofed, informally designed buildings, some of them plastered, some plain cinder block. The only consistent feature was the bars on all their windows, both street level and upper floor. Several shops were open for business—a bodega, a cell phone shop, a man standing under an umbrella selling *carnitas* from a pushcart. Most of the vehicles traveling by were recent models. The sidewalk was in need of repair, and pedestrians skirted around large muddy puddles that remained from a recent rain. To Finn, they seemed like regular, middle-class people—women with strollers, guys in collared shirts, old folks. A couple of mangy-looking dogs trotted past, their ribs showing. Still, it didn't match Finn's idea of a slum. Grimy, unplanned, low income, sure. But why call it a slum?

Mona smiled. "The meaning of a word is its use," she said.

"What?"

"Something I learned in college. Half the people here don't have running water. No running water is one of the academic definitions of a slum."

Finn reflected on that. "I guess I was expecting something worse, the way the cabdrivers reacted," he said. "So, where do they get their water?"

"They buy it from those guys." Mona pointed at a donkey-drawn cart ambling down the street. The cart had a water tank on it. People were placing plastic drums on the sidewalk. "The city gives away the water for free, but the residents have to pay the middleman. They buy what they can afford, then ration it month to month."

Finn watched the man get down from the cart and attach a hose between the tank and a blue drum. Money changed hands. He looked up and noticed the water tanks perched on stands above the houses.

Mona pressed the security intercom button by the school gate. A woman in dark slacks and a cardigan appeared at the gate. Mona spoke to her in Spanish. Finn didn't catch everything, but he understood when Mona explained that a former pupil had died in the United States. They wanted to notify her parents, she said.

The woman, who Mona said was the principal, invited them in. Finn and Mona followed her through the yard, where kids in uniform stopped their playing to stare at them. In her office, the principal asked them to sit and went to a filing cabinet. "*Qué pena,*" she said, flipping through files. She said some more, which Finn didn't catch. Mona translated for him. "She says she remembers Carmen well. She was a spirited girl."

"*Ella quería ser actriz,*" said the principal.

The principal pulled out a file and hesitated a moment before opening it. A conversation ensued that Finn couldn't follow.

Mona said something, and then the principal nodded, relieved. "*Pobre* Carmucha," she said, writing something down on a piece of paper and handing it to Mona.

✦✦✦✦

Outside, Mona explained why the principal had hesitated. "Carmen has a little sister, Clara, who is a student at the school. The principal wanted to know whether she should tell her. I said no, wait for us to go to the parents first."

Mona followed the directions on the piece of paper that the principal had given her, and Finn followed Mona. After a five-minute walk, they came to a narrow house. Mona pressed the buzzer. A potbellied man with gray hair opened the door but not the grille. Through its bars, Mona asked if he was Señor Jorge Amado Vega. He nodded warily. "We're here about your daughter," she said in Spanish.

"Clara?" he said.

Mona shook her head. "Carmen."

He unlocked the grille. Jorge Amado Vega shook Mona's and then Finn's hand with a rough-skinned palm. They followed him through a lounge, down a lightless corridor, to a kitchen where a short, wiry woman stood at a counter, husking corn, dropping the husks into a bucket by her feet. Jorge Amado Vega introduced her as his wife, Maria Elena. Finn recognized Carmen in her features—the big, gleaming eyes, the golden skin stretched over high cheekbones. If Maria Elena was surprised to see them, she didn't show it.

Finn looked around the room. He got the impression that Jorge Amado Vega had built the house himself. There was a kitchen table with a plastic tablecloth, a crucifix on the wall, and a TV on a sideboard. At the back, a dutch door gave onto a tiny yard. The top half was open, and something squealed from the yard. He glanced over the half door and saw the biggest hog he'd ever laid eyes on—a great, pony-sized beast too large for the yard containing it. He wondered if it could even turn around in there. Maria Elena emptied the bucket of husks into the yard, washed her hands, and invited Finn and Mona to sit. She sat across from them and stared. Finn got the feeling that she knew what was coming and was steeling herself. He assumed she would react with the forbearing he'd come to expect on the faces of so many of the migrants he had intercepted. Yet when Mona broke the news, tears burst from Maria Elena's river-stone eyes. "*Lo siento,*" he heard Mona say.

Finn paid close attention. He wanted to follow the conversation with his limited Spanish. He was fortunate in that Carmen's parents spoke slowly.

"It was the telenovelas," said Jorge Amado, leaning against the doorjamb. He made no move to comfort his wife. He pointed at the television. "She watched that rubbish all day. It gave her foolish ideas."

Mona turned to Carmen's mother. "Señora Vega, when was the last time you heard from Carmen?" she said.

Señora Vega pushed herself up from the table, went to a drawer, and brought back a postcard. Mona read it, then handed it to Finn.

"She must've bought it at the commissary," said Mona in English. "She didn't tell me she'd contacted her parents."

Finn looked at the card. On the picture side was the California flag. The card had been postmarked in Paradise, California, on April 3—three weeks earlier, and the day before Carmen's arraignment before Judge Ross.

Carmen's last words to her mother, scribbled in a childish script, were in a Spanish basic enough for Finn to read: "Mama, I am in the United States. God willing, I will make a new life here. I am sorry for leaving you and Clara. One day I will bring you both here, I promise. I love you like the sky. Carmen."

Maria Elena asked how her daughter had died.

Finn noticed Mona hesitate.

"They think a rattlesnake bit her," she said.

"A rattlesnake?" said Carmen's mother, startled.

Mona put down the postcard and pulled a sheaf of documents from her bag. "These are copies of the reports from the hospital where they took Carmen, the coroner who examined her, and the police who investigated. I have translated all three into Spanish."

Maria Elena looked at the pile of documents with a defeated expression. She made no move to reach for them. "Tell me what they say," she said.

Mona nodded. "The detention center is in the desert, north of Mexicali. There are rattlesnakes there. The guards found Carmen unconscious on a bench. The doctor came, but it was too late. The snake had bitten her three times on the arm. Nobody saw it happen. They took her to the hospital, but she died in the ambulance."

"What will they do with her body?"

"I will arrange to bring her here."

Finn could feel the awkwardness. He heard Mona say, "The government will pay for it." She glanced at him. He knew it wasn't true. Mona presented another piece of paper.

"This document authorizes me to represent you in the United States," said Mona. "It means I can arrange to have Carmen's body sent back to you."

She handed Maria Elena a pen and pointed where to sign. The mother made her mark. The father did the same. Mona put the paper in her briefcase. Then she put another one in front of Maria Elena.

"Señora, it is my belief that the authorities at the prison should have done more to protect Carmen. I believe they should have treated her more quickly. I want to sue them for negligence. But I cannot sue them directly; I need to do it on your behalf. If I win in court, then they will be forced to do something to protect others. This document authorizes me to sue the prison in your name. I want to make sure no other family suffers what Carmen suffered. What *you* have suffered," she said. Her voice sounded strained.

"I don't understand. You want to sue the American government?" said Maria Elena.

Mona explained how the government had outsourced the detention center to a corporation. "We think you have a strong legal case against the Border Security Corporation of America—the company that the government paid to look after Carmen. We believe we can make the company pay compensation. For your loss."

Now it was the father's turn to speak. "How much?" he said.

Mona told him about the man from El Salvador whose family was awarded $2 million after he died in a detention center in Texas. Carmen's father looked at his wife, but Señora Vega did not meet his gaze.

She looked at Carmen's last postcard, pressed between her hands. "From when she was a little girl, Carmen always wanted to be on television. Everyone told her, 'Forget it, *muchacha*. People from Neza don't go on television.'"

"*Dos millones de dólares,*" said the father, to no one in particular.

"But I always said to her, 'Why not? You're so beautiful.'"

Mona nodded. "She looked like Dolores Romero."

"We are humble people," said Maria Elena. "I don't know how we can fight a big American company. We have nothing."

"You don't have to fight them. I will. All you have to do is sign."

"You?" said Maria Elena. She didn't sound convinced.

"*Dos millones de dólares,*" said the father again.

The pig grunted.

"I used to watch the telenovelas with Carmen," said Maria Elena. "If one of us missed an episode, the other would tell her what happened. She loved *Aprendí a Llorar.* She liked the romantic ones. She was young, but she tried to pretend she wasn't."

Maria Elena wept. When she was finished, she looked directly at Mona and said, "Do you think you can win, Señora?"

Mona said, "I don't have an answer, Señora. But I will fight with everything I have."

Maria Elena absorbed this. Then she said, "I have another daughter, Clara. This is going to break her heart."

"I know of no greater grief than yours," said Mona.

Maria Elena wiped her tears. "Women here don't live lives like they do on television. Carmen tried to live a different life. I will remember her for her courage."

She asked Mona where on the document she wanted her to sign.

Then, in a hard voice, she said to her husband, "If there is money, it will be for Clara. To take her away from here. It will be Carmen's final gift to her."

·····

Out on the street, walking back toward the bus stop, Finn—who didn't have a knack for languages but who was trying to improve his Spanish—said, "You told Carmen's mother, '*Creen que una Vibora de cascabel la mordiò*'; that's the third person, right? '*They* think a rattlesnake bit her'?"

"Correct."

"*You* don't?"

"No, I do think a snake bit her."

"But you don't think it was an accident?"

Mona let out a sigh. "I've got a thought going through my head I can't shake, Nick. What if Soto *had* found her? Like in the dream she told me about? What if he found a way to get into the detention center and put Carmen in a box with snakes, like she said he did to another girl? I know snakes bite people. But everything about this is wrong: the fact that it bit her three times, that no one noticed, that she *died* from it . . . I need to talk to someone who knows about snakes."

Finn thought for a moment. Then he said, "I know a guy at Fish and Wildlife who might be able to help you. Greg Wilkins, out at LAX. Last time I saw him, he was saying how they caught this one guy who flew in from Vietnam with ten snakes taped to his body. Live snakes, I mean. Venomous. Anyway, Greg told me how they weren't too sure how to handle it at the airport. None of them wanted to pull the snakes off the guy's body, and they couldn't figure out how to deal with the situation without hurting the guy or the snakes. One of them had a contact, a guy out in Pasadena, who's apparently a world expert on venomous snakes. They call this guy, this snake guy, he comes down, gets all the snakes off the smuggler. I can ask Greg for his name, if you want."

They passed the school again. It was lunchtime, and kids were crowded round the *carnitas* cart. Finn got the uneasy feeling that the guy under the umbrella was watching them, keeping track of their movements. Mona said she would very much like to speak to the snake expert. "How'd he do it?"

"What?"

"Get the snakes off the smuggler from Vietnam?"

"He got the guy to stand in a cold room for fifteen minutes. The cold numbed the snakes. Then he just picked them off him with his bare hands."

Mona smiled. The bus came and they got on it, heading back to the airport. Finn looked out the rear window and saw Carmen's mother standing at the school gate. A girl with long black hair came out. Maria Elena held open her arms.

A little farther down the street, Finn noticed the man at the food cart talking into a cell phone.

TWELVE

BACK home, Mona spent the weekend glued to her laptop, drafting her complaint. At midnight on Sunday, she printed out the final draft, put it in a manila envelope, and went to bed.

She was on the road to Paradise by 6:00 A.M. the next morning, the envelope in her briefcase on the passenger seat. It was still dark, and she turned up the volume on the radio, partly to pep herself up, and partly to cover the irritating rattle coming from the AC. It was a long drive, and she was tired of it.

She could have saved herself a lot of time and hassle by simply filing her suit downtown—the BSCA, though incorporated in Delaware, had a representative in LA. But Carmen had died in Paradise, and Mona felt strongly that justice must prevail even in that bright, burning place. And anyway, another task awaited her there, one that only she could do. Mona had arranged to meet the funeral director at the coroner's office. Felix Diaz had said over the phone that he had sent dozens of bodies back to Mexico. He knew the procedure.

•••••

The Paradise coroner's office was in a single-story building on the same block as the courthouse where Judge Ross
had refused Carmen bail. Everything was the color of
sand—the coroner's building and the crop fields beyond
it—except for the patch of lawn in front of the building.
The lawn had a towering flagpole on it, from which the
Stars and Stripes hung listlessly. Beneath the flag, sprin-
klers scattered water on the emerald grass.

Inside, a stocky man in a suit got up from the bench.
He introduced himself to Mona as Felix Diaz.

"I'm sorry for your loss," he said in Spanish.

"Can you tell me what the procedure is to send her
home?"

"First, I must embalm her—otherwise, the airline won't
take her. This I will do in my funeral home. Then I will
place her in a coffin and drive her to the airport. I will
liaise with the airline. They know me."

"What do I need to do?" said Mona.

"You have the authorizations from the family?"

Mona nodded.

"Then there is just one form from the consulate that you
will need to complete—it concerns the repatriation of
human remains—and the payment."

Mona told Diaz about the acid burns to Carmen's body.
"I don't want you to get a shock," she said. The sad look
on his face didn't change.

"I will make her look right for her family," he said.

A moment later, a young woman with straight bangs
and an unwavering gaze appeared. She introduced herself as Brigid Bauer, the coroner. In English, she greeted
Diaz by his first name. She thanked Mona for sending
through the authorization to release Carmen's body, then
led Mona and Diaz to the examination room: tiled floor,
stainless steel washbasins, adjustable overhead lights, no

windows. Along one wall were two rows of coolers. The room itself was very cold. For Mona, the worst thing was the smell: the sting of formaldehyde competing with the stench of decomposing bodies. In the middle of the room was a stainless steel dissection table on which lay a body covered with a sheet. On the toenails of the feet sticking out, Mona saw beige nail polish.

Bauer pulled the sheet back. She didn't uncover Carmen's whole body, where the acid burns were. Just her untouched face.

Mona looked at Carmen and tried to think of a way to describe what she was seeing. She could think of none. She remembered the person she'd met on April Fools' Day, the attractive young woman bearing a startling likeness to Dolores Romero, a character in a Colombian soap. A young woman who'd risked her life in order to come to the United States to escape a sadistic torturer and to find a plastic surgeon to repair the damage he'd done to her body. The parallels between truth and fiction struck Mona as uncanny. Except the ending. In *Aprendí a Llorar,* Dolores is cured of her disfigurement and marries the man she loves in a spectacular finale watched by millions. Carmen, her body burned and poisoned, was going home alone in a coffin.

Mona brought her focus back into the moment. She noted that the skin on Carmen's face and neck wasn't black, as she had expected it to be. If anything, it looked a little greasy, as if Carmen had applied skin lotion before she had died.

"I thought snake venom caused necrosis," she said to the coroner. Bauer pulled back the sheet a little further. Carmen's arm was entirely black. It looked like a shriveled limb belonging to a mummy Mona had seen once in the anthropological museum in Mexico City. Bauer replaced the sheet, then suggested Mona join her in her office to sign the release-of-remains document.

Diaz lingered by the corpse.

"There's a weird smell," he said. He looked at the coroner. "Like vegetable oil. Can you smell it?" The coroner said no, she couldn't. Mona said she could only smell antiseptic. After a moment, Diaz shook his head and said, "I've been doing this a long time. There's a weird smell."

+++++

Mona signed the necessary documents, left Diaz to arrange transport of Carmen's corpse to his premises, and drove over to the courthouse.

She sat in her car in the parking lot and read over her complaint one last time. On the final page, she had listed the compensation she was claiming on behalf of Carmen's family: $50,000 in general damages, and $50 million in punitive damages. Her argument was that the BSCA owed its inmates a duty of care, but that the corporation's cost-cutting program placed it in breach of that obligation. For lack of antivenin and adequate staff training, Carmen had died. The scale of the claim was far greater than any case she'd litigated before. She thought of Michael Marvin, with his fake tan and white teeth.

Mona strode into the clerk's office. The filing process took less than ten minutes—Mona handed over the complaint, paid a fee, received a receipt. Now she stepped back out onto the courthouse's steps and stood in the morning sunlight for a moment with her eyes closed. She could still see Carmen's blackened limb in her mind's eye. Suddenly, she felt very tired. She went back inside to ask the clerk where she might find a decent cup of coffee nearby. At the counter, she noticed a court schedule.

Mona checked which of the town's two judges was sitting today.

Judge Ross.

Mona drove about a mile down the road to the place the clerk had recommended, picked up coffee and a sandwich, and headed back to the courthouse. She sat on a bench in the main hall, drank her coffee, and ate her sandwich. In an alcove in the wall opposite her was a statue of Lady Justice, with her blindfold and scales.

She threw her empty cup and sandwich bag into a trash can and went into the courtroom. Inside, it was as chaotic and overcrowded as it had been at Carmen's arraignment. There were no spare seats in the gallery, so she stood against the back wall and scanned the room. She saw dozens of detainees in jumpsuits. Mona recognized Kristin Chase, the public defender she had sat next to at Carmen's arraignment. Next to her was a man in a suit that needed pressing. Mona surmised he was the no-show from last time. Both lawyers were staring at their mobile phones like teenagers at a bus stop. That made Mona angry. Couldn't they at least *pretend* like they had a hope?

The judge's door opened, and a hush came over the dark-paneled room. Perhaps because she was seeing him from behind the bar rather than in front of it, Judge Ross looked even smaller than she'd remembered. Were it not for his gray hair, she might've mistaken him for a boy. The judge sat down. Proceedings began. Three men, arrested together, were being arraigned for illegal reentry. The judge appeared to be doodling while the charges were read out. He never once looked in their direction, not even when they pleaded guilty. When he remanded them to twelve months in Paradise Detention Center, he sounded bored. A group of officers took hold of the men by their elbows and led them out, the men shuffling their shackled feet and looking bewildered. The whole procedure had taken no longer than five minutes. Mona felt as discombobulated as she had the first time, as though she had again entered some parallel universe where all the rules and protocols of court no longer applied, where the judge ruled with absolute authority like some despot from ancient history. What disconcerted her most was not so much the judge—who was nothing but a bully, a trivial and cruel man—but the near-conspiracy among all the other legal and law-enforcement professionals in the room, people she considered her peers. Not just the public defenders but the court officials, the clerks, the police officers, even the ICE agents and assistant district attorneys prosecuting the undocumented immigrants. All of them were witnessing the same thing Mona was witnessing. All could see that Judge Ross was brushing aside any semblance of due process, wasn't even bothering to make a show of it, yet none of them displayed any of the shock that Mona felt. They were like fish who couldn't see the water they were swimming in.

That evening, utterly drained, Mona got in her car and headed west. The sun set. The vents rattled. She pictured Carmen lying on the stainless steel table. For long stretches, her headlights were the only ones she could see.

THIRTEEN

TUESDAY morning, Mona slept late. At noon, she made her to-do list for the day. She put only three things on it. The first was to locate Michael Marvin, the CEO of BSCA, and serve her complaint and the court summons on him. The second was to start building her case for court. The third was to book her car in for a service.

She got to the office, adjusted the tilt of the vertical blinds to deflect the afternoon glare off her computer screen, and got to work.

From Marvin's bio on the BSCA's slick corporate website, Mona learned that he had grown up in Orange County. He had been with the company for twenty years. Prior to getting the top job, he had been vice president of new development and quality assurance, which made Mona laugh out loud. She wondered whether the vice president of quality assurance had ever smelled the stink of twenty-eight backed-up lavatories out in Paradise.

The corporate website didn't give his home address, of course, but the company was now headquartered in Washington, D.C., so Mona presumed Marvin was based out there. Serving the papers on Marvin herself would've given her enormous satisfaction, but she didn't have the time to fly across the country, so she contacted a process server she sometimes used to find elusive defendants.

Next, she started prepping her case for court. Ordinarily, Mona would've waited until hearing the defendant's answer, but she expected this to go to trial. More than expected. She *wanted* it to go to trial. She pictured the statue of Lady Justice she'd seen in the hall of the Paradise County courthouse. Court was where she would fight for justice for Carmen. Not around a negotiating table.

Mona's case depended on her being able to prove that the BSCA had cut costs with criminal disregard for the well-being of the people in its care. She needed to find evidence supporting her argument. She was an adherent of the adage "Follow the money," and her first step was to download a copy of the BSCA's annual report. She wanted to comb through its budget statement. She knew evidence of a crime would be easy to miss—the slick website and glossy annual report told her that the BSCA spent a lot of money projecting itself as a responsible corporate citizen—but she had faith in her own diligence and was confident that she would know it when she saw it: some business practice of dubious legality, some statutory irregularity, some calculation that seemed off—anything that gave her purchase on the corporation's slippery carapace; any weak spot where she could begin burrowing.

Four hours later, she rushed into Joaquin's office.

"I've found something," she said.

Joaquin put down his pen.

"Shoot," he said.

"The BSCA subcontracts its services, including its catering. All the meals they serve out in Paradise Detention Center are actually preprepared in Anaheim by a company called AmeriCo Food Services. You know how much the BSCA paid AmeriCo for the year ending December 31?"

Joaquin shook his head.

"It paid $5,837,700," said Mona. "You know how much it costs the State of California to feed three meals a day to the inmates in its prisons?"

Joaquin shook his head again.

"Two dollars and fifty cents."

Now Joaquin adopted a shocked look.

"For *three* meals? Jesus. What do they eat for two bucks fifty?"

Mona remembered the drums of cooking oil and trolleys of blast-frozen food she'd seen going into the center during a visit to Carmen.

"I did some calculations," she said. "Two-fifty per prisoner, per day, equates to $912.50 per prisoner, per year. The occupancy of PDC last year, averaged over twelve months, was 450 migrants. That means that the actual cost, at a rate comparable to other prisons, to feed 450 inmates three meals a day for a year is a little over $410,000."

Joaquin raised an eyebrow.

"Which means this Anaheim outfit earned itself an almost five-and a-half-million-dollar margin," he said.

Mona nodded. Her heart was thumping, the way a fisherman's heart thumps when something big takes the hook and the line starts racing off the reel.

"Seems excessive, even by government procurement standards," said Joaquin dryly. "What do you know about AmeriCo?"

"Almost nothing. It's a private company. It doesn't even have a website. All I have is their address, the name of their agent, and the date they incorporated."

"When did they incorporate?"

"In 2016—the same year that PDC opened."

"What's the name of the agent?"

"Edward Maws. He's listed as the CEO and founder."

"Five million dollars. I wonder what that buys you in the migrant-detention business."

"I don't know. But I bet Edward Maws does."

Mona checked her watch; it was six o'clock—too late to get to Anaheim and visit AmeriCo Food Services. It would have to wait until tomorrow.

She had completely forgotten about the third item on her to-do list.

✦✦✦✦✦

AmeriCo Food Services was located in a business park wedged between the interstate and the Santa Ana River, in a putty-colored building with smoked-glass windows. There was no sign out front, and Mona could only be sure she was in the right place because she could see guys loading pallets of food products and drums of cooking oil into two trucks backed into the loading dock.

She sat in her car a moment and watched them. It was almost 9:00 A.M. She couldn't see anything that seemed out of the ordinary. Just the daily grind in a business park, one of hundreds sprawled through Orange County. And yet she felt nervous, like an archeologist about to open a tomb.

Mona got out of her car, climbed the steps to the side of the loading dock, and passed through the sliding glass doors leading into the reception area.

"Can I help you?" said the young woman behind the counter.

"This *is* AmeriCo Food Services, right? There's no sign anywhere," said Mona.

The receptionist, with a forced smile, said it was.

"Is Edward Maws available?" said Mona.

"I'll check," said the receptionist in a tone that suggested she wouldn't. "Who are you?"

"My name is Mona Jimenez," said Mona. "I'm a lawyer with Juntos Para una Frontera Mas Segura." She handed the receptionist her card. The receptionist invited her to take a seat on a nearby bench.

A minute later, a man emerged from a door behind the reception counter. He was of medium height. His suit and tie looked expensive. So did the blow-dried whoosh of his hair. He looked fit the way rich people look fit—like he played squash at a fitness club that had a sauna and a wood-paneled dining room. Mona straightaway pegged him as a guy born to wealth.

He greeted her and held out his hand. It had an oily feel, like he'd just moisturized. Then he invited her to follow him into his office. There was something oily about the invitation, too.

In his office, Maws sat first without waiting for Mona. She sat down, crossed her legs, and tugged down her skirt.

"How may I be of service to you?" he said with a flourish of his hands. Mona groaned inwardly. Maybe he thought he was being cute. But he sounded like a waiter.

"I mentioned to your receptionist, I'm a lawyer with Juntos."

"Yeah, she said. I had to Google it. Tell me what it is you guys do, exactly?"

"Essentially, what we do is help migrants stuck in the immigration system."

"I see. And you want my help with that?"

"Not exactly. I understand that AmeriCo Food Services has the catering contract for Paradise Detention Center?"

She phrased it as a question, inviting Maws to start talking.

He took the bait.

"Yes. You see, we already have something in common: you represent illegals, I feed them," said Ed Maws, sounding like a guy who liked the sound of his own voice. "We both help them in our own way."

He smiled an unctuous smile, then went on.

"It's a huge contract. Paradise is the biggest migrant detention center in the state. Did you know that? They started out with five hundred beds; now they're up to seven hundred. We feed them two hot and one cold meal a day. It's a big logistical operation. We send out two trucks a day, seven days a week, stocking their canteen. You probably passed a couple of them on your way in."

"How long have you been in the catering business?"

"I used to be a restaurateur. I had a restaurant in Santa Monica, called the Dining Room on Wilshire, down near the beach. Did you ever go there?"

Mona said she hadn't.

"Too bad. People raved about it. *LA Weekly* loved it. You like salmon? We had a salmon dish, if you died and went to heaven, it would be the one thing you'd miss about Earth. Amazing dish. Anyway. I had to give it up when I won the contract for the detention center. No one thought I would win it, but I did. A quality restaurant like the Dining Room, probably the best restaurant in Santa Monica at the time, maybe ever, you needed to be there. You had to stay on top of things, or else the standard dropped. So I had to give it up. It was too much even for me, you know? And I'm a workaholic. But I wish you could've tried it. I bet you would've loved it."

"How did you get from running a fine restaurant to catering to a detention facility?"

Maws assumed a serious look.

"Oh, it wasn't easy, believe me," he said. "I had to beat the biggest names in the business to win it. The big multinationals. Huge corporations. It just goes to show, size doesn't always matter"—that oily smile again—"sometimes, it pays to be agile. Or dexterous. It means the same thing. That's what I am. Dexterous."

"Was there a tender process?"

"Yes. And no one gave us a chance. Everyone said we would never win it, the other guys were too big. Even my wife said it. My ex-wife, now. She said don't do it. I did it anyway. I said, what've we got to lose? And guess what? We won it. *I* won it. She didn't believe I would, but I did. She was sure glad I'd won it when we got divorced, believe me. Her and her lawyer. Both very glad."

He fell silent and lost his smile.

Mona coaxed him along. "I'm impressed, Mr. Maws. What do you think the clincher was? That won you the contract?"

His smile returned.

"You know, people ask me that and I always say the same thing. It's not complicated. What it is, is price. Price and quality. Nobody could beat us on price and quality, and that's why we won the contract."

Mona tried to keep the skepticism from her face.

"I see. Price and quality," she said. "Mr. Maws, there's something I'm struggling to understand, and I was hoping you could help me."

He smiled like he could think of nothing he'd like more than to help an attractive young woman like her understand something. Mona dead-eyed him and said, "The BSCA paid you almost $6 million last year to fulfill the catering contract for their Paradise operation. I just can't figure out how you reached that number, especially since you say you won the contract on price."

She left a space for him to say something incriminating. For once, he was at a loss for words. Mona kept digging.

"Every other prison subcontractor in the country charges the government between two to three dollars per detainee. You say that there are seven hundred migrants in Paradise. That means you're charging the taxpayer more than thirty-three dollars per migrant. What does the extra thirty dollars buy you?"

The smile had slid from his face. Mona was glad about that.

"First of all, we're not charging the taxpayer anything. We charge the BSCA."

"They pass on the cost to the taxpayer."

"Second of all, that's proprietary information."

"The BSCA is a public company. It's in their annual report."

"Third, your numbers are wrong."

"Well, you see, Mr. Maws, that's what I was hoping you could help me with. Which numbers? The $5.8 million I got from the BSCA's annual report, or the two-to-three-dollars-per-person figure I got from the ACLU?"

"They must've made a mistake."

"Who? The BSCA or the ACLU?"

Maws looked like his tan was about to melt off.

"It's not just the food," he said. "It's the distance. Trucking costs. Paradise is way out in the desert . . ."

"I know where it is, Mr. Maws. I've been there many times. But many prisons are in out-of-the-way places. Calipatria, Corcoran, Ironwood—all those institutions feed their inmates three meals a day for two to three dollars a person. But you're charging thirty-three dollars per person. What do you give them in return?"

Maws sniffed. He was trying to look stern, but his face was flushed. He forced a smile and said, "Let's change the topic, Miss Jimenez. I can think of many other things I'd rather discuss with you."

At this point, she knew that any serious negotiator would've seen that there was no upside for them in continuing the conversation and would've put an end to it. But there was something off about Maws. She sensed he was unwilling to leave it there. Like she'd pricked his pride, and now he had to reinflate himself.

"It's *Ms*. Jimenez. Are you avoiding the question, Mr. Maws?"

"I like you too much to avoid your questions, Ms. Jimenez. What I'm saying is, my business is *my* business. I'm damned good at what I do, but I can't just give away my secrets. You look confused."

"I'm not confused."

"Fine. You want to know why I got such a great deal with the BSCA? I'll tell you in a nutshell: I'm a tremendous negotiator. You're sitting across from the greatest negotiator in California, maybe the greatest negotiator in the whole country. You should be impressed. Paradise is just one of my customers. We cater to institutions all over the state. Frankly, I can't give you the details you're looking for. It's proprietary, and anyway, I'm the big-picture guy. I'll get my finance department to see if there's any non-commercially sensitive information they can share with you. In the meantime, here's my card. And please"— his chair squeaked as he leaned forward—"that's my personal cell on there. Call me anytime."

Mona walked out of her meeting with Ed Maws certain of three things: one, that Edward Maws was a slime bag; two, that Edward Maws was hiding something about the inflated payment; and three, that Edward Maws felt protected enough to both lie to her and to hit on her while doing it. After the initial shock of discovering that she knew about the inflated payment, Maws had recovered. Clearly, Maws had decided she couldn't hurt him.

But she *could* hurt him. The numbers were damning. She could go to the attorney general. She could tell her friends at the ACLU. She could go to the press. That Maws was so unfazed by her probing only raised new questions in her mind.

Mona walked out of the AmeriCo lobby. Instead of going down the steps back to her car, she went over to the workers loading the trucks at the dock. She walked past drums of cooking oil, sacks filled with rice, beans, flour, sugar, giant cans of fruit in syrup, cardboard boxes packed with processed products like breakfast cereal, and a Mexican brand of lime-and chili-flavored chips she liked called Papas Santas. She didn't see anything that warranted the thirty-dollar markup. They weren't eating marbled rib eye out at Paradise Detention Center.

The workers looked tired. They didn't have whooshy hair. Their smiles weren't oily.

"I guess you cover a lot of ground, huh," she said to one of them in Spanish. "Delivering to customers all over the state?"

"Customers? Señora, we have only one customer: the prison out in the desert. We don't go anywhere else. Just the desert."

•••••

Because Mona and Finn had both grown up near the beach, they tended to take it for granted. The sunset that night, however, was too spectacular not to appreciate. They were walking along the water's edge on Redondo Beach, Mona's Roman sandals dangling from her right hand. The horizon was red and yellow, and the water separating them from it was gleaming. The evening colors, the give of the wet sand beneath her bare feet, the sound of the water lapping at the beach restored Mona's equanimity. She felt like she was finally emerging from the whirlwind that had followed Carmen's death; finally getting some perspective on things. She was telling Finn about how she had challenged Maws about the vastly inflated cost his company was charging the BSCA for the catering contract to Paradise Detention Center.

"What did he say?" said Finn.

"He said he couldn't remember the exact details. He made it sound as if he had more clients than he could keep track of. But on the way out, I spoke to one of the workers loading the trucks. He told me they only go to one place. Paradise."

"They have no other customers?"

"Nope."

Finn gave her a quizzical glance.

Mona continued, "None of it makes sense. A company like the BSCA, the first thing it does once it locks in a government contract is *cut* costs, not inflate them."

"Right," said Finn.

"That's what I went looking for in the financial statements. Evidence I can use to demonstrate that Carmen died because she did not receive the care due to her. And sure enough, I found all the usual stuff about cost-cutting initiatives, rationalizations, good management. In fact, the BSCA has been ruthlessly cutting costs in every area except one: its catering contract with AmeriCo. Why?"

"Some kind of kickback," said Finn.

"Exactly. And now I'm digging, asking questions. And now Maws knows I know. So why isn't he worried?"

"Maybe he is; he's just good at hiding it."

Mona shook her head. "No. I got a good read on him. He's a real slime bag, but he wasn't scared. The opposite, in fact. He wanted me to be impressed. He told me he was brilliant at making deals."

"Maybe he feels confident you won't find anything."

"Maybe."

"And maybe it's a job for the DA," added Finn.

Mona gave him a peevish look.

"Look, all I'm wondering is what any of this has to do with Carmen's death," said Finn.

Mona shrugged. "There's no direct link. But still . . .

I can't shake this feeling that there's something there, something bigger, you know?"

She was about 80 percent sure her gut feeling was right, but the 20 percent was niggling away at her.

Finn nodded. "But if it *is* something big, Mona, if it's kickbacks, corruption, anything like that, you should tell the attorney general. Let them investigate it. Whatever it turns out to be, you stumbled on it by accident. It's separate from what happened to Carmen."

They stepped over a large jellyfish abandoned by the tide.

"I left Maws feeling like I'd stepped on one of those," said Mona.

"Will you tell the attorney general?" said Finn.

"If I do, it's not my case anymore, is it? The attorney general takes over."

"You'll still have your lawsuit. You'll still be fighting for Carmen."

Mona looked out to sea. "If this kickback thing turns out to be as big as my gut's telling me, I could force the BSCA to shut down Paradise Detention Center. Can you imagine, Nick? What greater justice could there be for Carmen than shutting down the prison where she died?"

They walked in silence for a while. Mona kept glancing at Finn. She could tell from the set expression on his face that he was worried.

"I know I'm sticking my neck out, Nick. But if I can shut down PDC, the world will be a better place. But to do it, I'll need all the help I can get."

Finally, Nick said, "All right. Message received. How can I help?"

"Can you run Maws's name through the databases at work?"

As a marine interdiction agent with Customs and Border Protection, Finn was authorized to run names through the databases of various law-enforcement agencies, to check for outstanding warrants against people the agency processed at border checkpoints. But Maws was not trying to enter the country, nor was there any question about his citizenship or immigration status, which meant that what Mona was asking Finn to do was legally problematic. She knew Finn could get into trouble if he got caught.

"Okay," he said.

Mona smiled. "Thank you, Nick. Meanwhile, I'll try to find his ex-wife. He said he was divorced. Divorces tend to turn up a lot of dirt."

Finn returned Mona's squeeze when she took his hand. But his eyes still carried a worried look.

FOURTEEN

CALIFORNIA law mandates that almost all court records, including divorce cases in the family courts, are put on the public record. All Mona had to do the following morning was type Maws's name into the search box on the superior court's website to discover that he and his wife were divorced in Orange County.

Mona was in the Orange County courthouse by lunchtime. She found a seat at a wooden desk beneath a high window in the archives room. A clerk delivered a document box, and she began sifting. She learned that the marriage of Edward Maws to Katrina Wakefield had been consecrated at the Yorba Linda Golf Club on the September 3, 2011, and dissolved in Orange County superior court on November 15, 2018. He and Katrina Wakefield had two children. The divorce, Mona was not surprised to learn, had been far from amicable. It had taken almost a year of court action and had resulted in Maws forfeiting to his wife a house in Yorba Linda and committing to pay the mortgage on it. The house was valued at $4 million. On top of that, the court had ordered Maws to pay about $250,000 in alimony and child support a year. Katrina had custody. Maws had visitation rights. None of this surprised Mona. What did surprise her was that the court had forced Maws to surrender his 49 percent share of AmeriCo to Katrina. She must've had a terrific divorce lawyer. Maws was CEO but had no interest in the company he founded.

This guy is underwater, thought Mona. Between the mortgage and the alimony and the child support, he had an annual liability of $400,000. Without an interest in AmeriCo, and unless he had failed to disclose other sources of income during the divorce, which was a crime, Edward Maws was a desperate man.

Mona had learned in law school that most fraudsters don't see themselves as criminals. Usually, they see themselves as victims. They see the money they steal as compensation for some perceived wrong. Mona remembered how Maws had presented himself to her: as a victim of a vengeful wife and a savvy divorce lawyer.

With the BSCA annual statement, Mona had her money trail. With Maws's divorce records, she had her suspect's motive. Two big questions remained in her mind: What was the BSCA paying Maws kickbacks for?

And what did any of this have to do with Carmen's death?

⋯⋯

While Mona shifted through court records, Finn went out to sea. It was a gloriously blue-sky, day, and the pleasure yachts were out in numbers, making the most of the steady, onshore breeze, the horizon dotted with their billowing white sails. Finn was in his element. It was the kind of day that made doing any other kind of work unthinkable, but his mind was elsewhere. He kept thinking about his wife. He worried that her fury against the BSCA was consuming her. He worried about where it was leading, of things spiraling out of control.

Back at the station at the end of patrol, he quietly sat down at one of the station's computers. First, he ran the name *Edward Maws* through the DHS's database. It came up blank. Next, he ran it through the FBI's. Another blank. He tried the DMV. Nothing. The United States has a reciprocal treaty with Canada, and he tried the Canadian border authority database. Still nothing. Interpol: nothing.

Maws came up clean. No warrants, no lookout notices.

Just then, Finn sensed a presence at his shoulder. He looked up and was relieved to see that it was just Klein.

"Seems your stint at Riverside wasn't a complete waste of time after all," said Klein with a smile.

Finn laughed.

"I learned not to be scared of these things," he said, nodding at the computer.

Klein leaned over and read the name Finn had typed into the search box on the screen.

"'Edward Maws.' Who's that?"

Finn considered his answer. He didn't want to lie to his friend. But he knew that he couldn't tell him the truth. At least, not all of it.

"He runs a catering company out in Anaheim. I got a tip that he employs undocumented migrants, so I'm running some checks on him," he said.

Finn met Klein's gaze and knew straightaway that he wasn't buying it. But something in Finn's set expression must've made it clear to Klein not to push. After an awkward moment, Klein's smile returned.

"Undocumented migrants? Your wife's been schooling you, Finn."

Finn took a deep breath, then returned to his keyboard. He decided to search Immigration's database. Not for warrants but for Maws's travel history. He got a summary of Maws's comings and goings over the last three years. For the first year and a half of that period, Maws had exited and reentered the country thirty-four times. After that, nothing. Lots of people traveled overseas for work or vacation, thought Finn. But thirty-four times in a year and a half? He started clicking on each trip to bring up more information. The first trip had taken place on January 15, 2016. Maws had gone to Mexico by car, through the San Ysidro crossing. He had told the border guard that the purpose of his trip was leisure. He had returned two days later, on a Sunday. Finn clicked on the next trip: again to Mexico, again through San Ysidro. Finn clicked on all thirty-four trips. Every single one was a day or two in Mexico, sometimes over the weekend, sometimes during the week. Looking at the last entry, Finn saw something that made him sit up straight.

━━━━

Mona was in her car when Finn called.

"Wow," she said when he'd told her what he'd found: that the border agent who had waved Maws through the crossing during twenty of his thirty-four trips was none other than Antonio Figueroa.

They were both quiet for a moment.

"You know what I'm thinking?" said Mona.

"Yes," said Finn.

"All right, smarty pants. Read my mind."

"You're wondering whether there's a link between the five million Maws got from the BSCA and his trips to Mexico."

"You're good. Do you bend spoons as well?"

"Now your turn. Can you guess what I'm thinking?"

Mona smiled, even though she was alone in the car. "You're wondering whether it's a coincidence that it was Figueroa who waved Maws through twenty times out of thirty-four," she said.

"Do *you* think it is?"

"I saw Uri Geller bend a spoon on TV once. I knew it was a trick. I just didn't know how he did it. I still don't."

"Whatever was taking Maws down there, it must've been compelling. He was married, right?"

"Yep. Two kids. I've just come from the Orange County courthouse. That's where Maws got divorced. It was ugly. She got the house; he got the mortgage. She got the kids; he got the alimony payments. Unless he's got money stashed away that he didn't declare in court, he's deep in the hole."

"Why'd they get divorced?" said Finn.

"Infidelity."

"That could explain his trips to TJ. When I worked the border crossing, I used to see lots of men on their own heading south. It was obvious what they were going for."

"When was Maws's last trip?" she asked.

"Last summer. August 17."

"Carmen tried to come through San Ysidro on August 26," said Mona. She frowned, even though she was alone in the car. She had never asked Carmen if she had worked as a sex worker in Tijuana. It had made no difference to her case. But now she wished she had. Was it a coincidence that Maws had stopped going to Tijuana at the same time Carmen had left it?

She remembered Maws's oily hand and felt a bit sick.

"If we could get evidence of Maws soliciting, he might be more willing to help us," she said.

There was silence on the line.

"Nick? You there?"

"Yeah. Just thinking . . . you're the lawyer, but isn't that blackmail?"

"Blackmail is when you threaten to reveal damaging information and demand money to keep quiet. We want information, not money. Totally different."

"Oh, okay. I feel better now. I'll follow him around a bit, and see where he goes."

⁜⁜⁜

While Mona was at the Orange County courthouse, Finn drove from the CBP station at Long Beach out to the AmeriCo office in Anaheim. He'd changed back into civilian clothes. Now he parked in the lot of the business opposite—a truck-parts distributor—reclined his seat, and waited.

Finn thought back to that night on the water. He pictured Carmen helping the child up the ladder. Then the wave hitting, the boats parting, her hands slipping from his grip. Carmen hadn't panicked. It could've ended in disaster, that had been clear to everybody there that night, in the dark, with the swell, the rain, the panga sinking. But Carmen had stayed calm. Some people sometimes suffer a kind of inner bedlam that only returns to order in a time of crisis—as though they must encounter chaos on the outside before finding calm on the inside. Finn was one such person. He thought maybe Carmen had been, too. In any case, he had felt a kinship with her from the moment they had worked together to get the child safely aboard the Interceptor. Now Carmen was dead. She'd died in the system into which Finn had placed her—a system he helped sustain. The just-following-orders argument that had seemed convenient whenever Mona challenged him on his job felt hollow now.

Just then, Maws came through AmeriCo's smoked-glass doors, breaking Finn's train of thought. He headed for a silver BMW sedan parked in the spot nearest the entrance. Finn checked the time. It was ten past four in the afternoon. The boss giving himself an early mark.

The BMW headed out of the business park. Finn

followed. When he saw it get onto the I-5 heading north, he cursed. Maws couldn't have timed it worse. Sure enough, after a couple of miles, the traffic got denser, and instead of maintaining a regular speed, Finn found himself having to move forward in fits and starts. It was the kind of traffic in which anyone who knew what to look for would spot a tail—a car that stayed with him, no matter which lane he switched to, or which exit he took. Finn just had to hope that Maws didn't know what to look for.

Wherever Maws was going had to be important to him, thought Finn. Mona had told him that Maws had grown up in Yorba Linda; Finn, who was from Long Beach, took it as self-evident that nobody born and raised in Southern California got onto the I-5 at rush hour unless they had a gun to their head.

After an aggravating hour and a half behind the wheel, following Maws on the 5, then the 10, then the 101, Maws finally got off the highway system at Melrose. By then, the sun was on the horizon. Maws turned right onto North Western. A few hundred yards down the road, the BMW turned into a strip mall and parked. Finn drove past, turned around, and parked on the other side of the street.

The strip mall comprised a Korean BBQ, a nail salon, and a doughnut shop. Maws stayed in the car. After a minute, a woman emerged from the nail salon and approached the BMW. She was wearing short denim cutoffs, high boots, and a white halter top, even though the temperature was cooling fast. She opened the passenger door and got in like she was expecting him. The car's headlights went on, and Maws pulled out with the woman inside. Finn followed them to a quiet street nearby. Maws parked next to an elementary school, which was empty at that time of day. Finn saw the BMW's taillights go off. He pulled in a little way back and waited.

After twenty minutes, Maws pulled out and returned to the strip mall. He pulled over, and the woman got out of the passenger's side. Finn saw her drink from a bottle of water, rinse her mouth, and spit into the gutter. Maws took off, heavy on the gas. Finn had to push the speed limit to keep up. He was dismayed to see him get back onto the Hollywood freeway, this time heading south. After another twenty frustrating minutes in stop-and-start traffic, Maws took the downtown exit. Finn followed him to city hall. Maws parked in a lot next to the new glass-and-concrete courthouse on First and Broadway, got out of the car, and climbed the steps into the building. Finn followed, hustling not to lose him.

Inside the courthouse, Finn slowed. Someone had erected an easel near the entrance with a sign on it. The sign read PDP MEETING, 6:00 P.M.: ROOM 13. He saw Maws going through a metal detector, recovering the contents of his pockets from a tray on the other side. Finn waited a moment, then followed him through.

The officer at the metal detector asked him for ID. Then he said, "What is your business here tonight, sir?"

Finn said, "PDP meeting."

The guy nodded and, on a clipboard, wrote down Finn's name, driver's license number, and time of entry, then handed Finn the clipboard for his signature.

As Finn signed the clipboard, he noticed that Maws had used his real name. Next to both Finn's and Maws's names, in the space under "purpose of visit," the officer had written, "PDP." Finn made his way down the corridor. He found room 13. Through the window in the door, he could see Maws from behind, taking a seat in a circle of men. On the door, someone had Scotch-taped a sheet of paper with the words PROSTITUTION DIVERSION PRO-GRAM printed on it in large capital letters.

John school.

•••••

That night, back at home in Redondo, Finn was recounting to Mona what he'd seen.

"The guy leaves work early. He drives an hour and a half to pick up a hooker on Western Avenue. Then he goes to john school. Then, after john school, he goes to a strip club on Santa Fe called the Gentlemen's Club."

Mona was sitting on the sofa with her shoes off and her feet tucked under her. She thought again about Carmen in Tijuana, whether she might have done any sex work and whether she might've met Maws.

"He must've gotten caught propositioning an undercover cop," said Mona. "The court probably gave him a choice: john school or pick up freeway trash."

"Well, seems to me the freeway could do with some cleaning," said Finn, "because getting busted hasn't changed this guy. He doesn't care how long it takes, either. He took the five at five."

"What's a sex worker cost?" said Mona.

"Are you not happy with my efforts?"

"Shut up. I mean, what kind of money does Maws need to keep it up, forgive the pun? They say it's an addiction as powerful as heroin. So how much does a sex addict need to spend a day to feed his habit?"

"I don't know what a girl charges, but I know they charge ten bucks for a glass of lemonade in a strip club on Santa Fe."

"His divorce was expensive, too. If he's paying for sex addiction on top of that . . ."

Finn's phone rang. While he answered it, Mona

reflected. Now she had two reasons why Maws needed the money that the BSCA funneled into AmeriCo. She needed to find out what he was giving them in return.

She decided to pay a visit to his ex-wife, Katrina Wakefield.

Mona looked up. Finn's face was white.

"What's wrong?" she asked.

"That was Gomez. Leela's dead. Motorcycle accident."

"Oh my God, Nick. I'm so sorry."

Mona put her arms around him.

FIFTEEN

THE house in which Katrina Wakefield lived and for which Edward Maws paid the mortgage was a regal, three-story pile in the style marketed by Realtors as "Country Manor."

It was 10:00 A.M. the following day, a Friday. Mona knew Wakefield had kids, so she'd waited until they were sure to be at school. She walked up the path to the oak door. Inside, she could hear a vacuum cleaner running. She rapped the brass knocker. The vacuum cleaner fell silent. A peek window opened, and a woman's face appeared. Mona gave her name and asked for Katrina Wakefield. The window closed, and a moment later the door opened, revealing the owner of the face—a stout woman with a professional vacuum cleaner strapped to her back—and a thin, sweaty blonde in activewear, who looked like she had just stepped from a hot yoga class.

"Yes?" said the blonde.

"Ms. Wakefield? My name is Mona Jimenez. I'm a lawyer. Would I be able to have a word with you?"

"Is this about my ex-husband?"

Mona picked up an Australian accent.

"Yes," said Mona.

Katrina Wakefield looked unhappy. "My least favorite topic," she said.

She invited Mona in.

Katrina Wakefield led Mona through a vast foyer, around which spiraled a grand staircase, to a beautiful and meticulously decorated living room with a row of french doors opening onto a veranda and, beyond that, a lush and what appeared to be endless garden. She dispatched the woman with the vacuum cleaner to the "fitness room" to tell "James" that she was finishing early today.

"My personal trainer," she explained. Mona gave a little smile. Katrina Wakefield opened a bar fridge in the corner of the room and pulled out a bottle of coconut water. She offered some to Mona, which Mona declined. Wakefield poured herself a glass, took a big breath, and sat down opposite Mona.

"Before we start, do I need to call *my* lawyer?"

"I'm not here representing your ex-husband, if that's what you mean," said Mona. "Quite the contrary."

"Okay. Because, no offense, but I've seen quite enough lawyers for one lifetime," said Wakefield. "What can I do for you? Is Edward in trouble again?"

"I represent—represented—a young asylum seeker who was being held at the detention center in Paradise—"

"That's the one out in the desert, right? The one Ed has the catering contract for?"

"Yes. Last week, my client died inside the center. I am trying to find out what happened to her exactly."

"Wait a second. Was she the one bitten by a snake? The one that's been in the news?"

"Yes."

Wakefield looked genuinely upset. "How frightful," she said. "I grew up on a sugarcane plantation in Queensland. There are a lot of snakes where I come from. It's a terrible way to go. But what's this got to do with Ed? Or me?"

"Well, this is where I thought you might be able to help me, Ms. Wakefield—"

"Katrina."

"Katrina. I've been looking at the BSCA to see if they could've done more to try to save Carmen, my client. I noticed an unusual payment to your husband's company, AmeriCo."

"Unusual?"

"Unusually large. I asked Mr. Maws if he could explain it, but I feel he was not honest with me."

Katrina laughed. "What a surprise," she said.

"I thought you might be able to tell me what the payment was for."

Katrina Wakefield shook her head. "I can't, I'm afraid. I mean, I know Ed has a contract to supply the prison with food. If they're paying him for anything else, I don't know about it."

"Can I ask how you met?" said Mona.

"He owned a restaurant in Santa Monica. I got a job as a waitress there. I'd just arrived in the country."

"The Dining Room on Wilshire?"

"Yes. He was a decent bloke then. Although knowing what I know now, he was probably fucking all the other waitresses, too."

Mona remembered Maws's leer in his office. "I understand that this house is in your name—"

"Too right!"

"—and that the court decided that Mr. Maws has to pay the mortgage on the house, in addition to a substantial alimony."

"You know a lot, don't you?"

"I assume it's the money he receives from the BSCA that allows him to afford all that?"

Katrina took another sip of coconut water. "Frankly, I don't care where he gets the money as long as he pays it. But yes, the prison contract is his big earner."

After a pause, Katrina said, "You know he was spending a lot of money *before* we got divorced, right? Not just after?"

"Do you know what for?"

"I do, unfortunately."

Mona must've looked puzzled because Katrina elaborated, "He was spending hundreds of dollars a week on hookers. He is what people here call a 'sex addict' and what people back home call a 'dirty dog.' You want to know how I found out? He gave me herpes."

"I'm really sorry to hear that," said Mona.

"Not as sorry as I was. My gynecologist told me that *herpes* means *creep* in Ancient Greek. My gynecologist has a dark sense of humor."

"And all the money he was spending back then, where was he getting it? Before he made the deal with the BSCA, I mean," asked Mona.

"He was taking it from the restaurant. We were making decent money back then. Not like now, but still, we were doing well. But we kept running out of cash. I was doing the books by then, and for the life of me I couldn't figure out why. Now I know. I still don't know how he found the time to do it. Do you know how time-consuming it is running a restaurant? Anyway. When he got the catering deal, that's when the big money started flooding in. And that's when he really let loose."

"What can you remember about the deal?" asked Mona.

"I was pregnant with our first child. One day in the middle of my first trimester, Ed comes home from a boozy lunch and says we're selling the restaurant and setting up a catering operation. I said that didn't seem like a wise idea. We had worked hard to get the restaurant to where it was, and it was finally going well. But he was adamant. He told me that we would make ten times what we were making with the restaurant. 'We'll be in a different league,' he said. He said he'd worked out all the details already. I had morning sickness all day long, I had trouble thinking straight, so I didn't put up much resistance. But I was worried. He had this look about him. A weird spark."

She finished her coconut water and poured herself another before continuing, "Turned out, he was right. We sold the restaurant, he set up the catering business, and right from the start, we started making buckets of money. I mean, an absolute fortune. Within a year, we left our little apartment in Santa Monica and bought this house. Ed wanted to live near where he grew up, near his parents. And he wanted Archie—our son—to go to the same school he went to, Saint Ignatius, which is just down the road."

"Were you involved with the new business?" asked Mona.

"No. Archie was born, and I was busy looking after him. And then Vanessa, our daughter, came along, so that was it for my career. You have children?"

Mona shook her head.

"Well, I had no idea what was happening at the company, and I didn't really have the headspace to know, I was so busy with the kids," continued Katrina. "All I knew was that Ed was bringing home truckloads of money. I guess I figured, well, this is what's supposed to happen in America, right? People make loads of money fast? I suppose I could've tried to find out more, but why would I? I was busy with the kids, I had a beautiful house, my life was perfect. Then one day, my gynecologist told me I had herpes." She shook her head.

Mona asked, "Katrina, in January of 2016, your ex-husband starting making frequent trips to Tijuana. Do you know why?"

"Yes. That's when he started the catering business. He said he had to go to Mexico to see his 'suppliers.'" She put air quotes around *suppliers*.

"His last trip was in August of last year. Do you know why he stopped going?" Mona held her breath. Was there a link with Carmen?

"Yes. Because one of his 'suppliers' gave him herpes." Katrina laughed cynically. "Do you know what *bareback* means? In Mexico, Ed was paying women extra for unprotected sex. Apparently, hookers here insist on condoms, and that just wasn't good enough for Ed. That's how he got herpes. I got diagnosed in August last year. When he found out I had it—and that he'd given it to me—he stopped going. At least, he said he did. I don't know. I kicked him out of the house straightaway. We were divorced within a year."

She slipped into a moment of reflection.

"You know, he wasn't always like he is now. When he was getting the Dining Room off the ground, he worked really hard to make it work. I think to prove to his father he could do it. His parents are conservative people. Catholics. His dad was an engineer. Anyway . . . the money changed him. For one thing, he started working less. For another, he became showy. Like he was trying to make an impression on people, especially his father. I think that's why we bought this house. We never needed six bedrooms, you know. Even Michael thought it was over the top. Have you spoken to Michael yet?"

"Michael?"

"Michael Marvin? The CEO of BSCA? He was the one who came to Ed with the catering contract. Michael's the one you should talk to. He and Ed are old friends. In fact, they were at Saint Ignatius together."

Mona asked in what she hoped was a composed tone if Katrina had an address or phone number for Michael

Marvin. The sweaty blonde put down her coconut water and reached for her iPhone. Then a thought occurred to her.

"I'm not sure I should," she said. "Michael's the school's most generous donor. I don't want to get him into trouble. Also, to be quite frank, I depend on AmeriCo, you know. For my income."

"I appreciate your candor. I'll be frank, too; your ex-husband has some awkward questions to answer—especially if it turns out that Marvin doesn't know about the transfer. But this isn't about protecting Edward Maws or even Michael Marvin. This is about what happened to Carmen Vega."

Katrina Wakefield pondered this. Mona could almost see her weighing her self-interest against her desire to hurt Ed Maws. Finally, she said, "I'm sorry, but I don't think I can give you Michael's number. But I *can* introduce you to him."

"That would be fine, too," said Mona.

"Are you free tomorrow night? Saint Ignatius is having its annual fund-raiser, and Michael will be there. He's chairman of the school board. I can seat you next to him, if you like, at table 1, right by the stage. I'm on the organizing committee."

"I would like nothing better," said Mona.

Katrina smiled, obviously pleased with the compromise she had devised. "Then it's settled. I'll see you tomorrow."

Mona got up to leave. A thought occurred to her. "Will your ex-husband be there?" she asked.

Katrina's face clouded over. "Yes, unfortunately. But don't worry, he's on table 28. By the toilets."

•••••

Mona sat in her RAV outside Katrina Wakefield's Tudor mansion in Yorba Linda and processed what she had learned over the last four days: on Tuesday, she had spotted a suspiciously large payment made by the Border Security Corporation of America to its catering company, AmeriCo; on Wednesday, she had intuited that the boss of the catering company, Edward Maws, had something to hide; on Thursday, she had learned that Maws required a great deal of money to meet his divorce obligations, as well as the imperious demands of his sex addiction; today, Friday, she had learned that Maws had gone to school with the CEO of BSCA.

Katrina Wakefield had said that Marvin had brought Maws the contract. Mona remembered the picture of Marvin she had seen in the *LA Times,* with his white teeth and puffer jacket. Maws was a small-time restaurateur. Marvin was CEO of a multibillion-dollar company and had been nominated by the president to be secretary of the Department of Homeland Security. What did Maws have that Marvin could possibly want?

Mona knew what she *should* do next. She should take everything she had to the attorney general. What she should do, she thought, is drive straight downtown and see Marius Littlemore, an old friend from law school, now a prosecutor in the AG's office. She should tell Marius about the 5.8 million, about the lack of a legitimate tender process for the catering contract, and about the fact that Maws and Marvin were at school together. That's what she *should* do. Let Marius do his job and investigate the suspicious payment, while she did hers and prosecuted her wrongful death case.

It would be a huge story—the president's nominee for secretary of Homeland Security accused of corruption. The *LA Times* would run op-eds.

So why was she still sitting in her car, hesitating? She felt like a teen standing on a bluff, looking down at the lake below. Her friends were yelling for her to jump, but the water was dark. She couldn't tell if there were hidden rocks. On the face of it, there was no obvious connection between the $5.8 million and Carmen's death. But what if there was? She knew that if she took what she knew to the attorney general and this thing blew up, in the furor that would follow, Carmen would be forgotten. The story would become about Marvin, about the hubris of the mighty and their inevitable fall. No one would care about a dead asylum-seeker who may or may not have been a Tijuana hooker. The earth is crammed with the bodies of forgotten murdered women. Mona had made a solemn vow to Carmen's mother. She had to put the wrongful death suit first, to make sure that Carmen's sister, Clara, lived the life that Carmen never would. She had to fight for Carmen first; only then could she go after Marvin.

Mona decided on her course of action. She would not go to the attorney general today. Instead, she would write down everything she knew, and then she would file it away, ready to send to Marius all wrapped up in a nice red bow. Meanwhile, she would get on with her lawsuit. If it turned out that the payment to AmeriCo had something to do with Carmen's case, then she would know that she had made the right decision. If it didn't, if the two things weren't connected, then she would go to Marius and show him what she'd found. But until she had the answers she wanted, she would obey her gut.

Mona started her car and headed for Neiman Marcus. If she was going to attend a fund-raising ball at an elite private school, she needed something to wear.

SIXTEEN

ON Saturday evening, sitting in the passenger seat of Finn's truck, wearing a green velvet gown, Mona looked out at the vast lawns of Saint Ignatius Loyola Academy in Yorba Linda, the grass gleaming in the setting sun, and could see why the school needed to raise money. The school looked like England. Only the occasional eucalyptus stood as reminders that they were actually in Southern California.

"Imagine how much water they use to keep all this from turning brown," she said to Finn, who was wearing a tuxedo. Finn nodded, but said nothing. He'd been low-spirited ever since Gomez had called with the terrible news of Leela's death. Mona knew he hadn't wanted to come tonight, and that he wsa doing so for her sake.

According to the information sheet that Katrina Wakefield had sent Mona along with the tickets, the fund-raiser was taking place in the school's great hall. They drove up a graveled drive to a vast building built in a Gothic Revival style that wouldn't have been out of place at an Ivy League university, and pulled up under its portico. A young man in school uniform opened Mona's door. Finn walked around the back of the truck and gave her his arm. Mona stepped out. Heads turned.

They made their way up the stone steps. Mona stopped for a moment to read the quote scrolled in the stone over the doorway: *Go forth and set the world on fire.* They walked past a bust of a stern-looking man in clerical garb, whom Mona assumed was Saint Ignatius. Inside, people made a path. A complete stranger with champagne floating off her breath teetered up to Mona and said, "Oh my goodness, darling, you look ravishing!"

Mona gave the woman the kind of imperturbable smile she'd seen celebrities give the fans crammed behind the velvet rope on Oscars night. She and Finn followed the flow of people down a wood-paneled corridor hung with scrolled honor rolls and photos of schoolboys standing in neat rows.

Katrina Wakefield appeared in a long, midnight-blue gown so spectacular that for a moment Mona didn't recognize her. She looked like a film star, from her bare shoulders to the trailing hem of her dress. She seemed happy to see them. Mona felt a twinge of guilt about what she was planning to do that night.

"Come, I want to show you something," said Katrina in a conspiratorial tone. She led them over to a framed photo on the wall. The photo was of nine adolescent boys in a racing shell—eight big ones holding oars, and one small one facing the other way. Katrina pointed at the first boy holding an oar.

"That's Michael," she said.

Mona saw a good-looking teenager with dark, wavy hair holding an oar and looking directly at the camera. He was wearing a crew singlet, which revealed big biceps. Everything about the young man radiated assertiveness, from his steady, intelligent gaze to his pulled-back shoulders and puffed-out chest. Even his hair looked imperious.

"And that's Ed," said Katrina, pointing at another boy three seats farther toward the front of the boat.

Mona recognized a much-younger Edward Maws. He was also wearing a crew singlet, and his muscles were, if anything, even bigger than Marvin's. But there was a hesitancy in his face, a slump in his shoulders that belied the pumped-up brawn he was so obviously trying to project.

"Do you know how long Marvin and your ex-husband crewed together?" asked Mona.

"Oh, three or four years at least. They used to talk about it endlessly every time they got together. The way they talked, you'd think their time rowing that boat was the best time of their lives," said Katrina.

"They *did* win a lot of trophies," she continued as though to make up for the note of resentment she'd let slip into her previous comment. "I think rowing in a crew creates a tight bond. It's hard work."

Mona thought about that. "Did they continue crewing after school? In college?" she asked.

"Michael did. He was especially good. In fact, he won a crew scholarship to Stanford."

"Did Maws go to Stanford, too?" said Mona.

"Ed? God, no. He was just the muscle, I'm afraid. Michael has brawn as well as brains. That's why he rowed in this position, in what they call *stroke,* which means he set the pace. All those other boys followed his lead."

Mona pointed to the small boy at the back, the only one facing forward, whose face was not visible.

"What about this guy? He's not holding an oar. What does he do?"

Just then, Champagne Breath returned and accosted Katrina before she could reply. Mona and Finn gently edged away and continued into the great hall.

They threaded their way through beautifully decorated tables toward the stage, checking the numbers written in calligraphy on cards perched atop bouquets of flowers at the center of each table. Just like Katrina Wakefield had told her, table 1 was right by the stage. Mona recognized Marvin from the photo of him arriving at Davos—the wavy hair, the snowfields tan. He was sitting with a pair of reading glasses perched on his nose, looking over what Mona assumed was the speech he was due to give.

"That's him," she said. Finn gave Mona an encouraging press on the back. Then he reached into his inside pocket— Mona's dress didn't allow for pockets—and handed her an envelope. Seeing Marvin in the flesh dissolved any lingering pangs of conscience Mona felt toward Katrina Wakefield.

"Michael Marvin?" she said.

The man looked up over his reading glasses. He looked displeased at the interruption. There was a lull in the conversation. The other people at the table all turned toward the beautiful woman in the green velvet gown.

"Yes?" said Marvin.

Mona dropped the envelope on his lap.

"You've been served," she said.

SEVENTEEN

"WOLFESON, White. Jesus," said Joaquin. He hustled around the table in the conference room of the Juntos office in Boyle Heights and adjusted the spacing between the chairs. It was just before ten on Tuesday, the fourteenth of May. Ten days had passed since Mona had served Michael Marvin in front of three hundred people in evening wear. Eight had passed since Wolfeson, White had contacted Mona to say that the BSCA had appointed the firm to defend it against her suit.

"How many people did they say?" said Joaquin.

"They didn't," said Mona.

A cloud passed over Joaquin's face. "Maybe we won't have enough chairs."

"I've got chairs in my office. So do you. We'll bring them in if we need them."

She knew why he was anxious. At first, she had been anxious, too. Neither Mona nor Joaquin had ever encountered Wolfeson, White in court before, but they both knew the firm by its reputation for producing some of the most fearsome litigators in the country. The moment Joaquin had learned who was representing the BSCA, he had tried to persuade Mona to drop the case. He'd stood in the hallway of the poky, cheaply fitted-out Juntos office and moved his hands nonstop, running them through his hair, even clenching them into fists to emphasize how outmatched he felt they were against Wolfeson, White.

"They'll kill us in court. That's if the case even *makes* it to court," he said now in the conference room, speaking louder than Mona suspected he realized. "Because they're going to do everything they can to keep it from going to court. You realize that, right?"

Mona said she realized that. She wanted to say more, but Joaquin kept rolling. He was verging on manic.

"Wolfeson, White. Jesus," he said again. "Don't they represent Exxon? They probably represent Exxon. And Halliburton. Or Monsanto. Or Big Tobacco. One of those. Maybe all of them. They're gonna drown us, Mona. Like kittens in a sack. They'll depose and delay. They'll request endless documents. They'll get teams of lawyers to do nothing but draft things that you'll have to respond to. We'll have to work insane hours to keep up, and even then it won't be enough."

Mona smiled. If there was one thing she knew how to do, it was how to work insane hours. She wasn't worried about her ability to work.

"It's not even billable," said Joaquin. "Who would I bill? There's no one to bill. So you'll be costing us. Which means all those hours you put in will be paid for by our donors. Which means it's a violation of our charter. We're supposed to help *living* migrants deal with immigration law. Who's going to tell our donors we're spending all their money fighting a wrongful death suit? And what if you lose? What then? What if you lose and we're ordered to pay costs?"

Mona let him carry on, let him vent, bleed the steam from his pipes. He was a lawyer like she was, and like she had, he had chosen to work for justice not profit; but he was a boss, in charge of running a small not-for-profit with limited resources, of which she was one. She couldn't blame him for being worried.

Joaquin was now reciting some of the cases that Wolfeson, White had litigated—infamous cases, studied in law schools throughout the country. In one case, Wolfeson, White had successfully defended a billion-dollar building-material company from an asbestos-related class-action suit. In another, it had saved an oil company after one of its supertankers had hit a rock and coated the coastline of British Columbia in a million barrels of Alaskan crude.

Mona interrupted him.

"Can I tell you a story my father likes to tell?" she said. She didn't wait for an answer. "My father came to LA in 1972. He was seventeen years old. He started working on building sites, first casually, then he got some more permanent gigs. He needed to get around, but he couldn't afford a car, so he bought a little old Japanese motorcycle for a hundred dollars. After he bought it, he realized he didn't know how to ride it. So he asked the guy who sold it to him to teach him. The guy said, 'It's pretty basic. Wherever you point your head, that's where you'll go. So look where you want to go.' My dad asked the guy what he meant. The guy said, 'If you see a pothole on the road ahead, don't look at the pothole. Not unless you want to ride into it. Look at the path you want to follow *around* the pothole.'"

Joaquin stared at her. "Wolfeson, White makes pretty big potholes. Like, crater-sized," he said.

Just then they both heard the sound of voices at the front desk.

"So we'll go around them," said Mona. "We'll look for a way to get where we want to go."

✦✦✦✦✦

A moment later, Natalie brought in the "five people from BSCA"—they were all men. Hands were shaken, cards handed out. Three of the men were from Wolfeson, White. The fourth was the BSCA's in-house counsel. The fifth was from the BSCA's insurer, Chattel House.

The Wolfeson, White contingent was led by a trial lawyer named Morrison Scott. Like almost everyone in the legal profession, Mona had heard of Scott's fearsome reputation. He was supposed to be a rottweiler, yet meeting him now, Mona thought he looked more like an overfed Labrador. He had the doughy midsection of a man who routinely ignored health warnings. His suit, though obviously expensive, was cut too large, and it billowed on him like a wedding tent untethered by strong wind. His tie had loosened, and Mona could see his top shirt button clamping shut his too-tight collar. His jowls were blotched. His thinning gray hair flared up in unruly wisps. When he smiled, he did so heartily, his neck puffing out of the collar like a cake out of its tin.

Scott introduced his assistants, naming them as Anderson Page and Marshall Wilson III. Mona wondered whether Wolfeson, White only employed white men with last names for first names. The BSCA's in-house lawyer had a normal first name: Bill McCormack. The fifth man, from Chattel House, also had a normal first name: Lewis Anning. Strictly speaking, he didn't need to be there, but Mona knew why he had come: he was there to look after Chattel House's money. That meant preventing a payout if possible, and minimizing it if not. Chattel House, Mona later learned, had a market capitalization of $100 billion.

Everybody sat, except for Mona. In a strong voice, she said, "Thank you for coming. Our first task today is to establish deadlines for discovery. I think I'm speaking for all of us when I say that it's in the interests of all parties to avoid any unnecessary delays. I know that the Vega family want this to be over as quickly as possible. They've suffered enough already."

Scott looked at her apologetically, like he had something to say but didn't dare interrupt her. He looked like an old man out of his depth. She almost felt sorry for him.

"Yes, Mr. Scott," she said.

"I appreciate your sense of urgency, Ms. Jimenez. The death of Ms. Vega is, as you say, a great tribulation for her family. However, the matter that you have filed with the Paradise Superior Court is complicated. It has serious implications. I don't think it will do to rush through discovery. I think we ought to allow for the full period of discovery permissible under Rule 26."

Mona said, "Respectfully, three months is the best I will do."

Bill McCormack gave a snort of disgust. "Yeah, right," he said.

Morrison Scott silenced him with a look and said, in a voice soft as butter, "Ms. Jimenez, do you feel three months will allow you enough time to address the many complex issues I expect we will encounter in this matter?"

It was a challenge. He was saying, "You think you'll be able to handle everything we're going to throw at you in the next ninety days?"

Mona held his gaze. "I believe I will, Mr. Scott."

"Very well," said Scott. "Then let us look at the calendar."

They set an end date for the discovery. They set an end date for amendments. They set an end date for expert-witness disclosures. The two sides agreed easily. *Too easily,* thought Mona. She began to wonder whether it had been Scott's intention all along to set a short discovery period.

The meeting came to a close, and Joaquin and Mona walked Morrison Scott and his team to the elevator. While they were waiting for it to arrive, Scott sidled up to Mona and said, "When you have time, you don't need people. When you have people, you don't need time." He stepped into the elevator, gave Mona a big smile, and said, "You, Ms. Jimenez, have neither."

The doors closed.

EIGHTEEN

WHILE Mona was meeting with the five gentlemen from Wolfeson, White, Finn was standing at the back of a Catholic church in San Bernardino.

The church was small and crowded. The mourners around him were, for the most part, young. Around Leela's age. Although he was sitting in the last pew, Finn could still see the casket placed on trestle legs on the raised floor of the transept. It was a closed casket, covered in flowers. A plain white pall hung over the sides. Projected on a large screen hanging from the ceiling above the casket was a studio headshot of a smiling, well-dressed Leela—Finn figured it had probably been taken for a graduation yearbook. At the bottom was her name, and the dates: 12/27/1995–05/02/2019.

The service had started by the time Finn arrived. The priest was standing at the pulpit, speaking into a microphone. He was talking in generalities, about grief and consolation. He spoke about forgiveness. Finn got the impression that he didn't know Leela all that well; that she wasn't a regular at the church.

The priest introduced Leela's father, Tony Santos, to say "a few words of rememberance." Finn watched a big man in a black suit climb the steps to the pulpit. He had a clean-shaven head and a goatee. His eyes were visibly red, even from the back of the church. The microphone squealed when he leaned toward it.

"I taught Leela to ride," he began, his voice hoarse. "On a little 50cc dirt bike in our yard, when she was just eight years old."

Behind him, the photo on the screen changed. It showed a kid riding a little dirt bike coming off a jump on a motocross track. The next photo showed a beaming child, recognizably Leela despite the missing tooth, wearing a protective suit and holding a trophy up for the camera.

After the service, people clustered on the steps outside the church, consoling one another. Finn waited at the bottom of the steps for Leela's father to emerge. When he did, Finn approached him and said, "I'm sorry for your loss."

Tony Santos peered at Finn with his red eyes, obviously trying to place him. When he couldn't, he gave a curt nod.

"I worked with your daughter at AMOC," continued Finn. "I just wanted to say, she was exceptionally good at her job. I didn't know Leela long, but she taught me a lot. I was totally devastated when I heard."

Tony Santos blinked a couple of times, as though to hold back tears.

"Thank you. She was coming home from work when the accident happened," he said.

Finn shook his head.

"I wasn't there that day. Do you mind me asking, where did it happen?"

"On the ramp onto the 215 off of Cactus Avenue. A box truck cut in front of her, knocked her off her bike. The car behind her collected her."

Finn knew the on-ramp. It was near March Air Reserve Base, where AMOC was located. He'd taken it many times.

"The truck didn't stop," continued Tony Santos. "Just drove off. The police are still looking for the driver."

The priest appeared and started moving toward Finn and Leela's father.

Tony Santos looked off into the middle distance, as though the priest were invisible. "People talk about forgiveness," he said, his voice hard. "I drive a truck for a living. That kind of thing, on the road, I don't forgive."

NINETEEN

AFTER the conference with Wolfeson, White, Mona closed the door to her office and dialed the cell number on the card Maws had given her.

"I want to meet," she said.

"Wonderful! Do you know the Players' Club on Wiltshire? Shall we say eight?" he said.

"I'll be in your office in forty minutes," she said.

•••••

Maws was behind his desk, reclining in his big leather chair, smiling. He didn't bother getting up. "You're back," he said.

Mona nodded. "I'm back, Mr. Maws."

"I don't mean to sound arrogant, but I'm not surprised."

"You *do* sound arrogant."

Maws grinned like it was a compliment. "I've been thinking about you, too," he said. "Let me ask you something: Is Mona your real name?"

"No."

"I knew it! You're up to something, I can tell. I like a woman with secrets. What is it?"

"What?"

"Your real name."

"You can call me Ms. Jimenez."

He affected a crestfallen look. "Now that's not very friendly, is it?"

"Mr. Maws, last time I was here, I asked you about the $5.8 million that your company received from the Border Security Corporation of America."

"Ah yes, the detention-center contract. And I told you, Miss Mona, there was nothing unusual about it. It's just good business."

Mona said, "I've just met with the BSCA's legal team, Mr. Maws. They know they're in trouble. They're looking for someone to take the fall."

Mona's bluff worked. The smile melted from Maws's face.

"He didn't tell you about the meeting, did he?" she asked.

"Who?"

"Your old crew mate. Michael Marvin."

"You don't know what you're talking about."

Mona leaned forward. "Cards on the table, Maws. Here's what I know. I know that in the winter of 2015, Michael Marvin came to you with a scheme. He asked you to give up your restaurant and set up a catering company. He said he would make you rich. I know that you went to Saint Ignatius Loyola Academy with Marvin. The same school your son, Archie, goes to now. I know that the detention-center contract with the BSCA is a sham, a cover for something else. I also know that you solicit sex workers on Western Avenue and are a regular at a strip joint on Santa Fe. I know that you went to Tijuana thirty-four times between January 2016 and August 2018, and I think I know why. I know a lot, Mr. Maws. But the most important thing I know is this: Michael Marvin is not your friend. He is not going to protect you. To him, you're just muscle. Someone to row the boat. The minute you become a problem, he'll throw you overboard. And your sex addiction has become a problem, hasn't it?"

He kept leering at her as if it were a shield, like it was all that stood between him and annihilation. His face was defiant, but his body slumped under the weight of shame. She felt almost sorry for him.

"I heard about your stunt at the school fund-raiser," he said. "What did Michael do to you, anyway, that pissed you off so much you're trying to ruin his life?"

"A client of mine died in his detention center out in Paradise."

"The whore who got bitten by a snake? How is that his fault?"

Mona said nothing for a minute. She let the ugliness of Maws's words hang. She could see the desperation in his eyes.

"Here's my offer. I can get you a deal with the prosecutor. No jail time. You can go to rehab. There's a place in Arizona that specializes in helping people like you."

"And in return?"

"Tell me what $5.8 million buys Michael Marvin."

She shut up and waited for Maws to decide. He sat there for a long time, blinking, the corner of his mouth twitching. She wondered what the private terrors he was working so hard to conceal looked like. Eventually he said, "Ms. Jimenez, the money to which you refer is to feed detainees at the detention center out in Paradise. What else would it be for?"

She stood.

"You're making a mistake, Maws. One way or another, I'm going to get Marvin. I'll find out what the money's for. And when I do, believe me, you'll wish you'd taken the deal. You think he's a friend, but he's not. He's using you. Men like Marvin don't have friends. Marvin won't protect you. His every move is calculated. He's always in control. But you"—she pierced him with a stare—"you can't help yourself, can you?"

She walked out.

✦✦✦✦✦

Later that evening, Mona was on the couch alone, enjoying a glass of wine and watching a telenovela called *Flores Amarillas*. Finn had gone to bed early. The show finished, and Mona was about to do the same when her cell rang.

"Hey, Mona," slurred a man's voice.

"Mr. Maws."

"'Mr. Maws.' Why don't you call me Edward, Mona? Or Ed? Why don't you like me? Mona. Mona. Mona. Has anyone ever called you Mona Lisa?"

"Maws—"

"They should. You're pretty as the picture, *Mona Lisa*. Hey, Mona. I'll tell you, Mona, what I want to do."

He was singing now.

"You should stop now," said Mona.

"Build a house next door to you."

"You've been drinking, Maws."

"Yes. Yes, Mona. I've been drinking."

"I'm going to hang up now," said Mona. But she didn't. It was eleven at night. Maws had drunk-dialed her. She knew two types of drunks: the belligerent kind, and the maudlin kind. If he got aggressive, she'd hang up. But if he wanted to unburden himself of his secrets, she would let him talk.

"Unless you have something you want to tell me," she said, softening her voice.

"Yes. Mona, I have something I want to tell you."

She braced herself. "Okay, but I'm warning you, if I don't like what I hear, if you disrespect me, I'm hanging up—"

"Relax, Mona Lisa. I'm not gonna ask you to marry me."

"Okay. Glad to hear it."

"Although, now that I think of it, that wouldn't be a bad idea. Mona? Will you marry me?"

Mona physically moved the phone away from her ear. "Good night, Maws."

"Wait."

She waited.

"I know what happened in Paradise," said Maws.

Mona made an effort to modulate her voice. "What do you think happened?"

"I don't think. I *know*. I know what happened to that girl."

Mona's heart thumped like a kettledrum.

"That got your attention, didn't it? *Now* you're listening to me. See, that's all I want. Someone to listen to me."

Was he crying? Was that sobbing she could hear?

"I've done some bad things, all right, Mona? Some bad things. I know what I am. But I'm not like these guys. These guys, Mona. They're *animals*."

"Which guys? You mean Michael Marvin?"

She heard a wet laugh.

"Michael fucking Marvin. No, not Michael Marvin. I mean, he's an asshole, but he's not the one you want. You *think* he is, but he's not. But *I* know. *I* know what you want. I know everything, Mona, and it's bigger than Marvin. *Way* bigger than you can even imagine."

"Okay. So then, who?"

More sobs. "Oh, Jesus. I need help, Mona."

"Maws, where are you?"

"I'm at home."

"I don't think you should be alone right now. If you tell me where you are, I can come round."

There was a long silence.

"Maws? Are you there?"

"Aren't *you* alone, Mona? Isn't everyone?"

Mona bit her lower lip. She loathed drunks. Her husband was a recovering alcoholic. He'd been sober three years, but listening to Maws brought back the feelings she'd felt at the nadir of Finn's drinking—the way his lies and sneakiness and self-pity had darkened the sky like a storm that constantly threatened but never broke. She found Maws repugnant, but she needed him to tell her what he knew.

"Edward. Tell me what happened to Carmen Vega. Tell me what the money's for."

She heard a gurgling sound: liquid leaving a bottle. Then more sobbing.

Mona affected a consoling tone. "Edward, I can only imagine how you feel. I really want to help you. But to do that, I need to know what you want, and I need to know what you know. You understand?"

"I want to start my life over."

"I understand. Listen, I just had an idea. Ask me to be your lawyer."

"What?"

"If I'm your lawyer, whatever you tell me is privileged. And if I think it's strong enough, then I'll go to the prosecutor and, swear to God, I will get you a deal. And you can go to Arizona and stop the madness. If it's not, then as your lawyer, I can't tell anyone else. Either way, you're protected."

There was a pause while the logic worked its way through Maws's alcohol-soaked brain.

"You're really smart, aren't you?" he slurred.

"I'm going to press Record on my phone, and then you'll ask me to be your lawyer, okay?"

"Okay."

Mona pressed Record. "All right, go ahead."

"Ms. Jimenez, will you be my lawyer?"

"Yes, Mr. Edward Maws, I agree to act as your legal representative."

More sobbing. She rolled her eyes.

"I'm sorry," said Maws.

"Take your time," said Mona, wishing he wouldn't. She heard more gurgling; he was emptying the bottle.

"Feeling better? Okay, now, why don't you start by telling me what *you* want."

"I don't want to go to jail. I want a new name, a new life. They'll kill me if they knew I talked to you. You understand?"

"I understand. But who, Edward? *Who* will kill you?"

She heard the faint sound of a doorbell ringing.

"That's Honey," said Maws, his voice brightening. "She's early, for once."

"No. Stop. Edward, don't answer the door."

It was too late. She heard unsteady steps—Maws's, she assumed, stumbling down a hallway. She heard him say, "Honey, is that you?"

She heard a woman's muffled voice, as though from behind a door, answer, "Yeah, baby."

She heard the sound of a lock opening. She heard Maws yell, "Wait, no!"

She heard two loud bangs.

She heard Maws say something. It sounded like "lawyer is lost." Then another bang.

She heard a clattering sound.

A moment later, she heard different steps—stiletto heels on boards. She heard the sound of someone handling the phone. Then she heard a man's voice say in Spanish, "Turn it off."

The line went dead.

TWENTY

MONA dialed 911.

"Nine-one-one. What's your emergency?" said the dispatcher.

"I just heard someone get shot," she said.

"Are you in immediate danger?"

"No. You need to send the police."

"What's your name, madam?"

"Mona Jimenez. You need to send the police right now."

"Where are you located, Ms. Jimenez?"

"I'm in Redondo Beach. But it didn't happen here. I heard it over the phone."

"Where was the person located?"

"He said he was at home. His name is Edward Maws. I don't know where he lives. Somewhere in LA." Mona thought quickly. "I have his ex-wife's number. She might know. Hang on."

Mona scrolled through her phone for Katrina Wakefield's number. She gave it to the dispatcher.

"The police will want to speak with you, Ms. Jimenez. What is your location, please?"

Mona gave the dispatcher her address. Then she hung up and ran into the bedroom. She switched on the light and shook Finn by the shoulder. Finn looked at her groggily.

"I heard Maws get shot," she said.

Finn sat up straight. "What happened?"

Mona held up her phone. "Listen. I recorded it."

Mona played the recording she'd made. When it finished, she took a deep breath.

Finn got out of bed and started throwing on clothes.

The doorbell rang. Finn and Mona went together to the front door. Two uniformed police officers were standing there. They asked if they could come in.

"Please leave the door open," said one of the officers. The cops had left the lights on their car roof flashing. The red and blue beams now swirled through the open front door.

In the living room, Mona played them the recording on her phone. When they reached the end, one of the officers stepped out to respond to a call on his radio, while the other asked Mona questions: What time did the call take place? How long had she known Mr. Maws? What was he referring to when he said he didn't want to go to jail?

The other officer stepped back inside. "Anaheim PD are responding to a shooting at an apartment on Katella Avenue," he said. "The caller identified the occupant as Edward Maws."

The officer turned to Mona and Finn. "You want to ride with us?" he said.

Finn and Mona jumped in the back of the police car. The officer behind the wheel drove fast, using his lights and siren to clear the way. In just under half an hour, they pulled up at a six-story block of units on Katella Avenue in Anaheim. Several black-and-whites were clustered out front, along with two ambulances and a fire truck. All the vehicles had their lights flashing. Finn and Mona followed the two officers first into a lobby, up an elevator to the fifth floor, then along a long, carpeted corridor until they got to a door with a police officer standing guard. They weren't

allowed to enter the apartment, but over the police officer's shoulder, Mona saw people in white protective suits
moving carefully around Maws, who was lying on his back
in a pool of blood, legs splayed, his head tilted to the right.
He was wearing boxer shorts and a T-shirt. His T-shirt was
soaked red. Blood was still trickling out the side of his
mouth.

The sight triggered a wave of guilt in Mona. She had
treated Maws like dirt. He had been no more than a means
to an end. She had pretended to care about him in order
to get what she wanted. She had been careless. She was
the last person he had spoken to, apart from whoever had
killed him. Life suddenly seemed a nasty, empty thing.
She started to cry.

The Redondo PD officers were consulting with their
Anaheim peers. Now one of them peeled away and approached Mona.

"We're gonna need your phone," he said.

⁜

The next afternoon, Finn drove Mona back out to Anaheim
again to the police headquarters on Harbor Boulevard to
get her phone back. She asked the lead investigator what
he heard on the recording. "I hear 'lawyer is lost,' too,"
he said. He told her that the mobile-device forensics team
were running tests on the audio they had copied from her
phone. He would let her know what they found.

Mona and Finn sat in his truck outside the station and
listened to the recording again.

"There—right there. You hear that? What's that sound
like to you?"

"'Lawyer'?" said Finn. "I hear 'lawyer is lost.'"

"I hear that, too. 'Lawyer is lost.' Why does that mean?"

Finn shook his head. "Maybe he wants to say more, but
they finished him off."

"Who's he saying it to? His killer? Or me?"

Finn sighed. "We need to find Honey."

Mona snorted. "A sex worker in LA called Honey. Shouldn't take long." After a moment, she said, "Sorry. I don't mean to be sarcastic. I just . . . 'Lawyer is lost.' I don't get it. His last words . . ."

Finn started his truck. "I don't get it either."

While Finn drove, Mona kept playing the recording over and over. The stiletto steps. Then:

"*Turn it off.*"

TWENTY-ONE

ON Thursday morning, two days after Maws was shot dead, Mona met with Marius Littlemore, her friend from college who was now a district attorney. In the wake of Maws's murder, her resolution to investigate AmeriCo on her own had dissolved. She was in Littlemore's office to tell him all she knew.

At USC Law, Mona had found Littlemore arrogant and insufferably clever. She had also dated him. That's why he'd agreed to meet her now at such short notice. Littlemore had been a lesson for Mona: a man could throw up more red flags than a Chinese Communist Party Congress and still be attractive. Now, sitting in his office in the government building on West Temple Street downtown, looking at Littlemore behind his big desk and framed by a fine view of the city all the way out to the sea, Mona felt a twinge of jealousy.

"You're doing well, it looks like," she said.

"Don't be deceived. It's a shit show here."

Mona raised an interrogative eyebrow. Marius said, "Word is, Perez's days are numbered. Everyone's jockeying for position."

Over the weekend, a number of the country's top legal minds had participated in a televised town hall, organized by a news network, on the legality of the president's attacks on sanctuary cities. Esther Perez, the attorney general for the district of Los Angeles, had been particularly scathing.

"She reminded me of Edward Smith," said Littlemore.

"Who?"

"Edward John Smith? Captain of the *Titanic*? Went down with the ship. Everyone calls him a hero. I call him drowned."

"Is the ship going down, Marius?"

Littlemore smiled.

"Who's the smart money backing to replace Perez?" said Mona.

Littlemore's eyes darted to the ceiling. "Oh, there are various hats in the ring," he said.

"You?"

"Me? C'mon. I'm too young," said Littlemore unconvincingly. Then, like a true politician, he pivoted. "It could've been you, Mona Jimenez. Top of the class, summa cum laude. You were always the smart one. How's the not-for-profit sector?"

"Rewarding."

Littlemore flashed that confident smile that Mona remembered so well. His teeth seemed brighter than they had been ten years previously.

"I assume you mean rewarding for the soul. You always did like carrying the cross, Mona. I remember in college you sneaking off to volunteer at that legal-aid center."

Mona remembered it, too. At college, she'd made a standing commitment to volunteer four hours of free legal advice in a migrant resource center downtown. Unfortunately, her four-hour shift was on Saturday mornings, when, more often than she'd intended, she would wake up in Littlemore's bed with a hangover and last night's clothes strewn across the floor.

"I do it full-time now. And I object to 'sneaking off,'" she said. She had walked into the migrant-resource center proudly, with her head held high. But first, it was true, she had had to sneak out of Littlemore's room.

"Objection sustained. How can I help you, Mona? I assume you're not here for nostalgia's sake."

"One of my clients died in the detention center out in Paradise. I'm suing the operator for negligence leading to wrongful death."

Littlemore dropped his smile. He listened closely. "I heard about that. The one who was bitten by a rattlesnake?"

Mona nodded.

"Right. And now you're suing the BSCA."

"Yes."

He nodded. "Okay. So what can I do for you?"

Mona shifted forward to the edge of her seat. "I may have found evidence of a crime."

Mona explained to Littlemore how she had discovered how the BSCA was making inflated payments to its catering company, AmeriCo. She pulled the printout of the balance sheet from her briefcase and placed it on Littlemore's desk. She'd highlighted the budget allocation for catering services.

"It says, '$5,837,700,'" read Littlemore.

"To feed 450 detainees for a year."

"And you're saying the market rate is . . . ?"

"About a quarter that."

Littlemore nodded. "What else have you got?"

Mona pulled out a picture of Edward Maws. "This guy? His name is Edward Maws. He was CEO of the catering company, AmeriCo. AmeriCo didn't exist before the BSCA built the detention center out at Paradise. It's like it was set up just to win the catering contract. Before the BSCA built Paradise, Maws was running a restaurant

in Santa Monica. Then Marvin comes to him with a pro-
posal, and Maws goes from running a small restaurant
to a huge institutional catering operation. And here's the
kicker: Maws and Marvin went to school together. A private Catholic school in Yorba Linda called Saint Ignatius.
Doesn't that ring alarm bells, Marius?"

The expression on his face didn't change. "You say he
was CEO of the catering company?"

"Maws was shot dead on Tuesday night."

Littlemore leaned back. "Wow. Okay."

"I was on the phone with him when he got shot. He was
about to tell me what the money is for. I think that's why
he got killed."

"Where was he murdered?"

"Anaheim."

Littlemore intercommed his secretary and told her he
needed to speak with the homicide detectives at Anaheim
PD—whoever was investigating the murder of Edward
Maws. When he was done, he turned back to Mona and
said, "How long have you been sitting on this information?"

She told him.

"How come?" he said.

She shrugged.

"You should've come to me earlier," said Littlemore.

She looked at the view behind him and thought of Edward Maws, lying in his underwear in a pool of his own
blood.

"I know," she said.

*****

Mona drove from the DA's office to her own feeling
chastened. She had let things get out of hand, it was true,
and now a man was dead. She had become distracted by

a grandiose vision of bringing down a powerful institution. She had put her own ambition ahead of all else. She had forgotten who she was—a migrants' right advocate employed by a small not-for-profit with a tiny budget. She worked civil cases. She was *not* a criminal investigator with the resources of the federal government to draw on. It was up to the DA and the police to investigate corruption schemes, not her. She was glad she had gone to Littlemore, and she scolded herself for not going sooner.

She thought about her case against the BSCA. The truth was, she was more likely to lose it than win it. Joaquin was right; the resources that the BSCA had at their disposal were virtually limitless. Juntos was three people. Two on the days Natalie was at law school. Mona had told herself that justice would prevail, but now she admitted to herself that she had been willfully naïve. Carmen was dead. Nothing would bring her back. Mona could do more good by helping living migrants currently in the system. She parked the car next to the Porsche Macan and looked into her own eyes in the rearview mirror. She was going to go upstairs and tell Joaquin that he had been right. She would withdraw her complaint. In life, you have to pick your battles. She got out of the car and marched into the elevator.

The elevator went up. She stepped out.

"Thank God you're here," said Natalie, panic in her voice. Mona could hear Joaquin speaking loudly into the phone in his office.

"What's going on?" said Mona.

"Wolfeson, White have let loose," said Natalie. "They've filed a motion to move the case to Washington. They've demanded a truckload of documents as part of discovery: Carmen's birth certificate, school records, health records. They even want a copy of her employment record at the auto-parts manufacturer she said she worked at in Tijuana. It's in her statement, so they're proceeding as if it's real. Basically, they've asked for everything they could think of. Oh, and a process server is looking for you. Michael Marvin is suing you. You personally, I mean, not Juntos. I told him you weren't coming in today. But keep an eye out."

"Suing *me*? What for?"

"For defamation of character. Marvin claims that when you served him at that school fund-raiser, you compromised his reputation. He says you staged it to maximize the reputational damage you could do to him. He's very distressed, apparently."

Joaquin came out of his office at a near run. "There you are. They're coming at us, Mona. It's a full-court press," he said, speaking quickly.

"Listen, there's something I need to tell you," said Mona.

"Me, too. Lots," said Joaquin.

"I'm dropping the case," said Mona.

Joaquin stopped in his tracks. He and Natalie stared at Mona.

"You were right. We're too small. They're too powerful."

Joaquin shook his head vigorously. "Remember that little talk you gave me about the motorcycle? About looking where you want to go, not at what's in the way?"

She nodded.

"Well, guess what? You were right. I mean, we're not a motorcycle, we're a . . ." He ran out of words.

"Car?" suggested Natalie.

"No."

"Bus?"

"No."

"Boat?"

"We're a family. That's what our name means, really, right? That we're in this together?"

Mona felt her eyes tear up. But it wouldn't do. "They've outlawyered us already. We don't have the resources," she said.

"That's what I was coming out here to tell you. I just got off the phone with Joe," said Joaquin. "He's going to transfer $100,000 into our account today."

He meant Joe Rodriguez, the principal funder of Juntos, a millionaire who had made his fortune in recruitment. His parents were migrants.

"Bless him. But it won't be enough," said Mona.

"Wrong again. He owns his own recruitment company, remember? He's going to get his people to find us some lawyers. We'll have them tomorrow, he said. In the meantime, Natalie and I are putting everything else on hold. Wolfeson, White may end up winning in court, but not before we've pissed all over their territory. Juntos!"

Mona noticed Natalie looking at Joaquin with glowing eyes, and for a second, she thought Natalie was going to break into applause.

"So let's go," said Joaquin. "*You're* the lead on this, Mona. *You* decide what's most pressing. Game on!"

Joaquin's resolve and energy galvanized Mona. She felt a wave of gratitude. "Okay. I need someone to deal with the motion to move the case to Washington. We need to nip that in the bud."

"All right. I'll deal with that," said Joaquin.

"I need someone to dig out the paperwork they're asking for."

"On it," said Natalie.

"Okay. I'm going to make a list of people I want to get

depositions from. I want to get to them before Wolfeson, White do."

Mona could feel the blood pumping through her veins. Her remorse had evaporated.

"Joaquin?"

"Yes?"

"Thank you. Really. I mean it."

✦✦✦✦✦

For the next seven days, Finn and Mona barely saw each other. She was putting in fourteen-hour days at Juntos, and Finn was back on night patrols, which meant he was out on the water by the time she came home, and she was gone by the time he returned to shore. They left each other notes on the kitchen counter and sent each other the kind of ordinary texts that sustain the marriages of busy people: *Miss you. Don't overdo it. Dinner's in the oven.*

The Juntos office in Boyle Heights became a hive of activity. Everyone on the team knew that Wolfeson, White were waging a war of attrition. The mega-firm was counting on their vast resources and their client's deep pockets to bleed Juntos dry. You need armies of lawyers and vaults of money to fight legal battles against large corporations. "You, Ms. Jimenez, have neither," Scott had said. Mona was working to prove him wrong.

Through his recruitment agency, Joe Rodriguez seconded them three lawyers, on his dime. The expanded team succeeded in quickly having Wolfeson, White's motion to move the case to Washington dismissed. Natalie managed to find all the documents they had requested, except the employment record at the nonexistent auto-parts factory in Tijuana. Mona drafted dozens of documents, then sent them by messenger to Wolfeson, White's office downtown, insisting that someone there sign a receipt for every piece of paper she sent. It was an expensive but necessary move to prevent their crucial documents from mysteriously going missing—a classic delaying tactic.

And indeed, Wolfeson, White tried everything. They would delay responding to requests for documents for as long as they could get away with and would then bombard Juntos with boxes of completely irrelevant paperwork. Couriers delivered document box after document box to the Juntos office, until the corridor was lined with them. The team had to review thousands of pages of cases that Wolfeson, White claimed were pertinent—only to discover that the claimed pertinence was either tenuous or nonexistent.

Tempers frayed. There were squabbles. Joaquin slammed his door more than once. One of Rodriguez's seconded lawyers called in sick and never came back. Once, Mona went to the bathroom and found Natalie sobbing in a stall. She took her out for lunch. The days went by. Summer arrived. No one took a break.

Meanwhile, Michael Marvin's nomination for secretary of Homeland Security gathered pace. When Mona learned that he was scheduled to appear before a congressional confirmation committee on the twelfth of June, she called everyone she knew with even the slightest influence in Washington and told them about Carmen's death and conditions in Paradise Detention Center. She asked them to get a committee member to press Marvin on deaths in custody. She watched the hearing on C-SPAN, first with anticipation, then disappointment, before switching off the TV in disgust. The committee members threw Marvin questions so soft, they may as well have been pompoms. It wouldn't have surprised her to learn that the committee members were reading questions drafted for them by Wolfeson, White. They were handing Marvin the nomination on a platter.

The next day, Mona called Marius Littlemore to find out what progress he had made with the $5.8 million that the BSCA had paid AmeriCo. He said they hadn't yet figured out what the money was for.

"Without the quid pro quo, we don't have any crime to prosecute," he said. "Michael Marvin's got a lot of powerful friends. There's a lot of pressure on us to drop it."

"What about from AmeriCo? Can't you find anything on that side?"

"We've talked to their financial officer. Maws was the only one who was there when the deal was made. With him dead, no one knows anything."

Mona had called the lead detective working on Maws's murder every week since she'd witnessed it over the phone. She called him again after speaking with Littlemore.

"We're not getting anywhere on the corruption angle," said the detective. "So now we're interviewing pimps and sex workers, see if anyone had any dealings with him. The theory is, Maws did something to a girl and a pimp decided to do something about it."

"What makes you think that he did something to a girl that warrants getting killed?" said Mona.

"We went through his porn viewing history on his computer. He was into some pretty nasty stuff," said the detective.

Mona remembered Maws's clammy hand.

"What about the recording from my phone?" asked Mona. "Why did he say 'lawyer is lost' before he died?"

"I don't know what that means. The forensics techs couldn't come up with anything conclusive from the audio. There's no database of voices that we can use to identify the voices."

Mona hung up in frustration. Neither Littlemore nor the police had made any progress. She reminded herself to focus on her own job. She knew Littlemore was competent, and she had no reason to believe the cops weren't. It was frustrating, but that's how things stood.

Right then, Natalie came in. "I finally got you a meeting with your snake guy," she said.

TWENTY-TWO

THE snake man's name was Stewart Butterfield, and Mona had been trying to see him since April. He was the guy Finn's Fish and Wildlife colleagues at LAX had called in to get the snakes off the trafficker from Vietnam.

Turned out that snakes were an enthusiasm rather than a vocation for Butterfield; his day job was designing robots for the Jet Propulsion Laboratory. He explained apologetically that he'd been in Tokyo at a robotics conference, and then he had had to fly to Chile for a satellite launch, and anyway he was sorry it had taken so long to schedule a meeting. Butterfield was obviously a busy man, but Mona found that he was more than happy to talk to her about snakes—she got the impression he could talk to her for hours, so long as the subject was snakes. They were seated in comfortable armchairs in his office on the JPL campus in Pasadena. Mona had her yellow legal pad out. Butterfield wore an open-collar Oxford shirt and tortoiseshell spectacles. On the wall behind him was a framed blueprint for some kind of space vehicle.

"Is that the one that went to the moon?" asked Mona, being polite.

"Actually, that one we sent to Mars. The *Sojourner*

rover. It's interesting, the *Sojourner* ended up with traditional wheels, but one of my early designs was based on the sidewinder."

Seeing Mona's incomprehension, Butterfield elaborated, "You have to remember, Mars is a sandy planet, and if you want to design a robot that moves efficiently over sand, you could do worse than mimicking *Crotalus cerastes,* the sidewinder rattlesnake. The sidewinder undulates across the sand like a sine wave." Butterfield waved a finger in the air to illustrate. "The sections of its body that touch the ground don't move; only the sections lifted off the ground are in motion. That way, it never disturbs the sand. Wheels, on the other hand, move. Wheels can dig themselves in if the sand's really soft. We didn't know then how soft the sand was on Mars, and it doesn't seem very clever to spend billions of dollars sending a robot to another planet just for it to get stuck."

Mona nodded as though she followed. She was worried that if she admitted to not knowing how a sine wave moved, he'd illuminate her by making use of the whiteboard by his desk. Right at that moment, she was more interested in snakebites than sine waves.

"Sorry, I don't mean to bore you," said Butterfield, seeing through her polite smile. "I find snakes really interesting from a design point of view. How can I help?"

Mona told him about Carmen. He listened intently.

"I'm suing the corporation that operates the detention center for wrongful death," she explained. "My case is based on the demonstrable fact that they built the detention center in known rattlesnake country, yet took no steps to either protect their detainees from the snakes or provide adequate treatment in the case of being bitten. I'm hoping you'll be willing to go on the record as an expert witness on rattlesnakes."

"Paradise is right in the heart of snake country, there's no question. Hikers *do* get bitten out there, predominantly by western diamondbacks. Still, what happened to your client is extremely unusual," he said when she had finished.

"Why?"

"Most rattlesnake bites occur late in the summer. Yet in your email, you say that your client was bitten on April 22."

Mona sat up straight. "Do snakes hibernate?" She hadn't even thought of it.

"Well, some species of rattlesnake *brumate* when the temperature drops. It's a type of semidormancy, not unlike hibernation, except they wake up for a sip of water every now and then. But in April, they are beginning to be active anyway."

"So they're not fully asleep?"

"It's not impossible that the snake that bit your client had come out of its den, for instance, to bask in the sun if it was unusually warm. It's just extremely unlikely."

Mona didn't remember the day being unusually warm, but she made a mental note to check.

"And then there are some species—like the sidewinder, as a matter of fact—that aren't dormant at all," continued Butterfield. "They're nocturnal in summer and diurnal in winter. But the sidewinder's pretty shy. When people get bitten by rattlesnakes in California, most of the time it's by a diamondback, as I said. And you hardly ever see a diamondback outside of summer."

"Is there a way of telling what kind of snake bit her? From the venom, I mean?" asked Mona.

"Did they do a toxicological analysis?"

Mona had brought the coroner's report with her. She handed it to him now. While he read it, her gaze drifted to a framed photo hanging by the door. It was of a rocky, rust-colored sand hill. It looked like rattlesnake country. The plaque read *Mount Sharp*. Mona realized, with some wonderment, that it was photo of a mountain on Mars.

"This is odd," murmured Butterfield.

Mona turned her focus back on him. Butterfield removed his spectacles. "Like I said, most envenomations in California are by diamondbacks, and that's what I would assume bit your client, even if it was strangely out of season. But the thing is, diamondback venom is primarily *hemotoxic,* rather than neurotoxic. It poisons the blood, not the nerves. If they found neurotoxin in her blood, it couldn't be from a diamondback," he said.

"Is there a kind of snake that would have neurotoxin in its venom?"

"Oh sure, many. The Mojave rattlesnake, for instance, has neurotoxic venom."

"So maybe that's what bit her?"

Butterfield put his glasses back on and read some more. After a moment, he said, "No. Definitely not a Mojave." He leaned forward and pointed out to Mona a chart consisting of numbers and chemical symbols. Like many nonscientists, her eyes had skipped over the complex-looking chart when she'd first read the document and had gone straight to the prose summary.

"See this? It's a chemical analysis of the toxins they found in her blood. This is the neurotoxin they found. It's a type called *dendrotoxin,* and there's only one snake in the world that produces it." Butterfield touched the tip of the arm of his spectacles to his lower lip. He was clearly pleased with himself for connecting the dots. "The world's most dangerous snake," he said. "The black mamba." He paused another moment, then added, "Endemic to central Africa."

Mona's heart raced. "How would someone get hold of a black mamba?" she asked.

"Legally, you mean? With great difficulty," said Butterfield. "It's easier to buy a semiautomatic rifle in this country than it is to buy an elapid. There's no constitutional amendment for cobras."

"What about illegally?"

"Well, there are ways," said Butterfield vaguely. "Traffickers and so on. But I'm afraid I'm not involved in that world and can be of no help to you there."

"You've been immensely helpful to me already, Dr. Butterfield."

•••••

The first thing Mona did when she left Butterfield's office in Pasadena was call Finn. She told him what she'd learned.

"If it's from Africa, that means someone brought it into the country. I'll call Wilkins, my buddy at Fish and Wildlife, see if he's heard anything about a black mamba," said Finn.

"Thanks," said Mona. She hung up. Then she dialed Paradise Detention Center and asked to speak to the warden.

"It wasn't a rattlesnake that bit Carmen," she told Pischedda. "It was a black mamba, from Africa. Someone brought it into the center. I want a log of everyone who entered PDC on April 22."

There was a long silence on the phone. Finally, Pischedda said he would be happy to release the visitor log to Mona.

"All you have to do is submit a request in writing to our legal department in Washington," he said. "I'll send you the log as soon as I get a green light from legal." Pischedda hung up.

Mona reached her office when her phone started to ring again. She checked the screen. It was Finn.

"Wilkins said he hadn't heard of anything like that, but he'd keep an eye out," he said.

Mona thanked him. She tilted back her office chair and looked out the window at downtown. "Carmen dreamed Soto had found her," she said.

"I know."

"Maybe he found a way to get into PDC."

"Yeah."

"Nick?"

"Yeah?"

"Before she died, Carmen said she got a prison job in the canteen."

"Okay."

"Maws said AmeriCo sends two trucks a day out there, delivering food. To the canteen."

A long silence.

"I'll pick you up in twenty minutes," he said.

TWENTY-THREE

WHEN Finn arrived to pick her up, Mona noticed that he was still in his utility uniform, the words CBP FEDERAL AGENT stenciled in large letters across his back. They drove to the AmeriCo office in Anaheim and pulled in next to the loading dock, where five or six workers were loading a truck.

Mona considered them for a moment. She turned to Finn.

"Some of those guys, if they see you dressed like that, might get a fright they don't deserve," she said.

Finn leaned on the steering wheel and watched the workers. "You need me, just wave."

Mona got out of the truck and climbed the short flight of stairs to the loading dock. She waved at a young guy pushing a pallet jack—the same guy she'd spoken with last time she'd visited. He took out his earbuds.

In Spanish, Mona said, "Remember me? I'm looking for someone who I think might work here."

"Who?" said the young guy.

Mona took out her phone, brought up a picture of Soto, and showed it to the guy. The guy nodded.

"I've seen him. One time only," he said.

"When?"

He scratched the side of his head.

"Not long after Easter, maybe the end of April? He came with us in the truck."

"Where to?"

"Out to the desert, to the prison out there."

"You mean Paradise?"

"Yeah. We usually go in pairs. But that time we were three, with that guy in the middle."

"Who told you to take him?"

"The boss. He died."

"Had you ever seen this guy before?"

"No."

"Have you seen him again since?"

"No. Like I said, just the one time."

"What did you talk about in the truck?"

"We didn't talk."

"It's a four-hour drive. You didn't talk?"

"We didn't talk."

"What did he do when you got there?"

"He helped us unload. He acted like one of us. He was wearing overalls like us."

"Then what happened?"

"He told us to wait in the truck, he had something to take care of."

"Did you?"

"Yes."

"Where did he go?"

"Into the prison."

"How long was he gone for?"

The guy shrugged. "Maybe one hour? I slept in the cabin."

"What happened when he came back?"

"We drove back here."

"Then what?"

"Then I went home. I don't know where he went."

"Anything else stand out about him? Anything you remember?"

The guy thought for a moment. "He carried a stick."

"Like a walking stick?"

"No. With a hook on the end, like they have on boats."

"Do you remember what he used it for?"

The guy shook his head.

"I don't know. It was creepy looking, though," he said.

* * * * *

Mona got back into Finn's truck. They drove out of the business park. She dialed Marius Littlemore. She had promised to let him know as soon as she found out anything relevant to the suspicious payment or Maws's death.

She told him what the worker on the loading dock had told her about the passenger in the truck.

"I'll ask the judge for a warrant to get the PDC's visitor log for that day," said Littlemore. "And I'll get their surveillance footage, too. It'll take a few days. I'll keep you in the loop."

Mona thanked him. Then she asked him what he'd learned about AmeriCo.

"There are only two shareholders," said Littlemore. "Maws's ex-wife has 49 percent. The rest is held by an entity called Loyola Holdings, in the Cayman Islands. Maybe the ex-wife knows more than she's saying."

"I've met her. I don't think she's involved. Can you find out who owns Loyola Holdings?"

"Not easily. That's why people have companies in the Cayman Islands. *Not* to get found out."

They agreed to stay in touch. Mona hung up. Finn suggested they head home. Mona shook her head.

"I have to go back to work," she said.

* * * * *

Mona worked till midnight. She was the last to leave the office. She switched off the lights and rode the elevator down to the parking garage.

She got in her RAV and started up the ramp to the street. Her phone started vibrating, rattling around in the dash recess. She picked it up. No caller ID. Nobody calls with good news at midnight. She answered, holding her breath.

A man's voice said, "Jimena Jimenez." He knew her real name.

"Who is this?" said Mona.

"You are the lawyer for Carmen Vega," said the voice in Spanish.

Mona recognized the voice. The one who'd said, *"Turn it off."*

"You drive a red Toyota RAV," said the voice. "Your license plate is 1AEG972. You have just left your office."

Mona scanned the street. There were no people about. No other cars on the road. Both curbs were lined with parked cars. Was he sitting in one of them, watching her? She gripped the steering wheel so tightly her knuckles turned white. She hit the gas—her tires squealed.

"Drop your suit," hissed the voice. "Or what happened to Carmen will happen to you."

The line went dead.

✦✦✦✦✦

Mona drove straight to the nearest police station and reported the phone call. The night-shift officer at the counter took notes. Mona gave her the time of the call, the duration, and what was said. The officer advised Mona to report the call to her phone company. Then the officer explained that there wasn't much the police could do but that Mona had done the right thing reporting the call.

"It gives us something to go on, should anything happen."

Mona shuddered. *Should anything happen?* The officer suggested that if Mona was really worried, she should go to a safe location.

Mona gave her a withering stare. She said she would call the phone company first thing in the morning.

She was relieved to see Finn's truck outside the condo when she got home. It was 1 A.M., and she had expected him to be home, but she was relieved nonetheless.

Inside, she turned on all the lights as she made her way through the living room, down the hall past the bathroom and the spare room, to the bedroom. Finn was asleep. She climbed into the bed on his side and curled up next to him.

Mona and Finn had been married long enough to develop certain routines. Mona never climbed into bed from Finn's side, for instance. She always got in from her side, even the nights he was out on patrol. When they made love, each came to the other from their own territory and met in the middle, a kind of erotic commons. And if they fell asleep holding each other, it was always in the same configuration: Finn on the left, Mona on the right. So although Mona made no noise when she lay down next to him, Finn sensed her body on the wrong side, and it sent a signal to his slumbering brain.

"What's wrong?" he said.

She told him about the phone call.

He sat up, instantly wide awake. He looked at Mona's shape lying in the dark. His mind raced. He was angry with the police for doing nothing.

"We have to set up a phone trap," he said. "If he calls again, we'll trace the call."

"God, please tell me he's not going to call again."

Finn looked in the dark in the direction of the closet. On the closet floor was a gun safe. Inside the safe was a

Glock 19 semiautomatic that Finn had bought three years earlier for Mona, after she'd been kidnapped by a murderous human trafficker that Finn had intercepted.

"To protect yourself," he'd said when he'd given it to her, which had made her laugh.

"Nick, how long have you known me? I hate guns," she had replied.

After that, he'd put the gun away in the safe and hadn't mentioned it again.

Until now.

"You think maybe it's time to reconsider the Glock?" he said.

"I'm not carrying a gun, Nick."

They lay in silence for a while.

Then Finn said, "I'm going to take some time off."

"No. I don't want a bodyguard."

"What, then?"

Mona rolled onto her back. "You know when you go out on patrol, and you're on your boat out on the sea, out beyond the cell phone towers, out where I can't reach you?"

"Yes?" said Finn.

"What you're feeling now is what I feel every time you do that. Anything could happen to you out there."

Finn sighed. "This guy. If I find this guy . . ."

"Forget about him," said Mona. She pulled his head toward hers. "Focus on me."

TWENTY-FOUR

MONA woke at 6:00 A.M. as usual. She remembered the phone call. Finn was still asleep. It was Saturday morning. Usually on Saturdays, she went to Pilates down by the beach. This morning, she decided to stay in bed, curled up against her husband.

Finn woke an hour later. "This is a nice surprise," he said.

Mona kissed his forehead. She didn't bring up the phone call, and neither did he.

"I start my shift at nine," he said. He got up and went to shower. Mona went to the kitchen and made coffee. When she came back to the bedroom, she found Finn sitting on the floor next to the closet, peering into the chamber of the handgun he'd bought for her.

"I don't want it, Nick."

"Just checking it hasn't jammed up."

Finn put the gun away in the safe, hugged his wife, and left for work. Mona stood in the doorway and watched him walk to his truck. She scanned the cars parked on the street. Then she closed the door. Normally, when she was home, she simply pressed the button on the door handle. This time, she used her key to double-lock it.

◆◆◆◆◆

Mona sat down on the sofa and called Littlemore on his cell.

"You're becoming a pest," he said, but not in a way that indicated he minded.

"Listen. Someone threatened me last night."

Littlemore dropped the jocular tone. "Who?"

Mona told him about the phone call.

"All right. I'll put a wiretap on your phone. If he calls again, we'll locate him."

Mona had never imagined the day would come when she would *want* her phone to be tapped.

"I'm making this case my priority, Mona. I'll put my best people on it," continued Littlemore. "Listen. If you want, I can get you some protection from the Marshals' Service. A couple of guys. I can do that. All right?"

"Thanks for the offer, but I'll be fine."

"At least until the trial is over."

"Really, no."

"All right, well. If you change your mind, just call, okay?" He sounded disappointed.

"Okay. Have you found who's behind Loyola Holdings yet?"

"I've got nothing. What's your best guess?"

Mona hesitated a second. "Michael Marvin," she said.

"I thought that, too. But it doesn't hold."

"Why not?"

"Five point eight million dollars goes from the BSCA to AmeriCo to Loyola. Why? It would mean Marvin is effectively paying himself. Why would he do that? Also, 5.8 million is a lot of money to you or me, but it's peanuts to Michael Marvin. I checked up on it; the guy is loaded. The BSCA gave him a stock option deal. Their stock price has quadrupled since he took over. He's worth at least a hundred million. There's no upside for him to risk a rack-eteering charge for what for him is chump change."

"Find out what the money's for. Then everything will fall into place."

"I'm working on it."

"Sorry. I didn't mean—"

"Don't apologize. You know, if you ever want a job, say the word. You'd make a great investigator. But for now, please, stay out of it, okay? And stay safe."

"Okay. I will. Thanks."

"One more thing," said Littlemore.

"What?"

"Do you own a gun?"

TWENTY-FIVE

SIX days later, at 7:00 A.M. on June 20—a Thursday—Mona kissed Finn goodbye, got into her RAV, and headed for Paradise.

She was going to a dispute-resolution session mandated by the court. She had tried to get it moved to LA, but the judge wouldn't countenance it. "*You* are the one who wanted to have this case heard in my court, Ms. Jimenez," she had said. So now Mona was on the road again, driving her little RAV into the ground. The only consolation was that Wolfeson, White had to send someone, too. She anticipated that they would send a junior lawyer rather than one of their high billers. She doubted they expected any more from the session than she did; in the mercenary world of corporate litigation, the judiciary's attempt to encourage cooperation through alternative dispute resolution was a quixotic boondoggle.

It was still cool when she left Redondo, but a heat wave was predicted. They were forecasting temperatures were over one hundred degrees out in the desert. By 10:00 A.M., Mona had reached the 215 at Riverside, and she didn't need her cardigan anymore. An hour later, driving past Palm Springs on the I-10, Mona could taste the heat in the air flowing through the open windows. She put them up and switched on the AC. Immediately, the vent started rattling.

For the last hundred miles, through city and suburb, desert and mountain, the defective air-conditioning rattling constantly in the background, Mona mulled the same questions over and over, worked them over in her mind the way a kid works over a Rubik's Cube in his hands, looking at it from all sides. What happened to Carmen? What did $5.8 million buy the BSCA? Who was behind Loyola Holdings? What had Maws been trying to say when he had shouted, "Lawyer is lost"? How was it all linked?

＊＊＊＊＊

Mona reached the Paradise courthouse at 1 P.M. She stepped out of her air-conditioned car and into the baking heat and made her way inside.

The court had set aside a conference room for the session. Mona was surprised to see that the Wolfeson, White contingent had arrived early. She was even more surprised to see that Morrison Scott himself was there.

"Mr. Scott, this is an unexpected pleasure," she said.

"My dear, I am a firm believer in mutually beneficial accommodation," he said with an avuncular grin.

The mediator—a man who affected thick-rimmed spectacles, an open collar, and stubble—began by introducing himself (his name was Gerard Mellon, a Paradise native), listing his qualifications (he had a community college certificate in general mediation), and the practical aspects of the day: the schedule, the confidentiality agreement, the rules of conduct.

Then he invited everyone to close their eyes and visualize their ideal outcome.

Mona groaned inwardly. *This is going to be a long afternoon,* she thought.

*****

Four hours later, she headed back to her car. Her intuition had been right: neither she nor Morrison Scott had budged on any point of contention. The case was going to trial.

She turned on the ignition and set the air-conditioning to maximum when there was a knock on the glass. Morrison Scott was standing outside her door. She rolled down the window.

"Would you do me the kindness of meeting me for a drink, Ms. Jimenez?"

Mona considered. To avoid having to drive back to LA the same day, she had booked herself a room again at the Eden Inn. She had nothing planned that evening but an early night.

"I noticed a bar on Main Street called Paradise Karaoke," said Scott. "I'm sure that if we go early enough we can avoid the karaoke component."

Mona smiled. "I'll see you there in an hour."

*****

Mona drove to the Eden Inn, ten minutes outside town, and took a shower. She consolidated her notes from the mediation session. Then she headed back into town.

She found Paradise Karaoke in a commercial court off Main Street near the intersection with the old highway. A few vehicles were parked outside the bar, all pickup trucks. Mona found a vacant spot next to a gleaming black Ram crew cab. Even its tires sparkled. In contrast, her RAV was covered in dust. The windshield had two angel wings on them, where she had used her wipers and washer jet to clear away the grime and smashed insects.

She went inside. Scott had taken up residence in a booth. He stood when Mona appeared and waited for her to slide onto the bench opposite him before sitting again. A cheerful young person poured her a glass of ice water before she'd asked for it.

"Could I have a vodka martini, please?" said Mona, pushing away the water.

"Martini. What a good idea," said Scott. He ordered one, too. The young person skipped away.

"I've been authorized by the Border Security Corporation of America to make you an offer," said Scott. "However, it wasn't convenient to make the offer during the mediation session, due to Mr. Mellon's rather tedious insistence on keeping a detailed record."

"I see. So it's an off-the-record offer?" said Mona.

Scott smiled. He took a piece of paper from his pocket, unfolded it, and put it on the table in front of Mona.

"More than I'd expected," she said. "You must be expensive."

Mona understood now why Scott had made the trip all the way to Paradise. The BSCA's insurance company, Chattel House, was hoping to reduce its exposure. If they could reach a settlement that amounted to less than the fee that Scott would charge for taking the case to trial, they would consider it a win. She knew also that the offer came with strings attached; the BSCA would insist that the settlement would in no way signify legal accountability. They would pay money, but they would not accept any responsibility for Carmen's death. They wouldn't want to set a precedent.

The waitperson brought their martinis. Or what the barkeep thought passed for a martini. The vodka was barely chilled, and Mona couldn't taste any vermouth.

Scott took a sip, screwed up his eyes, and put down his glass. "Goodness, California is overrated. If you ever come to Washington, I hope you'll let me make up for this abomination," he said. "The man behind the bar at the Willard InterContinental is a friend of mine. Nobody in the world makes a better martini than Jim at the Willard InterContinental."

"We're a long way from Washington, Mr. Scott."

He chuckled. "It would be a mistake to think that *anywhere* is a long way from Washington, Ms. Jimenez. Even Paradise."

Mona ate the olives from her martini. The rest she left in the glass. Scott was right; it *was* an abomination.

"If that's some kind of oblique threat, you've picked the wrong woman, Mr. Scott. Don't think I don't know who Michael Marvin is. But I'm not afraid of him. You know why?"

Scott smiled, shook his head.

"Because I'm too busy to be scared," said Mona.

Scott laughed. "I admire your moxie, Ms. Jimenez."

Mona held up the piece of paper. "Would you take this deal, Mr. Scott?"

"Certainly not."

Now it was Mona's turn to smile. "There's another thing we have in common," she said.

"What is the first thing?"

"We both know what a proper martini should taste like."

He laughed. "You won't beat me in court, you know. You may be an excellent litigator, but you have no friends. You've spent your career representing the powerless, and now you have no power. Me, on the other hand—when powerful people need a lawyer, they call me. And now I am the most sought-after trial lawyer in this country."

"I bet you drive a white Porsche," she said.

Scott affected a look of distaste. "Goodness, how vulgar. I don't drive anything, Ms. Jimenez. I have a driver.

He picks me up in my Bentley. In British racing green. Now, what answer shall I give the company?"

Mona shook her head. "It's a no, Mr. Scott."

......

After Scott left, Mona stayed in the bar and ordered a burger and beer for dinner. Paradise Karaoke may not have been able to produce a proper martini, but they could do the basics. Feeling restored and ready for bed, Mona checked the time on her phone. It was a quarter to eight. She settled up and got out of there just as they were turning on the karaoke machine.

Out in the parking lot, she saw the Ram pulling out. She glanced at the driver. He had a black mustache and black hair. He was staring at her. Mona's blood froze in her veins. *Soto.*

The truck exited the lot and was gone.

Mona ran to her car, got in, and locked the doors. There was no one in the lot but her, but she still locked the doors. Her hands were shaking.

"It wasn't him," she said out loud. "It couldn't have been him."

She told herself that she was exhausted, that it had been a long day, that the heat was oppressive, that her nerves were frayed, that she should've skipped the beer.

Mona picked up her phone to call Finn. But she put it down without dialing him. "What are you going to say?" she said out loud. "You just saw Carmen's psycho boyfriend in a parking lot?"

She started the car and exited the parking lot. By the time she was on the interstate driving back toward the motel, her hands had almost stopped shaking. She kept her foot steady on the gas, the RAV moving along with its unambitious, reliable engine. She drove out of Paradise and then through the few miles of desert between

the town and the Eden Inn. Soon the repetition of road-
side electricity poles, the rhythmic thump of her wheels
passing over the joins in the asphalt, the desert shrubs
merging into one, the stars coming out, put her almost in
a meditative state. The adrenaline surge now dissipated.
Either side of her, the highway dipped away a bit, and
then it was desert, sand and scrubs as far as she could see.
Soon, she thought, it would be dark, and desperate people
would emerge from the dunes and hollows and start moving north, while border agents with night-vision goggles
would search for the heat coming off their bodies. She
kept the radio off. She didn't want to break her somber
state of mind. She saw the neon sign for the Eden Inn
up ahead. The *E* was flickering, so that one second the
sign read *Eden,* the next just *den.* Mona heard a rattling
sound. Irritated, she glanced at the vents in her dash. She
really needed to get that fixed.

Then she realized she hadn't turned on the AC. The
rattling wasn't coming from the vents.

It was coming from under her seat.

Her throat went dry. Her heart banged to get out. Headlights from a vehicle heading the other way lit up the
inside of her car.

Something smooth and strong and cold brushed against
her leg.

She panic-slammed the brakes.

The RAV skidded, careened into the drainage ditch,
and pitchpoled into the air. The last thing Mona felt before blacking out was a momentary lapse of gravity and
then an earsplitting crash as the car landed on its roof.

TWENTY-SIX

AT 5:00 the next morning, Finn was piloting the Interceptor back into Long Beach after a long and uneventful patrol. When the boat reached a point about five miles from shore—the outer limit of the reach of the shore-based cell towers—he felt his phone, which he had zipped up in a waterproof pouch deep in a pocket of his utility overalls, vibrate. A moment later, it vibrated again.

And again.

He pulled out his phone. He saw he had seven missed calls from the same unknown number. A chill rippled through him. He slowed the boat down to quiet the outboards, then stepped away from the wheel.

"Take over," he said to Chinchilla.

He called the number.

"Paradise General Hospital, good morning," said a voice. It sounded faint. They were still far from shore, and the signal was weak.

Finn's stomach felt hollow. "I'm looking for my wife, Mona Jimenez."

"One moment, please."

He was put on hold. He heard music.

"Mr. Finn?" said a voice. "I'm Dr. Aguirre. I have bad

news, I'm afraid." The doctor told Finn about Mona's accident. "How soon can you get here?" he asked.

Finn hung up and turned to Chinchilla. "Mona was in a car crash. She's in intensive care in Paradise."

Finn's legs felt weak. He propped himself against the control console. He saw Chinachilla pick up the mic and heard her request a chopper.

After she hung up, she said, "Strap in." Then she pushed down on the throttles, and the Interceptor took off toward the sunrise.

At fifty knots, it took them a little over five minutes to cover the five miles. Chinchilla barely slowed when they passed the breakwater. She pulled up alongside the dock. Finn jumped ashore. He hustled to a waiting CBP vehicle. The vehicle switched its lights and siren on and rushed him to the helicopter pad. A CBP light helicopter was waiting for him, its blades already turning. Finn hauled himself up into the seat next to the waiting pilot; the pilot handed him a set of headphones, gave him a thumbs-up, then fired up the rotors; the chopper left the ground.

Finn watched the cranes lifting containers on and off the ships. The chopper passed over the giant round white tanks of the oil terminal. They flew over the waking city. He saw the streetlights go out. Through the headphones, he heard the pilot's voice tell him it was seventy-five minutes' flight time to Paradise. He nodded. Soon, the suburban sprawl gave way to mountains. Finn watched cars traveling along the road in a valley below. They left the mountains behind and flew over the Salton Sea. They flew over endless rectangles of emerald green—the crop fields of Imperial County. They crossed the main canal irrigating all those fields, and the green turned to brown. They passed over the interstate, then saw a cluster of lonely-looking, flat-roofed buildings surrounded by desert.

Paradise.

The pilot put the chopper down on a patch of sand next to the hospital. The rotors kicked up a sandstorm. Finn covered his mouth and nose and jumped to the ground. Staying in a crouch, he hurried to the hospital.

Dr. Aguirre met him at reception. "Follow me," he said.

While they walked, the doctor talked. "She was choppered in last night at 8:30," he said. "She's fractured the femur in her right leg, where she got trapped under the dash. They had to cut her out. She's broken four ribs. She's got bruises all over her face from the airbag. She looks pretty beat up, but we scanned her and didn't find any fractures in her skull, neck, or spine, so that's a lucky break, if I can call it that. We're keeping her in a brace just to be safe. She's got a fair amount of internal hemorrhaging, but it could've been a lot worse. She was lucky that the highway patrol responded as quickly as they did. With accidents like this, every second counts."

The doctor led Finn through a pair of swinging doors.

"Do you know what happened?" asked Finn.

"Just the basics. She was traveling west on the I-8. A truck coming the other way saw the car she was driving veer off the road, hit the embankment, and flip onto its roof. He radioed it in to the CHP from his truck. The first responders got to her within ten minutes. They made sure she was breathing, cut her out, and brought her in."

"What made her veer off the road?" said Finn.

The doctor shook his head. "I don't know. There was no other vehicle involved. We're testing her blood alcohol."

Finn shook his head. "It's not that. She wasn't a big drinker."

"We still need to run the test," said the doctor.

The doctor had given Finn the first of the two things he needed: information. Now he needed the second thing.

"I want to see her," he said.

Dr. Aguirre pushed open a door. "This way," he said.

◆◆◆◆◆

When Finn saw that Mona was conscious, his adrenaline flow briefly ebbed, only to surge a moment later when he saw the bruises all down the left side of her face. Her head was in a brace, her left leg in a cast and hoist, and on the dark screen of the EKG monitor next to her bed, he saw three green lines peaking regularly. Next to that was a plastic bag hooked on the stand, clear liquid dripping from it through a tube leading into a cannula embedded in her arm.

"You're here," she said, her voice an opiated murmur. She tried to smile.

Finn sat down next to her, kissed her on the unbruised part of her forehead, and said softly, "I'm here." He took hold of her right hand and didn't let go.

Mona asked Finn to come closer. He leaned in.

Even inches from her lips, he wasn't sure he'd heard her right.

Something about a snake.

He shushed her. "You don't need to talk," he said.

But she wanted to talk. She looked at him as insistently as her injuries and the morphine would allow.

"I heard it rattling, Nick. Under my seat. I *felt* it."

He saw an expression pass over her face that even morphine couldn't kill: terror.

Finn's mind raced. "Maybe it came through a vent. Looking for heat," he said.

"No. Somebody put it there," she said. She glanced anxiously at the door before continuing. Finn leaned even closer. He could feel her breath on his ear when she whispered, "Soto."

Finn's stomach hollowed out. He remembered what Mona had told him about Soto, how he'd put a girl in a box filled with snakes. He thought about what Mona had told him about the dendrotoxin in Carmen's body. Then another part of his brain—the reptile part, the part that controlled for aggression and territoriality—unleashed a fresh wave of adrenaline. He tightened his grip on Mona's hand.

She continued, "I *saw* him, Nick. I went cold all over. Like being in a nightmare . . ."

The EKG machine beeped. Mona's pulse was quickening, but her voice was becoming weaker, like she was about to pass out.

"Carmen said she saw him, too, in a dream, but I didn't believe her. I should've believed her, Nick. I should've . . ."

He squeezed her hand. He said everything was going to be all right. He told her to rest.

"I should've believed her," said Mona again. Maybe she was hearing what he was saying, maybe she wasn't. Either way, her eyes were closing now, and the machine was beeping in an alarming way. Finn fetched the nurse, who adjusted the pump on the painkiller being drip-fed into Mona's blood.

"Your wife needs to rest," she said.

Finn pulled a chair up next to Mona and watched her sleep.

While she slept, Finn sat. In his younger days, whenever he'd felt this level of anger, this level of fear, he would either sweat out the feelings through intense exercise, or he would drown them in alcohol and drugs.

Now that he was older and sober, he'd learned a third way: to sit with them.

He did this now. He didn't try to do anything more than sit in the chair by his sleeping wife, counting his own breaths.

Eventually, his breathing slowed and his pulse settled. His vision softened and his eyelids started to droop. He felt himself on the verge of falling asleep.

Before letting himself succumb, he made a vow. He knew it was a profane vow, but he made it anyway.

He vowed he would find the man who had hurt Mona, and he would kill him.

TWENTY-SEVEN

MIDMORNING, two accident investigators from the California Highway Patrol showed up at Mona's bedside. She was still asleep, so Finn shepherded the officers into the corridor. They said they had a few questions.

"Do you know if she takes any medication?" asked one.

"No," said Finn.

"Is she a regular drinker?"

"Not to excess."

"Has she been particularly fatigued?"

"Listen, she told me something," said Finn.

Finn told the investigators about the snake.

"Under the seat, she said?" said one. He had his notebook flipped open.

"You hear about them getting under the hood sometimes," said the other. "But inside the *cabin*?"

Finn told them about Soto. The whole story, from the beginning.

They looked at him dubiously.

"So what you're saying is, you think this guy came up from Mexico to kill your wife by putting a rattlesnake under her seat in her car? Is that what you're saying?"

"Yes," said Finn. "Mona saw him next to her car, in the parking lot outside Paradise Karaoke."

Again, the dubious look.

"There are easier ways of killing a person," said the other officer.

"This guy, Soto, is a psychopath," said Finn. "He doesn't just want to hurt people. He wants to *enjoy* hurting them. He threw acid on a girl. He put another in a box with snakes. He's a herper."

"A what?"

"A herper. A snake collector. He did this."

Finn caught the glance between the two investigators. He saw that they had already made up their minds about what had happened.

Fuck you guys, he thought.

"Well, the first responders who pulled her out didn't say anything about any snakes," said one of the officers. "But we'll make a note of it. Are you *sure* she's not on any medication?"

⁘

Over the following week, Finn and Mona quickly fell into a rhythm. Little rituals that brought them both great comfort. At Mona's insistence, Finn took up residence in her room at the Eden Inn.

"I want you to shower and change your clothes. For my sake," she said. Finn rented a car, brought a change of clothes, and slept in the room, but he was always at the hospital before Mona woke and always the last visitor to leave. He got to know all the night nurses. He brought her treats and magazines; her cell phone had been destroyed in the crash, so he went out and bought her a new one. He got in touch with the phone company to set it up. He coordinated with the insurance company about the car. He called her office. Joaquin said he would file a motion to delay the trial.

After a week, the CHP accident investigators completed

their report. They brought Finn a copy. The investigators had written that it was a single-vehicle accident caused by driver error. They put it down to something called trucker syndrome. They noted Mona had been driving long distances over the past few months, back and forth between the coast and desert. People with trucker syndrome become complacent. They forget how fast they're going. They imagine things. Finn saw that the investigators had not included in their report Mona's assertion that there was a snake under her seat, causing her to panic. He threw the report in the trash.

He got into his rental and drove out to the spot on the interstate where Mona had flipped her RAV, pulled over to the shoulder, and got out. Near where he had parked, a large white polyester bag caught on a thorny bush fluttered in the breeze. The RAV was a good thirty feet from the road, lying upside down, tilted forward onto its hood, its back wheels high. It was so far from the road that the highway patrol did not deem it a hazard and hadn't pressed Finn to organize removal.

Finn walked up to the wreck. Up close, the ground smelled of fuel. He stepped over a dark patch of sand where gas had spilled from the ruptured tank. He walked round the front, and the smell of gas gave way to a sweet scent— coolant spilled from the radiator. He kicked aside some wreckage and glass to clear a space, carefully got down on his hands and knees, and peered into the wrecked cabin through the driver's side. Amid all the shards and broken bits lying on the ceiling of the car, he saw a tube of Mona's lipstick. He reached for it now. Then he saw a high-heeled shoe, which he also recovered. He looked around until he located the other. It was poking out from under the driver's seat above his head. Finn reached for it and pulled it out. A thought occurred to him. He reached under the driver's seat and felt around.

His fingers touched something cold, smooth, scaly. He took hold of it, pulled it out, and stood.

He looked at the dead snake in his hand. It was maybe six feet long. It was surprisingly heavy, weighing about the same as a bowling ball. Its head was the size of a cat's. He examined the gray-green diamonds down its back. He turned it over and looked at its white belly. He ran his fingers along the segments of its rattle. They were, he realized, hollow, like shells.

Finn walked back to his car. He untangled the abandoned bag from the bush and dropped the snake in it. He put the snake and Mona's shoes on the passenger's seat of his rental and her lipstick in the dash. He drove to the CHP office in Paradise. He asked the receptionist for the accident investigators. The two officers appeared.

He pulled the snake out of the bag and smacked it down on the counter.

"She didn't imagine it," he said.

TWENTY-EIGHT

THE hospital released Mona on June 29, nine days after she had flipped her car. They gave her a pair of crutches and a script for OxyContin. Finn drove her home on the interstate. They passed the spot where she had flipped her car. The wreck was gone.

"The insurance company took care of it," Finn explained.

"I'm glad I didn't have to see it," said Mona.

After a minute, Finn said, "What are you most looking forward to when you get home?"

"Washing my hair."

Finn's phone beeped. It was Wilkins, his contact at Fish and Wildlife, sending him a text: *Have lead on mamba.* When they stopped for gas, Finn texted Wilkins back, setting up a meeting.

Four hours later, they arrived home in Redondo. Mona got out of the rental car, hoisted herself up on her crutches, and filled her lungs with ocean air.

"Gosh, it's good to smell the sea again," she said.

Someone had left a bouquet on the front steps. While Mona leaned on her crutches, Finn opened the little envelope and pulled out the card.

"'From all of us at Wolfeson, White, wishing you a speedy recovery,'" he read.

"Bless their hearts," said Mona.

••••

Wolfeson, White weren't the only ones to send flowers. At ten the following morning, the doorbell rang. Finn opened it and saw Chinchilla, Gomez, and Klein. Klein was holding a huge, expensive-looking bouquet.

Finn waved them all in. Mona was sitting on the couch in the living room, her broken leg up on a cushion. Her face lit up at the sight of the visitors. Finn handed her the card. She read it out loud.

"'To Mona Jimenez. Get well soon. From your friends at CBP Air and Marine, Long Beach.'"

Mona smiled. "Thank you. First time I got flowers from the Customs and Border Protection."

Finn took the bouquet to the kitchen, searched for a vase, found none, so he put the flowers in a jug, which he carried back into the living room and set on the sideboard.

Everybody was sitting around the coffee table. Finn asked if anyone wanted tea or coffee, but they all declined. There followed an awkward silence, then some equally awkward attempts at humor. The conversation veered to movies featuring snakes.

"My wife loves horror," said Chinchilla. "She made me watch *Anaconda*. I get shivers just thinking about it."

"The original?" said Gomez.

"There's another?"

"You're too young to have seen it, Mona, but in the first Indiana Jones movie, he gets thrown into a pit of snakes," said Klein.

"Now I'll never see it," said Mona.

"No one's mentioned the greatest snake film of all time," said Gomez. "*Snakes on a Plane.*"

"Ella made me watch that one, too," said Chinchilla, shaking her head.

"Did you know it's based on a true story?" said Gomez.

"Stop it," said Chinchilla.

While Chinchilla and Gomez argued, Klein turned to Finn and said he'd take him up on his offer of coffee after all. He followed Finn into the kitchen. Finn filled the filter machine with ground coffee and switched it on. The machine started hissing.

In a low voice, Klein said, "What happened?"

"She was on the highway. A snake came out from under her seat. She veered, hit the bank, and the car flipped."

Klein shook his head. "How'd the snake get in the car?"

"Someone put it there."

If Klein was dubious, he didn't show it. "Who?" he said.

"Mona's suing the BSCA. Someone wants her to drop the suit. It was a message. Not the first."

Klein absorbed this. "Some message," he said. "She must've gotten the fright of her life."

Finn nodded. The coffee was ready. He poured Klein a cup. "You want cream?"

"Sure."

Finn fetched the half-and-half from the fridge.

"I'm putting you on compassionate leave," said Klein. "Two weeks, full pay, not counting the time you've already taken. You need more time, you let me know."

"Thanks," said Finn. He handed Klein the cream.

"Not a problem. We need you, but she needs you more."

Klein poured cream into his coffee. He glanced quickly back into the living room, then turned to Finn and, in a near-whisper, said, "I've been speaking to the commissioner. He says the FBI think they have him. The mole."

"Who is it?"

"I don't know. But he told me that they're going to make an arrest soon. Maybe as soon as next week."

"That's good news," said Finn.

"That's not all. I started putting Interceptors in the corridor. We've busted two drug boats so far."

"Even better," said Finn.

Finn glanced over Klein's shoulder. From where he was standing, he could see Mona sitting on the sofa in the living room. She was laughing at something Chinchilla had said. Finn quietly closed the door and turned to Klein.

"Listen. There's something I didn't tell you. I think I know who put the snake in Mona's car," he said, lowering his voice even further. Klein leaned in.

"Who?"

"A Caballeros enforcer named Soto. The woman Mona was representing, the one who died in Paradise?"

"The one you rescued from the sinking panga?"

"Yeah. Carmen Vega. She was mixed up with the Caballeros in Tijuana and ran with Soto for a while. But she left him, and he didn't like that. When he found her, he burned her with acid. She got away again. That's when I found her. Mona says she saw him."

Klein looked shocked. "Here in the United States?" he whispered.

"Yes. In the parking lot of a bar in Paradise. The day she crashed."

"She tell this to the cops?"

Finn nodded. "Yeah. I don't think they believe her."

Klein looked thoughtful. "What's this cartel guy got to do with Mona's lawsuit against the BSCA?" he said.

"I don't know," said Finn, thinking but not saying that he intended to find out. He liked Klein and trusted him, but he intended to kill Soto, and he didn't want to put his friend in an awkward situation. Still, his expression must've given him away, because after a moment, Klein put his hand on Finn's shoulder, fixed him with his intelligent eyes, and said, "I know sometimes Mona doesn't get what we do, Finn, but right now that doesn't matter. Today, she's one of us. You understand? You need help, anything at all, finding this son of a bitch, you let me know. Not just my help. I mean the whole of Customs and Border Protection. You've got sixty thousand CBP agents backing you up."

Emotion welled up in Finn.

"Thanks," he said. He used the pretext of putting the cream back in the fridge to turn away.

◆◆◆◆◆

Later, after everyone had left, Finn went to the bathroom and ran a bath. While the tub filled, he foraged through Mona's clutter in the cabinet under the sink until he found the fancy bath salts he'd seen her use, then poured them into the steaming water. He fetched a broom from the kitchen closet, taped a towel around its handle, and put it across the tub. He went back to the kitchen, got a large, extra-strong trash bag and some masking tape, and went to Mona.

"Ready?" he said. She nodded. He helped her out of her clothes, wrapped the trash bag around her cast, then taped it shut to her thigh. He helped her into the bath, making sure to keep her broken leg out of the water.

She pointed at her cast resting on the broom handle.

"Clever," she said.

"Put your head back," he said.

He used a saucepan to pour water over her hair. He massaged shampoo into her scalp.

Mona closed her eyes. "This is nice."

Finn washed his wife's hair. The day after Mona had been threatened over the phone, Finn had cleaned the Glock 19 semiautomatic he had given her but which she had refused to take. Now, kneeling on the hard bathroom tiles and looking at the bruises on Mona's naked body, he decided he would keep the gun loaded and on him. It was no use in the gun safe. Klein had given him compassionate leave. He would stay close to Mona, and he would carry a weapon. Not that she could go far on crutches and with no car, but Finn wasn't going to let her out of his sight. Not until he had found Soto.

"What are you thinking about?" she said.

"Who said I was thinking?"

"I can tell. Your fingers don't lie. Something's on your mind."

He rinsed out the shampoo. "I want to get this guy," he said.

She opened her eyes and met his gaze.

"I may have a lead," he said.

She reached out and held his forearm. "Give it to the police. That's their job."

He shook his head. Mona looked uneasy. Like something was bothering her, but she wasn't sure how to articulate it.

"Nick," she said.

"Yes?"

"I need some conditioner."

While she waited for the conditioner to work, she said, "Soto is a killer. I mean, that's his job. The thought of you coming face-to-face with him terrifies me, Nick. I want you to know that."

Finn had been so scared for Mona, it hadn't occurred to him that she might be scared for *him*.

"Don't worry. I'll have backup."

"Who?"

"You remember my Fish and Wildlife buddy? Wilkins?"

"Can't you ask your colleagues? Chinchilla, Gomez, Klein?"

Finn considered this. "I thought about asking them. They'd help if I asked."

"So why didn't you?"

Finn chose his words carefully. "It might go a certain way that would mean the end of their careers."

"Nick. Please don't say things like that."

"I'll speak to Klein. He's retiring anyway."

She nodded. "Thank you," she said. "Joaquin called. The trial's been rescheduled to next week."

"So soon? Isn't it too early?"

Mona lay back in the tub. "Don't worry, I'll have backup," she said.

TWENTY-NINE

THE next day, Finn went out to LAX to meet Wilkins at a coffee-chain outlet in the landside food court. Wilkins, who was in his Fish and Wildlife inspector uniform, had the physique and demeanor of a high school football coach: a barrel-chested man with close-cropped hair and good humor twinkling in his blue eyes. At Glynco, he and Finn had bonded after figuring out that they had both grown up by the beach in Southern California—Wilkins was from Carlsbad. They sat down at a table looking out at the crowded departures hall.

Finn told Wilkins what had happened to Mona. How she'd veered off the highway when a rattlesnake slithered out from under her seat. How a cartel enforcer, Soto, had put it there. Unlike the accident investigators, Wilkins didn't hesitate.

"There are some crazy sickos in this world," he said. "Speaking of which, that's why I texted you. Last week, we busted this guy trying to smuggle a dozen king cobras. So we're interviewing him, seeing if he could fill some gaps we had with other cases, other animals we'd intercepted, and he starts talking how last April, this guy paid him $10,000 for a black mamba."

Finn put down his coffee.

"We're holding him in Torrance," Wilkins said.

·····

The California base of the United States Fish and Wild-life Service is located in a business park out by the refinery in Torrance. Wilkins led Finn into an interview room, then went off to get the reptile trafficker. He'd given Finn the guy's background: his name was Zhao Wei, originally from Laos, ethnically Chinese, a naturalized U.S. citizen, currently living in Garden Grove. "But on the forums, these guys never use their real names," Wilkins said. "His herper handle is Ofis."

·····

Zhao Wei, a.k.a. Ofis, was a slender man in his midthirties who didn't waste time. As soon as he sat down, he looked directly at Finn and said, "So we make a deal?"

Wilkins sat down next to Finn. "Slow down, Ofis. Let's see what you've got first. Tell Agent Finn what you told me about the mamba."

Zhao nodded. "Last year, beginning of April, one of my clients sends me a message. He says he wants a black mamba. No one ever asked for one before. I knew it was hard to get, but he's one of my best clients. I said I would try and that it would be expensive. He said he didn't care; he needed a gift for his girlfriend."

Finn felt a chill.

Zhao went on, "I said okay, whatever. I'll find one. Then I say it will cost $10,000, because I figured it's so much money, he'll drop it and save me a lot of trouble. But he said okay, fine. Money's no problem. So then I have to find the snake. Not easy!"

"Why not?" asked Finn.

"Because the black mamba is so dangerous. Nobody likes handling them. It's so quick, you know? The fastest striker. Also, my suppliers are all in Asia. The black mamba is an African snake. It cost me money to find someone I could trust there."

"What was the buyer's name?"

Zhou shook his head. "I want a deal first."

"Where did you meet him? For the handover."

Zhou shook his head again and made a loud smacking sound with his lips. "I never meet clients face-to-face. He wires the money. I mail him the snake. Usually, they use temporary post boxes. Never the same one twice."

Finn was incredulous. "You sent a black mamba in the *mail*?"

Zhou seemed to think it was nothing unusual.

"What service do you use?" said Wilkins.

"Delta. Delta's very good. The animals usually arrive alive."

"I'm curious, how do your customers find you? Online, I mean. Is it on the dark web or something?" asked Finn.

Zhao shook his head. "My customers don't know how to use the dark web. They're not weirdos. When I want to sell a snake, I put an ad on Craigslist. Herpers know where to look."

Craigslist. Finn thought, *What a world.*

"So we make a deal and I give you black mamba guy, yeah? No jail time?" said Zhao.

Wilkins looked to Finn. Finn shook his head.

"You haven't given me anything, Ofis. All you've told me is about some person you met on Craigslist. No name, no address, nothing. How do I know if it's my guy?"

"If you're looking for someone who has a black mamba, this is your guy. No other herper in the country has one."

"What, you know every herper in the country?"

Zhou gave Finn a look that said, *Pretty much.*

Finn said to Wilkins, "Can I talk to you outside for a moment?"

✦✦✦✦✦

In the corridor, Finn said, "You trust him?"

"He's facing a solid decade in jail," said Wilkins. "I think he's legit. And anyway, if he's feeding us BS, we just prosecute as we would have for the cobras."

"Okay. So how would we set it up? I need to actually locate Soto, not just mail him a package."

Wilkins thought for a moment. Then he said, "You ever collect trading cards?"

Finn shook his head.

"Stamps? Marbles? Anything?" said Wilkins.

Finn said no. He hadn't had that kind of a childhood.

"Okay. Well, I did. And the thing I remember about collecting cards is that even when I got the card I wanted, the one I'd wanted all semester, I'd feel happy when I got it. But not for long. After a while, my treasured card became just another card, and then I'd start craving another. That's the thing about collecting. Your collection is never complete. You never have enough. There's always one more out there."

Finn nodded. That kind of craving was something he could understand.

"Your guy, Soto. If he's really one of these guys, one of these collectors, then my guess is he's always adding to his collection. He's always on the lookout. There's always a snake he doesn't have, a rarer snake, a prettier one, a deadlier one, whatever. You want to catch this son of a bitch? You need to bait him with a prize. Dangle something in front of his eyes. Something that he'll risk anything to have."

"So, what, I advertise a snake on Craigslist?"

Wilkins shook his head. "Not you. Zhao. The herpers know him; they trust him. *Zhao* advertises the snake. *You* deliver it."

Finn considered this. "Okay. So where do I get the bait?" he said.

"Remember that guy I told you about, that Mona spoke to? Butterfield? Go see him. He has snakes."

⁕⁕⁕⁕⁕

The next morning, at 7:30, Finn went to meet Stewart Butterfield. Butterfield lived with his wife in a modest-sized house surrounded by a huge garden in South Pasadena. The exterior was standard Spanish Mission; the interior was more unexpected—in the entrance hall was a display cabinet containing scores of snake skeletons. Butterfield introduced Finn to his wife, Jen, who greeted him warmly and asked with genuine concern about Mona. It was Tuesday morning, and she offered Finn coffee, which he declined. Then Butterfield took Finn down to a vast basement area where most anyone else with the money for that kind of house in that neighborhood would've put a home cinema or a pool table or a bar.

What Butterfield had built down there was nothing less than a private reptile breeding program. Finn saw five rows of trestle tables; on each table, he saw white boxes with perforated PERSPEX tops. Power cords ran from each box to power boards located in the middle of each table. Inside the nearest incubators, Finn could see, through the perforated PERSPEX lids, eggs resting upon little piles of wood shavings.

"You mentioned on the phone that your target has a weak spot," said Butterfield. "Well, welcome to mine."

Finn absorbed everything he was seeing. "Wow," was all he managed to say.

"I hasten to point out that this is all perfectly legal," said

Butterfield. "Well, it's legal as per the law as it stands now. They're always changing it. It's hard to keep up." There was a hint of irritation in his voice.

"I wouldn't know," said Finn. "Not my area."

"Well, I don't show this to many people," said Butterfield. "Especially not federal agents. It's just a hobby, you understand. But I was shocked to hear about your wife, whom I've met. I've been able to be of service to the Fish and Wildlife people on one or two occasions, so when you called about your plan to trap the perpetrator, I thought I may be able to help."

He started showing Finn through the room. "Here, you have the incubators," he said, waving his arm over the white boxes on the trestle tables. "Each one is temperature controlled to ninety degrees."

"These are all rattlesnake eggs?" asked Finn.

Butterfield shook his head. "Rattlesnakes don't lay their eggs. They keep them inside themselves until they hatch. These are python eggs, mostly. Some other kinds, too," Butterfield said vaguely. He led Finn to some terrariums lining the wall. "And here they are hatched."

The front of the terrariums were made of glass, the sides were made of plywood, with air vents in them. Each terrarium was about six feet long, two feet wide, and about four feet high. Some contained a floor of gravel, others of sand. Many contained green plants, branches, small hollow logs, and even small ponds, as well as wooden bars across the top for the snakes to hang from. And indeed, Finn observed several serpents coiled around them. Above each terrarium was a heat lamp.

"It's like being at the zoo," said Finn.

"Actually, I had these custom made. The zoo doesn't give them this kind of space," said Butterfield with a sniff.

Finn heard a scurrying sound from a large plastic box on the ground that looked a bit like a pet carrier.

"Sounds like one of your pets is keen for a walk," he said.

Butterfield laughed. "My pets don't walk," he said.

He opened the top of the plastic box to show Finn what it contained: scores of mice.

"I'm afraid their next walk will be their last," said Butterfield. A chill ran down Finn's spine.

"Let's move on," said Butterfield. He led Finn to the other side of the room, where a terrarium stood all on its own, in pride of place.

"Here's what I wanted to show you. The White Queen."

Finn looked inside. At first, he couldn't see any animal—just white gravel, branches of what looked like eucalyptus leaves, a couple of big sticks, and a couple of pale rocks. After a moment, he realized that the larger of the pale rocks was in fact a snake—except this snake was entirely white. It was coiled up on itself, but Finn could tell it was a big animal. At least four feet long. Then he noticed the flare behind the head.

"Is that . . ."

"A cobra, yes it is," said Butterfield. "In fact, a king cobra. One of the most beautiful snakes, but quite common in India and Sri Lanka and therefore not particularly sought after by collectors. Unless, of course, it's an albino."

"Albino. Right. That's why you call her the White Queen."

"Yes. She's a king cobra, but she's a female."

"Why 'king'?"

"I'll show you."

Butterfield opened the lid of a nearby terrarium and with his bare hand reached in and pulled out a small, thin green snake.

"What's interesting about the king cobra, the *Ophiophagus hannah,* is that its diet consists mostly of other snakes. It's at the top of the serpent hierarchy. That's why it's the king. In fact, *Ophiophagus* means *snake-eater* in Latin."

With his right hand, Butterfield slid open a hatch on the side of the terrarium and then thrust in the little green snake with his left. Finn saw the little snake slither into the terrarium and look around anxiously, tongue twitching.

The White Queen began to uncoil. Soon, it had raised its top third, flared its hood. It was astonishingly big. Finn could see a white-on-white diamond shape on its back. Its belly was a faded pink. It stuck out a forked tongue and rose even taller. The smaller snake froze. Finn was fascinated and repelled at once.

"You think Soto would be interested in this snake?" Finn's voice had dropped to barely a whisper.

Without looking away from the drama unfolding in the terrarium, Butterfield said, "There's not a herper in the world who would *not* be interested in this snake."

The green snake started inching away toward the hatch. For several moments, the White Queen remained perfectly still, just flicking its tongue. And then it whipped itself down onto the smaller snake and struck it behind the head, lifted it off the ground, and flung it down. The green serpent was stunned. It curled up in a ball. Blood pearled on its neck. Finn could see its sides rising and falling with its rapid breath.

"The venom is already taking effect," said Butterfield quietly. "Working its way through the lymphatic system."

After about a minute, the White Queen started to draw near the dying snake. It darted its tongue in and out along the doomed snake's head, testing it, checking for a reaction. The dying snake, paralyzed but still alive, couldn't move away from the approaching cobra, which unhinged its jaws and, positioning itself in front of the now inanimate green snake, began enveloping its mouth around it, beginning with the snout.

Finn told himself it was nature's way of predator and prey. But he realized that he was trying to reassure himself. The lethal little drama that Butterfield had staged for him in the terrarium had left him strangely unsettled.

He straightened and turned toward his host.

"There's a theory that we're born with a fear of snakes," said Butterfield in a cheerful, professorial tone. "A sort of behavioral adaptation. Our fear makes us avoid them, which means we don't get envenomated as much as we might otherwise. That's why they get such a bad rap in our culture, starting with the Bible."

Finn could only nod in agreement. It made sense to him.

"What about you? You're not frightened of them?" He looked around the room. There must have been twenty terrariums in there, not to mention dozens of incubators.

"I prefer to say I have a healthy respect for them. I always treat them with respect. The most important thing, should you ever come across an angry snake, is not to move. Don't make sudden gestures. Don't shine a flashlight at it. A snake will only strike if it perceives you as a threat. Otherwise, it would prefer to slither away."

"Have you got a black mamba?" said Finn.

"Those are impossible to get," said Butterfield. Finn noticed that he hadn't actually answered the question.

"I'm curious—who would win in a fight between a black mamba and a king cobra?" asked Finn.

"Oh, that's easy," said Butterfield. "Both are highly venomous. A bite from a black mamba can kill a human within twenty minutes. But evolution has endowed *Ophiophagus* with a secret weapon: because its diet consists primarily of other snakes, it has developed an immunity to snake venom. So if a black mamba bit a king cobra, the cobra would survive. But if a king cobra bit a black mamba, the mamba would die."

THIRTY

AT the same time as Finn was leaving Butterfield's house with the White Queen, Mona was sitting in the passenger seat of Joaquin's Subaru Outback outside the U.S. District Courthouse in Paradise waiting for Natalie, who was in the back seat, to get out and hand her her crutches. Then she hauled herself up the stairs into the courtroom, while Joaquin and Natalie carried the document boxes.

They had arrived thirty minutes early. This time, there were no jumpsuited migrants filling every available space in the courtroom. Mona sat down at what in a criminal case would've been the prosecutor's table and rested her crutches against the bar. She got out her yellow legal pad. She set her pen neatly beside it. She made a tidy pile of the various documents she had brought for today's proceedings. Joaquin asked if there was anything she needed. He was her boss, but this was her case. She was the lead.

The public gallery started filling. Mona could pick out the journalists. She thought she recognized one from the *LA Times*.

Five minutes before the trial was scheduled to start, the Wolfeson, White team arrived. Like Mona, Morrison Scott came through the bar empty-handed. His seconds were doing the heavy lifting, pulling trolleys loaded with document boxes. Scott greeted Mona and Joaquin with a friendly hello, then looked at the jury box. Mona had claimed the table closest to the jury. It meant she was in a slightly better position to read the jurors' body language.

"Well, this will be just fine," said Scott with a big smile, pulling out a chair at the defense table. His seconds set things up around him. He turned to Mona. "Are you recovering well, my dear?"

"My doctor has confined me to light duties only."

Scott smiled. "Well, I will do what I can to comply with your doctor's orders. However, I suspect the judge will be more heavy going."

"Judge Estevez? She seems to me to be tough but fair."

Scott raised an eyebrow. "You don't know? We have a new judge. Estevez wasn't available for the rescheduled trial date."

Mona's stomach turned. "Who's the new judge?"

Before Scott could answer, the room went quiet and everyone stood. Judge Ross entered the room. He sat down and barked that he expected the two sides to complete jury selection by the end of the day.

"I will not tolerate any delaying tactics. Do I make myself clear?" he said. He looked displeased that the case was taking place at all.

The jury selection process began. Paradise was a small town—the jury pool wasn't large, and Mona and Joaquin had done their homework. The detention center was the town's biggest employer, and they quickly rejected three potential jurors after figuring out that they had family members who worked there. By four in the afternoon, they had whittled down the jury pool to sixteen—twelve jurors and four alternates. They had worked quickly and cooperatively. Neither side had tried to slow things down. Judge Ross seemed, if not pleased, at least less irate. He announced that the court would adjourn for the rest of the day. He told the jury to go to another room, where they would receive instructions. After that, they could go home. The trial would continue tomorrow, when he would hear opening arguments.

"Let me reiterate to you all that I will not tolerate over-long arguments. I'm sure the members of the jury want to get back to their lives as soon as possible," he said. He looked at Mona when he said it.

•••••

While Mona interviewed potential jurors in Paradise, Finn took the White Queen with him to Torrance. Butterfield had given him a carrier box with a clear perforated PERSPEX lid and a bedding of wood shavings.

"She's had her weekly meal, of course, so I won't give you any garden snakes to feed her," Butterfield had said, before adding anxiously, "Unless you think you'll keep her longer than a week?" Finn had said he hoped to have her home before then.

At the Fish and Wildlife station, Finn put her carrier carefully on a desk, and everyone stopped their work and came to see. Even Zhao had never seen an albino king cobra before.

"Wow. She's so beautiful," he said.

After five minutes, the crowd dissipated. Wilkins invited Finn to sit down on an office chair in front of a computer monitor. Zhao sat in the middle. Wilkins sat on the other side.

"All right, Ofis. Do your thing," said Wilkins.

Finn watched as Zhao logged into his Craigslist account, then went to the listing for snakes. Finn was astonished by how many snakes were for sale.

"Is this really legal?"

"This is America," said Zhou.

Wilkins had a more nuanced answer. "Some of these

animals being traded here are being traded legally. Some aren't. When a trafficker wants to sell something he shouldn't be selling, he uses code words. Isn't that right, Ofis?"

"Code words?" said Finn.

"*Rare* means endangered. *WC* means wild-caught, not bred. And so on," said Wilkins.

Finn saw that diamondbacks were selling for just fifty dollars. He thought of Mona, how close she came to being bitten by one.

"We need photos," said Zhao.

Wilkins took out his phone and snapped a series of photos of the White Queen. He transferred them to the computer, and Zhao uploaded the best ones to the advertisement he was composing.

"She's *so* beautiful," he said again, looking at the photos.

"How much do you think we ask for? It has to be believable," said Finn.

Zhou made the smacking sound with his mouth. "A snake like this, so rare and so beautiful? Fifteen thousand. Plus shipping."

"No shipping. Pickup only. LA area," said Finn.

Zhao turned to him. "That will make him suspicious."

"Tell him the snake is pregnant," said Wilkins. "She's too fragile to go by mail."

"Okay. Then the price is twenty thousand," said Zhou. "That price will weed out the time-wasters. Very few herpers have that kind of money."

He typed out the ad, then read it aloud.

"RARE! Bona fide, WC albino *Ophiophagus hannah*," said Zhao. "Gravid, so pickup only. LA area. Twenty thousand. Experienced elapidists only. No time-wasters."

"What's an 'elapidist'?" asked Finn.

"Someone who likes cobras," said Zhao.

"As opposed to?" said Finn.

"As opposed to crotalidists, who like rattlesnakes. Totally different type of person," said Zhao.

"I'd add 'Check your state laws,'" said Wilkins.

"Yes," said Zhao, typing. "Makes it seem legit."

Zhao hit the Confirm button, and the three men stared at the screen.

"Now what?" said Finn.

"Now we wait," said Zhao.

They kept staring at the screen. Zhao refreshed the page. The view counter read 004. A minute later, he did it again—013. Another minute—033.

A comment had already appeared. Someone called TheGreatElapidist had written, "Unicorn alert!" Followed by a unicorn and a coiled snake emoji.

Donttreadonme63 commented on that comment: "Yeah seriously. Who believes this is even real."

"There are always lots of wise guys in the comments. The real guys will get in touch by private message," said Zhao. He gazed lovingly at the pictures of the White Queen he had posted, then over at the carrier box.

"She really is beautiful," he said for the third time, in a tone that struck Finn as slightly unnatural.

Finn, realizing it could take some time for Soto to appear, saw there was nothing more for him to do here. He went home, taking the White Queen with him. She'd had her weekly feed. Butterfield had explained that there was nothing he needed to do.

⁕⁕⁕⁕⁕

The next morning, Wednesday, Finn was sitting at the kitchen table, eating breakfast and looking warily at the albino *Ophiophagus hannah* on the counter when his phone pinged. It was Wilkins: *We got a bite.*

Finn stopped eating and dialed his friend.

"What have we got?" he said.

"A guy says he wants the White Queen. Ofis here says it's the same guy who ordered the black mamba."

"How does he know?"

"Same herper handle. Once you have it, you can't change it."

"Will he meet?"

"He says yes, but he gets to choose the time and place."

Finn looked at the White Queen again. He could never be a herper, he decided.

"Fine," said Finn.

"Okay. I'll text you once I get a reply."

"What's the guy's handle?"

"Cascabel."

Finn hung up. He looked up *Cascabel* on his phone.

It meant *rattlesnake* in Spanish.

+++++

Later that morning, after locking the White Queen in the closet next to the gun safe, Finn drove out to Long Beach. In Klein's office, he noticed some flat-packed cardboard boxes leaning against a wall.

"It's my birthday tomorrow," explained Klein. Finn knew what that meant. Independence Day. Mandatory retirement.

"That's the bad news," said Klein. "The good news is, I got my wish. The FBI found the guy."

"Really?"

"Yep. Turns out it was a hacker, like Santos said, not a mole. They've tracked him to Mexico City, so they haven't been able to arrest him yet. They've requested his extradition. Meanwhile, the shit's about to hit the fan at Riverside. There's going to be a big review of all their data security. The place has more holes than a slice of Swiss cheese, apparently. Heads are going to roll."

Klein nodded at Finn. "You'll do well out of this, Finn. Your name is known to people in high places."

"It was Santos, not me."

Both men fell silent for a moment. Then Klein leaned back in his chair and looked wistfully around the office. "I fear that AMOC is the future, Finn. Sitting miles from the action, looking at video filmed from drones."

"Times have changed."

"Times have changed."

The two men shared a moment of silence.

Then Klein said, "How's Mona?"

"Recovering." Finn got up and closed the door. Sitting back down again, he said, "I've tracked down the guy. Soto."

Klein tilted forward in his chair. "Where?"

"I'm setting up a meeting with him. Here in LA. To-morrow."

"You need backup?"

"Before you say anything, I want to be absolutely clear: I'm not planning on arresting him, Keith."

Klein nodded. "If I were in your shoes, I'd do the same."

"If you get involved and things go wrong, it could mean your pension."

Klein looked offended. "Jesus H. Christ, Finn. Twenty years, and this is how they treat me? You think I care about the pension?"

Finn nodded. "Okay. Then I'll tell you my plan."

THIRTY-ONE

MEANWHILE, out in Paradise, the temperature was rising. By the time Mona got to court, it was in the nineties, and it wasn't even nine. Judge Ross arrived late. He made no apology. The jury was sworn in at 9:15 A.M. When the judge invited her to make her opening statement, Mona was ready. She reached for her crutches.

"You can make your statement sitting down, if you prefer," said Judge Ross, nodding at the cast on her leg.

Mona hauled herself up. "Thank you, Your Honor. I would rather stand."

She hobbled to a spot midway between the judge and the jury. "Ladies and gentlemen, this case is about a young woman who died because a billion-dollar company neglected her."

She paused and looked at each of the jurors one by one.

"Her name was Carmen Vega, and she was just twenty years old when she died. She died on the twenty-second of April, in Paradise Detention Center, a few miles east of where we are now. No doubt you heard about the incident—it was all over the news at the time. Carmen was bitten by a snake."

Mona nodded to Joaquin, who put a picture up on the projector. A school photo of a fifteen-year-old Carmen, wearing pigtails and in the uniform of the middle school that Finn and Mona had visited in Ciudad Neza, appeared on the pull-down screen. She looked more like a child than an adult. Mona looked again at the jury. She was glad to see they were all looking up at Carmen, not her.

"Paradise Detention Center is operated by the Border Security Corporation of America. The BSCA is the largest and most successful for-profit prison company in the world. Last year, it made a pre-tax profit of $700 million—$700 million, ladies and gentlemen, from incarcerating migrants. Yet when Carmen Vega was bitten by a snake, budget cuts meant there was no antivenin in the infirmary.

"Ladies and gentlemen, the BSCA exists for one purpose only: profit. The BSCA has no aim other than making money. It doesn't care about the people that we, the taxpayers, pay it to incarcerate. And it's banking on the fact that we won't care, either."

"You all live out here in snake country. Maybe you know someone who's been bitten. Maybe your dog has been bitten. Maybe you've been bitten by a snake yourself. No doubt about it, it's horrible. But how many people do you know that have *died* from a snakebite?"

Mona marked a long pause.

"I would bet not a single one. Now, I'm going to show you some statistics during this trial. I'm going to ask you to consider the odds of something happening versus it *not* happening. There's no way around it, I'm afraid, and I thank you in advance for bearing with me. But for the time being, let me give you just two pertinent numbers. Let me tell you what the odds are of getting bitten by a venomous snake. According to the literature, around 8,000 Americans are bitten by venomous snakes each year. Eight thousand people, out of a population of 325 million. Of those 8,000 people unlucky enough to get bitten, on average, 5 die. That means that, in this country, the odds of getting bitten by a venomous snake and dying from it are 65 million to 1. Do you know what the odds are of picking all five numbers in the state Powerball, ladies and gentlemen? About 11 and a half million to 1. In other words, you're almost six times more likely to win the lotto than to die from a snakebite. That's how unlucky Carmen Vega was."

Mona paused again and looked over the jury. They were hanging on her every word.

"Five people a year, ladies and gentlemen. I'm on crutches because I was involved in a motor vehicle accident. Last year, almost forty thousand people died in motor vehicle accidents in this country alone. Your chances of dying in a car crash are much higher than of dying from a snakebite. So why did Carmen die? Not because she was bitten. She died because she was not properly treated. She did not receive basic first aid. It's as simple as that.

"Here's the golden rule if you get bitten by a snake: Keep the bite location lower than your heart and get to a hospital. If you get bitten on the ankle, keep your ankle below your chest, and get to a hospital. If you get bitten on the hand, keep your hand down below your heart, and get to a hospital.

"In the coming days, you will hear evidence that the guards who found Carmen did not have even this basic first-aid knowledge. You will hear from the PDC's doctor that there was no budget for antivenin in his infirmary. You will hear that more than sixty minutes elapsed between when Carmen was discovered unconscious and when she was given first aid. You will hear of all the ways that the BSCA management, in pursuit of profit, made decisions that severely—fatally—compromised the company's duty of care to its inmates. All the small cuts that led to Carmen's death.

"My name is Mona Jimenez. I am here to show you that Carmen Vega's death was entirely preventable. I am here today to make sure that what happened to Carmen never again happens to anyone incarcerated in our name by the Border Security Corporation of America. I'm here, on behalf of all Americans, to ask you to hold the BSCA accountable. We must show the BSCA that, even if the company doesn't care about the people in its prisons, we do. Thank you."

•••••

Mona sat down and tried to read the jury. Two of the women seemed to be looking sympathetically in her direction. Most of the men were looking at the judge, waiting for instruction. It was the defense's turn to make a statement. Morrison Scott hauled his bulk off the chair. He looked as ruffled as the first time Mona had met him in the conference room at the Juntos office. He gave the impression of being completely inoffensive, like an affable, well-liked high school teacher. A wolf disguised as a dotty old man. Scott greeted the judge, then turned to the jury and smiled.

"Usually, I would be sitting where Ms. Jimenez is sitting," he began, "but my honorable colleague appears to be an early bird, which, I'm sure you'll agree, is a sign of admirable self-discipline. In that, she puts me to shame, I'm afraid; I'm a night owl, and early starts make me grumpy. Just ask my wife." He gave a little chuckle, and his blue eyes sparkled.

"Having said that, there are *some* advantages to being an owl. For centuries, the owl has been a symbol of a certain . . . what shall I call it? Prudence? Judgment? Let's just call it common sense. Now, I'm sure there's no need to define common sense to *you,* ladies and gentlemen of the jury. I know that folks out here in Paradise

County are levelheaded, practical, sensible—immune, I'm sure, to the fashionable notions that sometimes spread like contagions in our cities.

"Take, for instance, the belief among some of the younger, more impressionable members of my profession that proximity to the jury constitutes some kind of advantage. A decrepit old owl like me cannot help but believe that it's argument, knowledge of the law, and the inherent common sense of jurors—men and women like yourselves—that wins and loses cases, not the feng shui of courtrooms."

Mona saw wry looks on some faces in the jury box. She had a sinking feeling. Morrison was good. Not fire-and-brimstone good, but honey-and-milk good. He was painting himself as the sensible, patient elder, and her as some kind of young, hotheaded radical. She predicted he would use the phrase *common sense* over and over again.

"Now, I'm sure that we all agree that we live in the greatest country on earth. But let's be honest, we are living through difficult times right now. Divided times. There's a lot of anger. Our representatives in Washington seem to spend most of their time shouting at each other. So do the people on TV. It seems to me that many people today think shouting is the way to win an argument, rather than good reasoning. There seems to be no room for courtesy anymore—young people nowadays seem to be willing to fight by means fair or foul, even over matters of the least consequence, such as the customary seating arrangements in a courtroom."

Scott didn't look at Mona. He didn't need to. An older lady in the front row of the jurors' box glanced at her with disapproval. This was a deeply conservative part of the country. Scott was painting her as a punk. Mona glanced at Judge Ross. He had fidgeted throughout her opening statement, flipping through papers and shifting in his seat, giving the impression that he could not wait for her to finish. He wasn't doing any of that now. He looked comfortably ensconced in his huge chair, up there on his dais, hanging on Scott's every word.

Scott continued, "Now, my esteemed colleague has made much of the fact that the BSCA is a for-profit company. And there's no denying that there is a legitimate debate to be had over the role of private enterprise in securing our borders. But, ladies and gentlemen, that is not the argument you are being asked to resolve here. The only question you will need to answer in this courtroom is this: Did the Border Security Corporation of America *cause* the death of Carmen Vega?"

He paused and looked at each of the twelve jurors in turn.

"The key word here, ladies and gentlemen, is *cause*. What do we mean by that word, *cause*? What does it mean specifically in this case?

"Let's look first at what it does *not* mean. It does *not* mean that the BSCA killed Carmen, because, as my learned friend mentioned during her opening, Ms. Vega died after being bitten by a rattlesnake. Bitten three times, in fact. It was the serpent that killed Carmen; on that, we are in agreement."

Here, Scott directed a kindly look at Mona, as though he were a friendly uncle indulging a young niece's foolish diatribe at the Thanksgiving table. Mona bit her lip.

"No, there's no argument that it was the snake that killed Carmen," emphasized Scott. "So then, are we supposed to believe that the BSCA *caused* the snake to bite Carmen? Ladies and gentlemen of the jury, ask yourselves: Is it reasonable to hold a person or a company responsible for the actions of rattlesnakes in the California desert?"

A murmur of agreement from the jury.

"Now, I expect my learned colleague will tell you all kinds of things about how the BSCA should have stopped the snake. She will tell you that they should've built a snake-proof fence. She will try to tell you that the BSCA should stock antivenin at the Detention Center, on account of it being in the middle of snake habitat. Well, ladies and gentlemen, you all live here, too. Have any of you ever built a snake-proof fence?"

A pause.

"Of course not. And do any of you stock antivenin?"

Another pause.

"Didn't think so. Why not? Well, because, as my learned friend herself pointed out, the odds of getting bitten by a snake are tiny. Not impossible—tragically, for Carmen—but tiny nonetheless. And the preventative steps that my colleague thinks the BSCA should have carried out are in fact quite impractical, certainly not reasonable, and extravagantly expensive, given how long the odds are."

Mona's heart slid to her feet. He was using her own argument against her. He was making her look like an amateur.

"Now, the idea of causation has a rather narrow definition in law. For someone to *cause* an occurrence, legally speaking, two criteria must be met: the 'but-for' criterion, and the criterion of proximate cause. The but-for criterion is simply this: but for one event, a subsequent event would not have happened. But for an interception, the Rams would've won the Super Bowl. But for a love of sleep, I would be sitting in my rightful spot in this courtroom."

More laughter. Scott had the timing of a stand-up comic.

"You can see what the problem is here, can't you? With this criterion, you can take almost any event, no matter how remote, and argue that it is necessary for a subsequent event. I'm sure you've heard of the butterfly effect: a butterfly flaps its wings in Brazil, which causes a disturbance in the air around it, which builds into a larger eddy, which causes a breeze to blow, and so on and so forth until you get a hurricane in Florida. By this measure, the butterfly did *cause* the storm, but you can't *blame* the butterfly for the storm. In law, we would say that the butterfly was a necessary but not sufficient condition for the storm to occur. The butterfly was too remote. That's where the second element of causation, proximity, comes in."

He paused, Mona surmised to check that he still had the jury with him. He needn't have worried. They were rapt.

"*Proximate cause* means simply this: that for one event to cause another—I mean *really* cause it, in the way a sensible person would agree with—the two events need to be close to one another. A butterfly in Brazil is too far from a storm in Florida to be considered proximate cause. But if I pull out a gun and shoot you, then it is my action— firing the gun—that directly causes you to be harmed. Now, I know all this must seem painfully obvious to anyone with an ounce of common sense, but I will beg your forbearance here. This is the kind of gobbledygook that we attorneys eat up for breakfast, I'm afraid.

"To reiterate my point, my colleague will try to prove to you that, but for the actions of the BSCA, Carmen Vega would be alive today. She will try to say that, for the want of a snake-proof fence, for the want of antivenin, for the want of first-aid training, Carmen Vega would be alive today. Ladies and gentlemen, even if she manages to convince you of this, which would surprise me, it will not suffice. It will not suffice because she must prove *proximate cause:* that *because* the BSCA did not stock antivenin, Carmen Vega died."

He paused.

"Let me say that again: Ms. Jimenez will need to prove that, *because* the BSCA did not stock antivenin, or build a fence, or train its guards, the snake bit Carmen Vega, and she died. See how silly that sounds? *That's* proximate cause.

"It sounds silly, because it is. But what *you* have to do here is not silly. It's the opposite of silly, in fact. What you have to decide here is of great consequence, not just to the BSCA but to the entire country. Imagine if a court like this one decided to hold a company or person responsible for the actions of wildlife. Imagine the consequences. Where might it lead?

"Let me give you one example. Imagine you go camping in Sequoia National Park and, God forbid, you get eaten by a bear."

Giggles from the jury box.

"A sad outcome," said Scott with a smile. "And I can imagine that, naturally, your family might bear some rancor toward the bear. They may even seek to hunt it—with a permit, of course. But should your family be permitted to *sue* the bear?"

More laughter.

"Should they sue the Parks and Wildlife service? On what grounds? That there are bears in the forest?"

Scott let the question hang. Mona was absolutely enraged. None of Scott's statement was presentation of fact. All of this was argument. Why wasn't the judge intervening? She glared at Ross. He looked entertained, as though by some amusing anecdote being told by a member at his club.

Scott continued, "Of course not. It would be absurd. It would go against all common sense."

Scott paused, allowing a moment, Mona sensed, to let the psychological complicity build between him and his audience. Common sense is what binds us, he was saying. What we have in common is common sense.

"Now, let us consider for a moment the tragic case of Carmen Vega. I say tragic, because there's no other word for it. The plaintiff will tell you how she suffered in Mexico, and how, after enduring horrific abuse—torture, there's no other word for it—she fled in fear of her life. She was intercepted by our border security forces and was being held in the detention center here in Paradise pending her trial. All of which is tragic. It really breaks my heart. But the key question here is, *why* was she being held here, in Paradise? She was being held in detention because she broke the law. *Our* law. I'm not blaming her—in her situation, who wouldn't have fled?—but she was being held in detention while her case was under review, and the law is the law. We are a nation of laws—that is what makes us great. That Carmen died after encountering a snake is a tragic end. But I put it to you that the Border Security Corporation of America is no more liable for the actions of the snakes in Paradise than Parks and Wildlife is for that of bears in its parks, or the State of California for the earthquakes that occasionally devastate the cities built on its fault lines. The natural world is cruel, ladies and gentlemen, of that there is no doubt. But to hold people or institutions or corporations responsible for it is unreasonable. It's worse than unreasonable, in fact. It's preposterous. It's just not common sense.

"Now, as I said, you look like people who value common sense. You are being asked here today to decide whether the BSCA is responsible for the death of Carmen Vega. You are being asked to base your decision on the preponderance of the evidence. *Preponderance*—another big word we lawyers like, I'm afraid. A shorter word that means the same thing is *weight*. When you *weigh* the evidence that you are going to hear here in this court-room, you must decide, is it enough to hold the BSCA responsible? I will let you decide. I will avail myself of your common sense. If there is any doubt whatsoever in your minds that it was not the BSCA, but the snake, that killed Carmen, then you must say so."

THIRTY-TWO

"YOUR Honor, may I approach the bench?" said Mona.

The judge gave her an irate look as if to say, *If you must.*

Mona walked over to him. Morrison Scott ambled behind.

"Your Honor, out of professional courtesy, I did not object to Mr. Scott's opening statement. However, I feel obliged to go on the record to say that it was all argument, not statement, and therefore entirely inappropriate. The 'feng shui of courtrooms?' I mean, come on."

"Your Honor, I respectfully disagree," said Scott. "I was being persuasive, not argumentative."

"Oh, please," said Mona. "None of what he said was founded on evidence. He went directly after my case. He was extremely loose with the facts, and that's putting it nicely. It was blatant argument." Mona was speaking quickly, furious. Scott smiled a large, slow smile that only infuriated her more. He turned to Judge Ross.

"Your Honor, I believe I mentioned in my opening statement that I have discerned among young people today a disconcerting tendency to try to win arguments with sound and fury rather than with reason—"

Mona wasn't going to put up with any more of this crap.

"Your Honor, the court should immediately declare a mistrial and—"

"Hold on, Ms. Jimenez," said Ross.

"Your Honor, this is a gross—"

"Goddamn it, one more word from you and I will hold you in contempt. Do you understand? Now listen to me: I think you're confused about who's in charge of this trial."

Mona had been a summa cum laude student. She had either topped or come near the top of her year at junior high school, high school, college, and law school. She was educated. She got Scott's sound and fury reference. She had, more than once, told men who had condescended to her that she did not get confused. But standing there in front of the bench in Paradise courthouse, Mona actually *did* feel confused. Her own opening statement had been textbook; it had been entirely founded on fact, brief, and to the point. She had given the jury a preview of the evidence they were going to see. For Mona, a good opening statement was like the jacket blurb on a novel; it provided the jury a succinct feel for the story they're going to hear, without spoiling it. Hers had been the kind of opening that was held up as a benchmark in law schools. Morrison Scott, on the other hand, had inveigled the members of the jury not with facts but with imputations and inferences. He had meandered. Any other judge would have called Scott out on it, but there had been not a peep from Ross. The judge's bias was so obvious, it sent questions tumbling through Mona's mind. Was Judge Ross not aware of how obvious his bias was? Was he aware, but simply didn't care? It was clear to her that Ross was not even going to pretend. She had naïvely convinced herself that, given how much media attention the case had attracted, Ross would've thrown a blanket over his despotic disposition and *feigned* impartiality for the press gallery at least. But

no. If anything, he had doubled down. He was proudly
partisan.

He was also visibly angry. He swiveled in his chair,
and Mona could see the skin around the diamond-shaped
birthmark on his neck flushing red. His wasn't a general-
ized hatred, either. It wasn't intransitive. It had an object.

Her.

That was the part that confused her the most. Judge
Ross, she sensed beyond any doubt, hated *her* personally,
and she had no idea why. He *hated* her. She could feel it
in her gut, his hatred, the inevitability of it, the way the
bell in a church tower knows, once it's been swung, that
it can't avoid the clapper. There's an impact, and then an
echo, to feeling hated. She'd felt it first in high school,
with a boy whose feelings she hadn't reciprocated. She'd
felt it many times since. Always from men.

Mona collected her thoughts, focused on what the judge
was saying. "Ms. Jimenez, you are overruled. I am more
than satisfied with Mr. Scott's opening statement. Now
you listen to me, and you listen carefully. You are in *my*
court, Ms. Jimenez, and you *will* follow my rules. I will
not have you calling sidebar conferences every time you
have some trivial grievance. In fact, I don't want to see you
up here at my bench again. You hear me? Now get back
down there and do your goddamned job."

His lip quivered as he spoke. Even Morrison Scott
seemed taken aback by the violence of Ross's words.

"Yes, Your Honor," said Mona.

♦♦♦♦♦

The court started hearing witnesses after lunch. Mona's
first witness was Jared Davies—the younger of the two
prison guards who had found Carmen, and by her reck-
oning the weak link. The guards had done nothing right
when they had found Carmen. Nothing that might've

saved her life. Mona wanted that fact to resonate with the jury. Still, she knew she'd have to find the right balance between aggressive and sympathetic; Jared had been born and raised in Paradise, and he probably knew some of the people in the jury. She knew they wouldn't take kindly to one of their own getting thrown under the bus. Especially if they thought of her as some kind of urban radical.

She began by getting Jared to walk the jury through events the day Carmen had died.

"You started your shift on the twenty-second of April at four in the afternoon. Is that correct?"

"Yes."

"And it was a fourteen-hour shift?"

"Yes."

"Do you normally do the night shift?"

"It's a rotation. Sometimes we do nights, sometimes days."

"Thank you, sir. But according to your deposition, you actually requested to be rostered with your uncle, Jim Davies, on the night of April 22. Is that correct?"

"Yes."

"Why did you and your uncle request to work that night?"

"You work nights, you get night-shift pay. I needed the extra money."

"Prior to the night of April 22, had you ever requested to be rostered on with your uncle?"

"No."

"And have you ever since?"

"No."

"Not once?"

"Objection! Asked and answered, Your Honor."

"Objection sustained."

"Mr. Davies, why did you request to be rostered with your uncle that night?"

Jared Davies looked uncomfortable. "Jim's a good talker. Fourteen hours is a long time. It's good to have someone to converse with."

"Mr. Davies, was there any matter in particular that you wished to discuss with your uncle on the evening of April 22?"

"Objection! Irrelevant."

"Sustained."

"Do you see much of your uncle outside of work, Mr. Davies?"

Scott leaped up with surprising speed for a man of his girth. "Objection! Your Honor, this question is immaterial to the matter under consideration here."

"Objection sustained. Cut to the chase, Ms. Jimenez."

Mona turned back to Jared. She glanced at the jury. She was pleased to see a few puzzled faces. Even if they did know the Davies family, she had planted a seed of an idea. She shifted tack.

"Mr. Davies, is it true that your position as prison guard at Paradise Detention Center is your first job?"

"Objection. Inflammatory and irrelevant."

"Sustained."

"Mr. Davies, you stated in your deposition that prior to beginning at Paradise Detention Center, you were looking for work. Is that correct?"

"Yes."

"You stated that you applied for the job after your uncle informed you that the BSCA was recruiting. Is that correct?"

"Yes. Uncle Jim told me."

"You said in your deposition that you underwent training for your job. You said that your training did not include any first-aid training. Is that correct?"

"Yes. No."

"Mr. Davies?"

"I mean, we were told in a medical-type situation to call the infirmary. They said we had to wait for the nurse or doctor to come."

"So you were not trained in any first-response actions?"

"No."

"You weren't told to check if the person was breathing?"

"No. They told us not to touch the prisoners."

"Even in a medical emergency?"

"No."

"Thank you, Mr. Davies. Mr. Davies, you said that on the evening of April 22, you and your uncle began by doing a head count. Is that right?"

"Yes. We do five head counts a day."

"And this was the fourth one for that day, April 22, is that right?"

"It was the first one *we* did, but yes, it was the fourth count of the day. The inmates were coming in from the yard for dinner."

"And when you did the head count, you found you were one short?"

"Yes."

"And that was when you went out into the yard?"

"Yes."

"And you saw Ms. Vega lying on this bench?"

"Yes."

Mona put up a plan of the yard on the projector. The bench in question had a circle around it. It was the farthest away from the doors that led into the canteen.

"Was the bench visible from the doors to the canteen where you did the head count?"

"No. On account of the tent in the yard."

"You mean the tent that was erected to accommodate the extra migrants? That tent blocked your view of the bench where Ms. Vega was?"

"Yes."

"So you had to walk around the tent?"

"Yes."

"You stated in your deposition that you believed she might be sleeping. Is that right?"

"Yes. Sometimes they sleep out there. They don't sleep so well in the cells, sometimes."

"I'm sure. What happened next, Mr. Davies?"

"We went over to the inmate. Jim spoke to her."

"What did he say?"

"He said, 'Get up.'"

"Did Ms. Vega respond?"

"No. Then we noticed that she didn't look right."

"In your deposition, you said her head looked like it was twisted too far. Like it would not be comfortable to lie like that. Do you still remember it that way?"

"Objection!" said Scott. "Leading the witness."

"Sustained."

"Mr. Davies, at what point did you realize that Ms. Vega was unconscious?"

"When she didn't respond to Jim."

"Mr. Davies, did either you or your uncle check whether Carmen needed help?"

"Objection! Inflammatory."

"Sustained."

"Mr. Davies, do you know what you're supposed to do if someone has been bitten by a snake?"

He scratched his head. "Suck out the venom and spit it out?"

"No further questions, Your Honor."

＊＊＊＊＊

After Mona sat down, Scott stood. If he'd been wearing suspenders, he would've hooked his thumbs under them.

"Mr. Davies, your family's been in Paradise a long

time, hasn't it? Your great-grandpa came out before the Second World War?"

"That's right."

"How would you describe the atmosphere in Paradise before the detention center opened?"

Mona got up and stamped a crutch on the floor. "Objection! Your Honor, this is opinion, not evidence."

"Overruled. Sit down."

"Thank you, Your Honor," said Scott with a look of forbearance. "Mr. Davies?"

"Well, we were all pretty worried, on account of the water drying up."

"And you yourself, you were considering leaving town, is that correct?"

"I heard they needed people in the orchards outside Bakersfield."

"Even though your family's been here for almost a hundred years, you felt obliged to leave?"

"When there's no water, there's no work. At least, it used to be that way."

"Mr. Davies, when the Border Security Corporation of America announced it was opening a 500-bed detention center that would employ fifty people, how would you characterize the reaction of people in Paradise?"

"Relief."

"Would it be fair to characterize it as a lifeline, Mr. Davies?"

Mona hauled herself up on her crutches. "Objection. Leading the witness."

"Overruled."

"A lifeline is a good way of telling it," said Jared Davies.

"Thank you, Mr. Davies. Now Mr. Davies, I want to bring your attention to your work at Paradise Detention Center."

"Yes, sir."

"Mr. Davies, apart from the defense, I believe you are the only person in this courtroom who knew the deceased. I think I'm right in saying that. Do you recognize her in this photo?"

On the projector, Scott put up the photo that Mona had showed during her opening statement, the one that Maria Elena had given her.

What's he doing? thought Mona.

"Sure, I recognize her, but that's an old photo. She didn't look like that by the time I knew her."

"How does she look to you in this photo, Mr. Davies?"

"Innocent."

"And when you knew her?"

"More grown-up, I guess."

"Like this?" said Scott. He put up another photo. It was the photo from Carmen's Facebook page—the one showing her on a beach, in a bikini, her breasts pushed out, her arm around a much-older man, a smile on her face.

"Yeah, like that," said Jared.

Mona saw the looks of disapproval on the faces of the jurors. Especially the women.

"Objection! Your Honor, this is an outrage—"

"Overruled! Sit down, Ms. Jimenez."

Scott carried on. "Mr. Davies, you said under oath that when you found Ms. Vega on the bench, you believed she had nodded off. You believed she was under the influence of drugs. Is that right?"

"That's what me and Jim thought first, yes."

"Mr. Davies, can you tell me why you thought that?"

"Well, some of the inmates take drugs."

"Do you mean to say that they can get drugs *inside* the detention center?"

"That's right."

"Goodness. And how do they do that, Mr. Davies?"

"Well, we try to stop it, obviously. But sometimes their family members or friends visit and smuggle things in for them. And sometimes the women offer things in return for drugs."

"What things, Mr. Davies?"

"Favors."

"You mean, the women offer sexual favors? Is that what you're saying?"

"I guess so, yes."

Scott pointed at the photo of Carmen on the projector. "Mr. Davies, to your knowledge, did Ms. Vega ever do such a thing?"

"Well, not to me personally, obviously. But I heard rumors. She was pretty messed up sometimes."

"Objection! Hearsay."

The judge could hardly overrule her. Jared Davies had actually used the word *rumors*.

And yet he did. Mona couldn't believe it.

"Overruled."

Joaquin wrote in big letters on her yellow legal pad: *WTF? What is going on?*

Mona wrote, *Welcome to Paradise.*

Morrison Scott continued, "Messed up?"

"Acting crazy, like she had taken a bad trip. I remember one morning in the canteen, she said snakes were crawling over her in her sleep. She went crazy over it. Dropped her tray."

"I see. And did you report this?"

"No."

"Why not, Mr. Davies?"

"I felt bad for her, on account of the scars she had. I didn't want her to get in trouble."

"What kind of trouble?"

"For taking drugs. And for, you know, the other thing."

"What other thing?"

"That other thing you said. Offering favors."

"Soliciting?"

"Soliciting. That's it."

Mona processed what she was witnessing. She was looking at three men annihilating the reputation of a young woman who had already been literally annihilated. The attorney asking the leading questions, the witness playing along, the judge turning a blind eye. The trinity of male privilege: the stern patriarch, the condescending uncle, the entitled young buck. The three of them trampling all over the reputation of a dead woman, with no one to defend her but Mona.

"Objection," she said.

"*Again,* Ms. Jimenez? On what grounds?" said the judge.

Mona shrugged. What did it matter? He would overrule her no matter what. This trial was a farce.

"Speculation. Is the witness saying he *knows* Ms. Vega was soliciting? Is he saying he *knows* she was taking drugs?"

"He's *your* witness, Counsel," said the judge slowly. "Overruled."

THIRTY-THREE

AFTER Scott finished cross-examining the guards, Mona expected the judge to adjourn. It was the third of July, and she expected that he would send everyone home for the holiday. But instead, he asked her to call her next witness.

Mona called Dr. Woods. After he was sworn in, she gave him a long, hard stare. *Here we go*, she thought.

"Dr. Woods, how long have you been working at the Paradise Detention Center?"

"Since it opened."

"And where were you before that?"

"At the San Clemente Detention Center, in West Texas."

"That's another BSCA institution, correct?"

"That's right."

"How long have you been on the BSCA payroll, Dr. Woods?"

"Since 2005."

"You earned your medical degree from the University of Oklahoma. Is that correct?"

"Yes."

"And when did you graduate from medical school?"

"2005."

"Thank you. Can you tell the court what your role is at PDC?"

"I'm the chief medical officer. I'm responsible for the health and well-being of all our inmates."

"How many inmates are currently in your care, Dr. Woods?"

"Seven hundred."

"And how many doctors do you have on your team?"

Dr. Woods hesitated. "Well, it's just me. But I have two full-time nurses, plus two more part-time."

"One doctor for seven hundred patients. Is that the ratio recommended by the BSCA, Dr. Woods?"

"I don't know."

"You've worked for the BSCA since 2005. For your entire career, in fact. Can you recall any other situation, working for the BSCA, with that doctor-to-patient ratio?"

"Well, you know, there's been a surge at the border. That's why we're over capacity. PDC was built for 500 people."

"So PDC is significantly over capacity?"

"That's right."

"Okay. In your opinion as a medical professional, Doctor, do you believe one doctor is enough to look after seven hundred people?"

"Well, as I said, we're over capacity . . ."

"Please answer the question, Dr. Woods."

"It's not optimal, no."

"So you *don't* believe one doctor is enough for seven hundred patients?"

"Objection! Asked and answered," said Scott.

"Sustained," said Judge Ross.

"Have you asked the BSCA to recruit more doctors, sir?" said Mona.

"No," said Dr. Woods.

Mona left the answer hanging.

"Can you tell the court what you were doing when you first heard that an inmate was unwell on April 22?"

"I was at home, having dinner."

"Do you live alone, sir?"

Scott stood. "Objection! Immaterial."

"Sustained."

Mona continued, "Dr. Woods, can you tell the court what happened on the night Carmen died."

"My cell rang. It was Gemma, the duty nurse. She told me that they'd found an inmate unconscious."

"Did she say which inmate?"

"Yes. She said it was Carmen Vega."

"Thank you, Dr. Woods. Can you tell us what you said?"

"Yes. I asked the nurse if Carmen was breathing, and she said yes. I told her that I'd be right out."

"Okay. According to the PDC's call log, a call was placed to your cell from the infirmary at 6:14 P.M. Does that sound about the right time?"

"I guess so."

"You're not sure?"

"It sounds right. I didn't note the time."

"Okay. Let the record show that only one call was made to Dr. Woods's cell phone from Paradise Detention Center on April 22, at 6:14 P.M. Dr. Woods, according to the entry log, you scanned yourself into the center, using the fingerprint scanner, at 7:04 P.M."

Dr. Woods didn't say anything.

"Why did it take you fifty minutes to reach an unconscious patient, Dr. Woods?"

"Well, I live in town."

"In Paradise, you mean?"

"Yes."

"It's a ten-minute drive from Paradise to PDC, Dr. Woods."

"I felt that the situation was in hand."

"'In hand'? Dr. Woods, your patient was unconscious. She died."

"I realize that. But I didn't know that at the time, did I? She was breathing."

"You didn't think that the situation was critical?"

"I didn't know she'd been bitten by a snake. No one did. Not the nurse, not the guards. Everyone thought she had nodded off. I figured by the time I got there, she'd have come to. When I saw that she hadn't, I gave her a shot of epinephrine. When that didn't work, I called nine-one-one."

"Dr. Woods, to your knowledge, had Carmen Vega nodded off before?"

"No."

"Had you treated Carmen Vega before, Dr. Woods?"

"Yes."

"For what?"

"Well, that's confidential."

"Carmen Vega is dead, sir. We are here to determine whether she died because of negligence. You can tell us what she needed treatment for."

Dr. Woods looked at the judge for direction. The judge gave a little nod.

"Okay. Well, she had severe chemical burns that caused her pain."

"How severe?"

"It's hard to . . ."

"Dr. Woods, on a scale of one to ten, how bad were Carmen's burns?"

"They were the worst I'd ever seen."

"Thank you, Dr. Woods," said Mona. "And Carmen came to you complaining about pain?"

"Yes. She said she had severe pain around her torso and that it hurt to breathe."

"And that was because of the acid burns?"

"Yes."

"Thank you, Dr. Woods. Dr. Woods, can you describe Carmen's burns to the court?"

Scott stood up. "Objection! Immaterial."

Mona saw Judge Ross hesitate. The jury, it was clear to everybody, wanted to hear what the doctor had to say.

"I'll allow it, so long as the doctor limits himself to the victim's medical condition on the night she died. We don't need her full medical history, Doctor, as tragic as it may be."

"Thank you, Your Honor," said Mona. "Dr. Woods?"

"They were severe."

"What were they caused by?"

"They were caused by sulfuric acid."

"The kind of acid found in car batteries?"

"Yes."

"Dr. Woods, can you describe the effects of sulfuric acid on human flesh?"

Again, he hesitated. At the periphery of her vision, Mona discerned people shifting uncomfortably in the jury box.

"It's pretty horrific," he said, keeping it vague.

That wasn't good enough. Mona wanted him to give details. Joaquin handed her a sheet of paper.

"According to Survivors International, these are some of the effects that battery acid has on human flesh: 'Sulfuric acid eats away at the skin, the layer of fat beneath the skin, and the bones beneath the fat. It causes coagulation necrosis, thrombosis, and third-degree burns. It causes lifelong physical and psychological problems.'" Mona turned to the jury.

"Ladies and gentlemen, I am going to show you a photo of Carmen's wound."

Mona switched on the overhead projector and showed

the photo she'd taken many months previously of Carmen's flesh. Shocked gasps from the jury. Several turned their faces away.

The judge intervened. "Take it down, Ms. Jimenez."

"Your Honor?"

"I said take down that photo."

"Your Honor, this photo illustrates—"

"Goddamn it, take it down right now or I will hold you in contempt!"

"Yes, Your Honor."

Mona took down the photo. She did not turn off the projector. The white square of light remained on the screen. Everyone stared at it, at the ghost image of Carmen's torment.

"Dr. Woods, what treatment did you give Carmen Vega?"

"I prescribed her a pain medication."

"What kind?"

"OxyContin."

Mona nodded. The doctors had prescribed *her* Oxy-Contin after her crash. She knew the peculiar bliss the drug gave, like laying your head on a cool, soft pillow. She understood why Carmen had it in her system.

"Dr. Woods, when you said earlier that you suspected Carmen Vega had nodded off, which drug did you think she had taken?"

"Well, I assumed she had taken OxyContin."

"The medication you had prescribed her, you mean?"

"Yes."

"Not a drug smuggled in, as Jared Davies suggested in his testimony?"

"No."

"Do you have any cause to believe Carmen took illegal drugs?"

"No."

"You don't think she was trading sexual favors for heroin?"

He shook his head.

"You're shaking your head, Dr. Woods. For the record, does that mean you *don't* believe Carmen Vega was trading sexual favors for heroin?"

"That's right."

"Thank you. So you assumed that she had nodded off from taking too much OxyContin? What dose did you prescribe Carmen?"

"Fifteen milligrams, immediate-release tablets, twice a day."

"How was it administered, Dr. Woods?"

"She presented herself to the infirmary twice a day. Either the nurse or I gave her the pill."

"Is it possible to overdose from fifteen milligrams of OxyContin?"

"No."

Mona took a long look at Dr. Woods. Late thirties, overweight, thinning hair. No wedding band. She remembered the last time she had seen Carmen, interviewing her in the yard. Carmen had said she'd been feeling unwell. Mona had asked her, "Did you ask to see the doctor?" She remembered Carmen hesitating before saying, "Yes. He gave me some medicine."

"Dr. Woods, given the severity of Carmen's wounds, and given the fact that she was unconscious, and given that this country is in the middle of an opiate epidemic, why didn't you tell the nurse to call 911 right away?"

Dr. Woods rubbed his face. He looked terrified. He looked on the verge of tears.

"I don't know."

"Why did you take almost an hour to reach her, Dr. Woods?"

"I don't know."

Very softly, Mona said, "Dr. Woods, were you angry with Carmen?"

He started crying.

"I gave her everything she wanted," he sobbed.

"Did you delay coming back to the center to punish her?"

"I gave her everything she wanted," he said again. "She wanted more drugs, I gave her more drugs. I told her I'd help find the best skin-graft surgeon in the country. All I wanted was for her to be nice to me, you know?"

Mona sat down and leaned her crutches against the bar behind her. She felt suddenly profoundly tired. She wanted to go to the Eden Inn and sleep for a week.

"No further questions, Your Honor."

♦♦♦♦♦

When it was Morrison Scott's turn to cross-examine Dr. Woods, he spent a long moment conferring with his colleagues before standing up. The doctor, sitting alone on the stand, looked pathetic. Mona wondered how Scott was going to play it. He couldn't argue that the doctor had followed protocol. Not now.

Scott stood up. He wore a concerned look.

"Dr. Woods, do you feel able to continue?"

The doctor nodded. "I'm fine," he said.

"Thank you, Dr. Woods, I appreciate it. It's been an emotional afternoon. I can understand the toll it might have taken on you."

"I'm fine."

"Very well. Then I'll get started." He turned to the jury and said, "I'm sure you all know what a preexisting condition is, but I believe it may be useful if I provide you with a legal definition. A preexisting condition is a medical condition that occurred before a person's health benefits went into effect.

"In September of 2018, Carmen Vega suffered a horrendous acid attack. Really, the most terrible thing. However, the attack occurred in another country and several months before she was placed in Paradise Detention Center. If Carmen had applied for health insurance on the date she was incarcerated, and failed to disclose on her application that she had third-degree burns to her torso, then the insurer would be within its rights to declare the policy void.

"Now, I can imagine how that might seem to you. It's hardly Christian charity. But that is in effect the situation we have here, legally speaking. When Carmen was placed in the care of the BSCA, she had already suffered the burns. They did not occur inside the prison. My point is, the BSCA is not liable for the burns to Carmen Vega's body."

Mona pulled herself up. "Objection. Your Honor, the defense is misleading the court. No one is arguing that the BSCA is responsible for the acid burns to Carmen's body. This is about what happened on April 22."

Scott said, "Your Honor, I apologize. I'm afraid I misspoke. I don't mean to assert that the defense is claiming that the BSCA is liable for the acid burns to Carmen Vega's body."

The judge raised an eyebrow. He looked at Mona and said, "There's your answer, Counsel."

"Thank you, Your Honor. Also, if the defense could ask an actual question, I'm sure it would be much appreciated by all."

Mona sat down and eyed Morrison Scott suspiciously. What was he up to?

Scott smiled. "Dr. Woods, why did you give Carmen Woods OxyContin?"

"To stop the pain."

"And how much did you give her?"

He shifted. "Like I said, fifteen milligram immediate-release—"

"No, I mean, how many pills did you give her? To take with her?"

Dr. Woods hung his head.

"I gave her a packet of thirty," he said.

"To be clear, you gave her a pack to keep? Not to be dispensed to her one at a time in the infirmary?"

"No. She said she needed it at night. So I gave her the pack."

"Is that allowed, sir? Giving inmates large quantities of drugs?"

The doctor shook his head. "No."

"Thank you. You must have felt strongly for the young lady to risk your career for her."

Dr. Woods started crying again.

"Dr. Woods? Would you like us to stop?"

"No."

"Dr. Woods, you gave Carmen OxyContin to mitigate her pain and suffering. Is that a fair way of putting it?"

"Yes."

"Did you read the coroner's report, Dr. Woods?"

"Yes, of course."

"So you know that the toxicology testing conducted by the coroner found high levels of OxyContin in her blood."

"Yes."

"Do you recall how much?"

"Not exactly."

"I have it here. The test showed that she had 2,012 nanograms per milliliter of OxyContin in her blood. In your professional opinion, Doctor, is that a high level?"

"Yes. It's a lot."

"More than you had prescribed her?"

"Yes."

"Enough to make her nod off?"

"It depends on her tolerance."

"Okay. Enough to make her feel no pain?"

"Yes."

"Okay. Dr. Woods, is it fair to say that OxyContin, in a high enough measure, will make you groggy?"

"Yes, certainly."

"Would it perhaps give you a sense of euphoria? Reduce your anxiety?"

"Yes."

"Dr. Woods, is it possible that Carmen Vega took too much OxyContin, to the point that she was so numb, she did not notice when she got bitten by the snake?"

Mona got to her feet as quickly as her cast permitted. "Objection! Your Honor, this is pure speculation—"

"Overruled! The deceased had OxyContin in her blood. It's a fair question."

"Your Honor, no one gets bitten three times by a snake and doesn't notice!"

"I said overruled. Sit down, Counsel."

Mona sat. She saw the concerned looks on the faces of the jurors. Scott addressed them directly.

"These are difficult truths, ladies and gentlemen, but they must be said, and I'm afraid it falls on me to say them. The plaintiff has claimed $50 million in punitive damages from the BSCA, on the basis that Carmen Vega endured horrible pain and suffering when she died. But as you've just heard, Carmen had an exceptionally high level of a powerful narcotic in her blood. She may well have felt nothing at all. She may have just nodded off like Jared Davies said and simply never woken up. Not even when the snake bit her. It is a terrible tragedy, what the poor young lady endured. Of that, there is no doubt. But, ladies and gentlemen, that is not the question you have to consider. What you have to consider is whether the BSCA is responsible for what happened to Carmen Vega. And the law is crystal clear: if there is even a 1 percent chance that Carmen contributed to her own death, then the BSCA cannot be held responsible. Carmen Vega arrived at Paradise Detention Center with a preexisting condition, one that made her vulnerable. Carmen Vega, of her own free will, took drugs that rendered her incapacitated, too groggy to avoid the snake the way a prudent person would. Carmen Vega was so high, in fact, that when she died, she felt nothing at all. No suffering, no pain. She just went to sleep and never woke up. Ladies and gentlemen, let me remind you of the odds of dying from a snakebite are vanishingly small. If Carmen hadn't taken so much OxyContin, she may well have alerted someone when she was bitten. She may even have noticed the snake, heard its rattle, and not stepped on it at all. I'm afraid we'll never know. All we can go on are the hard facts, the evidence we have before us: the high level of OxyContin in Carmen's blood."

✦✦✦✦✦

After the court had adjourned, Mona hobbled out of the courtroom on her crutches. Joaquin walked with her, carrying the document box.

He was fuming. "This is judicial misconduct, plain and simple," he said. "He's not getting away this."

Mona disagreed. She remembered what the public defender had told her at Carmen's indictment back in April.

"He's untouchable. He's the most popular person in Paradise."

She felt utterly defeated.

Joaquin and Mona passed Morrison Scott in the corridor. He was talking to Lewis Anning, the Chattel House lawyer. Scott broke away and approached her.

"Ms. Jimenez, the company has revised its offer."

He handed her a folded piece of paper.

She knew she shouldn't look at it, but she was so depleted after the day, she couldn't help herself. She glanced at it.

"Fuck you," she said.

She screwed up the paper and threw it in a trash can. Scott and Anning started laughing.

On the piece of paper, one of them had written ONE DOLLAR.

THIRTY-FOUR

AT eight in the evening of the Fourth of July, the headlights of Finn's truck illuminated a sign attached to a fence saying that the cement plant he had parked next to was patrolled by armed guards. Finn killed the engine and the headlights with it. Then he lowered the window. He was in an industrial park. There was no one around. He could hear the distant hum of cars traveling along the interstate. On the passenger's seat was the White Queen in her box. He said out loud, "I'm here."

Inside the box was a large, hollow rock made from resin, known as a *hide*. The hide gave the reptile a place to retreat to. It also gave Finn somewhere to plant the listening device. Klein had said, and Finn had agreed, that it was too dangerous to wire Finn. So they'd wired the White Queen instead.

Finn saw headlights approaching in his side mirror. A truck drove past, no logo on its white box. It was the same kind Finn had seen outside AmeriCo. It pulled over about twenty feet in front of Finn's sedan.

"A truck's just pulled up," he said. "A white box truck." He read the plate number out loud. "We might have to move."

Klein was sitting in his F-350 dual cab a mile down

the road, alone. Finn had refused Wilkins's offer to help. Wilkins had a wife, three kids. Finn didn't want to drag him into this. He hadn't mentioned it to Gomez or Chinchilla. Klein was the only person he felt was sufficiently unencumbered to help him do what he needed to do. The only one with the leeway to help him if things went wrong. Like Finn, he was ex-navy. There was a kinship there.

Klein had "borrowed" an M4 from the Long Beach Station. The plan was, if Finn did what he came to do on his own and got out safely, Klein would quietly slip away, return the rifle, and carry on with his retirement. If Finn needed assistance, he'd use a code word to call for help over the wire. Klein would then come in, kill Soto if necessary, and get Finn out. The code word was *corridor.*

For five minutes, nothing happened. Then two men jumped down from the cab of the white box truck, one from the passenger's side and the other from the driver's side. Finn could see their silhouettes walking quickly toward him. "Two men approaching from the truck," said Finn.

The guy who'd come from the passenger's side had something in his hand. Finn could not make out what it was. He reached under the seat for what he still thought of as Mona's Glock.

The guy got closer and pointed the thing in his hand at Finn. A beam blinded him—turned out, it was just a flashlight. Finn raised his hands. The guy said, "Please get out." He was polite.

Finn got out of the car, careful not to make any sudden movements.

"Are you Cascabel?" The flashlight guy didn't say anything. The other guy approached. "Raise your arms, please," he said. He was also polite.

Finn raised his arms, expecting a patdown. Instead, the guy scanned him with one of those wands security personnel used in airports. It beeped over Finn's hip pocket.

"Just my phone," said Finn.

"Leave it in the car," said the guy with the wand.

Finn dropped his phone on the driver's seat. The guy scanned him again. No beeps. "Okay," he said. The guy with the flashlight motioned to Finn to move toward the truck.

"What about the snake?" said Finn.

The guy shone his light on the plastic box.

"Don't do that. You'll upset her," said Finn.

The guy hesitated. "*You* carry it," he said.

Finn carried the box containing the White Queen to the back of the truck. The guy with the flashlight lowered the tailgate. Finn stepped on. The guy hit a button, and the hydraulics lifted Finn up, then shuddered to a halt when the tray was level with the cargo bed.

Finn stepped into the dark.

•••••

He sensed a presence.

"Hello?" he said.

A flashlight switched on, blinding him. Finn heard the hydraulic whine of the tailgate lift closing behind him.

"Cascabel?" said Finn.

The man holding the flashlight stepped forward and lowered the beam. Now Finn could see him more clearly. He wore black slacks, black boots, and a long-sleeved black shirt hanging loose. Finn recognized him from Carmen's Facebook photo.

Soto pointed at the box. "Put it down, please."

Finn put down the White Queen.

Soto squatted and unclipped the lid. Finn resisted an urge to step back. Soto glanced at him, then rested his flashlight on a pallet loaded with cartons of Papas Santas chips so that its beam passed over the top of the reptile box, rather than directly in it.

"My God. She is so beautiful. More beautiful even than in the photos," he said.

Perhaps it was because of the shadow cast by the indirect light, or perhaps it was the effect of looking down on her rather than seeing her side-on as he had through the glass of her vivarium in Butterfield's house in Pasadena, but the White Queen seemed much larger to Finn than he'd remembered. In Pasadena, Finn had figured her body was as thick as his wrist; now it looked equal in diameter to his forearm. And while in Butterfield's house she had lain coiled in a way that had disguised her true length, he had assumed she was around four feet long. Now, looking down at her body roped around the edge of the box, he could see that she had to be at least six feet. Her glossy white scales seemed brighter for being contrasted against the dull brown of the wood chips at the bottom of the container. He caught the glint of her strange blue eyes. She had her hood flared, the white chevrons faintly visible.

Soto stared at the snake, spellbound. Finn remembered what Wilkins had told him about the single-mindedness of collectors. He could see it now in Soto, the man bent over the serpent as if it were a holy relic. Finn knew he was looking at a sadistic killer. But right now, he saw only a pathetic figure.

Without warning, Soto reached into the box. Finn's heart skipped a beat when he pulled out the hide.

"This hide is way too small for a snake this size."

"It's just for traveling. She lives in a much bigger space, with a bigger hide."

Finn couldn't believe the way Soto had just reached into the box with his bare hand. If Soto turned over the hide, he would see the wire. Finn's weapon was all the way back in his truck, under the seat. Klein was a minute's drive away. A man could die inside of a minute. He had the word *corridor* on the tip of his tongue.

Soto held the hide in his left hand and looked back in the box.

"No water, either?" He handed the hide to Finn, then went to a gym bag sitting atop a cooking oil drum, unzipped it, and pulled out a bottle of water. He filled a cap with water and put it in the box. Again, the White Queen didn't react. She seemed to be in some kind of torpor. Finn decided to risk it; he reached in and put back the hide, careful not to make any sudden movements. His hand brushed against the White Queen. She felt cold and slick.

He slowly removed his hand, released his breath, and said, "Water would've spilled during the drive. Have you got the money?"

Soto went back to his gym bag. He held it open and shone the flashlight inside; Finn saw bundles of cash.

Finn took the bag and nodded. "You need anything else, you just let me know, you understand? Snakes, lizards, a crocodile, I can get it for you, all right?"

Soto banged on the side of the truck. The tailgate lift lowered, revealing the silhouettes of the two guys, the one with the flashlight and the guy with the wand. As his eyes adjusted, Finn noticed a third guy. Then he saw another vehicle parked behind his truck.

An F-350 dual cab.

He heard something behind him and turned. Before he could see what it was, he took a hard hit to his right temple, and everything went black.

•••••

Mona lay on her bed in her room at the Eden Inn and dialed Finn again. Still no answer. She had a bad feeling.

She knew he wasn't on patrol, and it was too late for an AA meeting. She left another message, telling him to call her.

It was the Fourth of July. She had spent the day working on the case with Joaquin and Natalie. When she'd asked Joaquin what he thought their chances were, he'd said, "Fifty-fifty."

She flung her phone down on the bed and scanned the ceiling. The ceiling was still vile. A thick layer of dust was visible on the top side of the ceiling fan's blades. The next day, she was putting Michael Marvin on the stand. It was supposed to be the keystone of her case. She would present him to the jury as the embodiment of personal greed, corporate callousness, and political indifference. She had thoroughly prepared for it. But now she felt like she didn't stand a chance. Over dinner at a booth at Paradise Karaoke, she'd told Joaquin and Natalie that she felt she'd lost the jury and would never win them back. She could already hear Morrison Scott's cross-examination in this solidly red district. This man is a friend of the *president;* he employs *dozens* of folks in this town; he lives in *Washington,* for goodness' sake. You honestly expect us to believe he's responsible for the death of this young woman out here in the California desert? Mona couldn't remember feeling so defeated. She wished Finn would answer his phone.

Restless, she hauled herself up on her crutches and started searching around for distractions. She considered the fruit basket on top of the minibar. Then she opened the fridge and considered a tiny bottle of vodka beckoning from its door. Mona vacillated for a moment, then decided vodka wouldn't mix well with the OxyContin she was taking. She shut the fridge door, grabbed an apple from the basket, and hobbled back to the bed. She took a bite; the apple was good—firm and sweet. Searching for the TV remote, she opened the bedside drawer and found the remote sitting on top of the Gideons' Bible.

Mona clasped the apple between her teeth and flipped open the Bible at random. She had only a flimsy grasp of scripture. Her parents had raised her Catholic, but the last time she could remember opening a Bible was during the preparatory classes she had been obliged to take for her confirmation at the age of fourteen. She read a random passage: "God said to Adam, 'You are free to eat from any tree in the garden; but you must not eat from the tree of the knowledge of good and evil, for when you eat from it you will certainly die.'"

Mona munched on her apple and read on. "The serpent said to Eve, 'You will certainly *not* die . . . when you eat from the tree. Your eyes will be opened and you will be like God, knowing good from evil.'"

Juice from the apple trickled from the corner of Mona's mouth. She wiped it with the back of her hand. She thought, had she been in Eve's position, she would've done exactly the same thing. "Your eyes will be opened"? Yes, please. Eve hadn't capitulated to temptation, thought Mona; she had seized the knowledge that was being denied her. The snake had spoken truth to power. No one had taught Mona *that* in school.

Mona put down the Bible and tried Finn again. She sent him an irate text. Then she switched on the TV and scrolled through the program listings. She was glad to see that the motel carried Spanish language channels. She searched for the telenovela she was currently invested in, *Flores Amarillas*. The title was a reference to a famous Spanish mondegreen, a misheard lyric: *flores amarillas* became *flores a Maria*.

It made her think of Carmen.

Flores Amarillas.

Flores a Maria.

She remembered Maws's last words.

Lawyer is lost.

An idea occurred to Mona, one so enormous that it sent an electric current surging through her nervous system.

She dropped the remote and reached for her phone.

THIRTY-FIVE

FINN woke to the stench of vomit. He realized it was his own. He could feel it down the side of his face. It was pitch-black. He tried to move. He couldn't. His hands and feet were bound with what felt like zip ties. He heard the warning beep of the hydraulic lift close and realized he was on the floor in the back of the truck. The truck started moving. His head throbbed.

The truck tilted, and Finn surmised they were going up a slope—probably onto an on-ramp. A moment later, the truck leveled out, and he heard the driver shift into top gear. It felt like they were traveling at highway speed.

Finn tried to make out his surroundings, but there was no point; he was in total darkness. To stay sane, he started counting breaths. It was a mindfulness exercise he'd learned from his AA sponsor.

Finn counted, and counted, and counted. His mind settled. An hour passed. Finally, he heard the driver gearing down, and then the truck slowed to a stop. A moment later, he heard the beeping sound that indicated the truck was backing up. Then the engine cut out, and the truck stopped rattling. He heard more beeping: the lift coming down, letting in light. Flashlight guy and wand guy appeared. Flashlight guy grabbed Finn's ankles. Wand guy grabbed his wrists. They weren't so polite anymore. They carried him out like a side of meat.

Finn immediately recognized where they were: the AmeriCo warehouse in Anaheim.

The two goons carried Finn into the center of the warehouse and sat him down on a chair set up on its own in the middle of the room on some black-and-yellow forklift markings on the concrete floor. LED lights high above filled the place with pasty light.

The two goons started walking away. Finn asked where they were going. One of them turned around, walked back to Finn, and punched him in the jaw—a big, heavy hook that knocked Finn off the chair to the floor and left him with a throbbing pain in his head. The goon picked Finn up, put him back on the chair, then walked off without answering the question. Finn's head throbbed. He closed his eyes. He heard steps. He opened his eyes. Then he closed them again and laughed. "You didn't need to dress up," he said.

Klein was wearing his dress uniform. His shoes were polished to a military gleam.

"It's my birthday," he said. "They're giving me my retirement dinner tonight."

He stopped in front of Finn, sighed, and shook his head. "Jesus H. Christ, Finn. Why'd you have to be so good? First, you intercept the go-fast in the corridor, so I take you off the water. Then I send you to AMOC to get you out of the way, and you find the goddamned corridor. You're the best damn marine interdiction agent I've ever seen, Finn. The best I've ever seen. That's what makes this so"—Klein paused as if searching for the appropriate word—"so regrettable. The agency needs men like you. Like us. Now more than ever. I mean, look who's coming up behind us. Kids like Leela Santos, God rest her soul, staring at a screen all day? Figueroa, who can't step off a dock without throwing up? This younger generation, they're too soft. They can't defend the line like you and I did, Finn."

Finn shook his head. "Figueroa never filed a complaint," he said.

"Can you imagine that bonehead writing a complaint to the OIG? I'd be surprised if he can spell his own name."

"There was never any investigation."

"Of course not. I just needed to get you off the water. You were about to ruin everything."

Finn thought of the box truck in which he had met Soto. "Santos . . ."

"Motorcycles are so terribly dangerous, aren't they?" said Klein with a sigh. "Such a tragedy. You think they'll ever find the driver of the box truck that veered into her?"

"A condo in Baja . . . that dual cab F-350 . . . how much are they paying you, Klein? To murder your colleagues?"

"I told you already, Finn, I don't care about the money. I'm doing this to stop the invasion. Our country is disappearing before our eyes, don't you see that? We're on the front line, you and me. The last line of defense. I did what I had to do. Do you know how many illegals we intercepted in the last twelve months at Long Beach Station? One hundred and twenty-nine. I turned us into the most effective border station in the country, Finn. And now they're making me retire. They're *forcing* me out. The most successful border station in the country. Can you believe that? It's not right."

Klein shook his head and sighed.

"At least when Marvin's confirmed, he's going to ask the president to give me the Medal of Freedom," he said. "It's the least they could do, if you ask me. After all I've done."

Klein looked at Finn as though an idea had just occurred to him. "You know what I'm going to do? I'm going to ask him to give you one, too. Posthumously, of course."

Finn's mind raced. "Marvin," he said.

"Yes, Marvin. Imagine what this country will be like when he's in charge. How great it will be again. Long Beach is just a trial run. He's planning to do the same thing from coast to coast. Isn't it beautiful? All those fucking subhuman beaners, paying the cartel to sneak them into our country, only to end up in our big, beautiful prisons."

Finn thought about Mona—about all she had said about Marvin. A terrifying truth was dawning on him.

"I can tell from the look on your face that you're beginning to see the whole picture now," said Klein. "It's really too bad, you know. You could've been part of it."

Klein fell into a moment of quiet reflection. Then he said, "Well, goodbye, Finn. It wouldn't do for the guest of honor to be late to his own farewell dinner."

Finn braced himself. He expected Klein to put a bullet in his head.

Instead, Klein walked away and disappeared through a door.

Finn felt an indescribable surge of relief.

Then he heard a forklift approaching.

On the fork was a skid. On the skid was a drum. The driver stopped a foot from Finn, then lowered the skid to the ground. Soto stepped out from the forklift's cabin. He fetched the White Queen's box from a little platform behind the driver's seat.

Soto stood in front of Finn and stared at him for a good minute like a scavenger watching a dead animal, making sure no other creatures were moving in on its kill. Finn could feel his jaw swelling from where the goon had socked him. Soto set down the White Queen on the floor a few feet to the left of Finn's legs. Then he walked over to the drum on the forklift—a standard, fifty-five-gallon steel drum stenciled with *cooking oil*. He unthreaded a bolt and removed the ring securing the drum head. He removed the head. Then he fetched a snake hook from the forklift's cab and reached into the drum.

Soto lifted up his hook. Coiled around it was a large, dark-gray snake with a coffin-shaped head, flicking a black forked tongue. Soto let her hang for a moment, a look of childish delight on his face. Then, with his left hand, he took hold of her tail and worked out the snake hook until she was hanging only from his hand. Soto lifted her, coiling and writhing, and held her inches from Finn's face. Finn didn't flinch. But he was clenching his fists, his wrists straining against the zip ties.

"You know what this is?" said Soto.

"A kitten?" said Finn.

Soto didn't smile. He placed the snake right at Finn's feet and let go. Then he whacked his metal hook into a nearby drum, making a sound so loud Finn would've jumped had he not been tied up. The snake reared up the top third of its body. It darted side to side with astonishing speed. It opened its jaws, revealing white fangs set well forward against the otherwise entirely black interior of its mouth. Finn knew what it was. He stared at the drum that Soto had taken the snake from. He remembered how Mona had told him about the oily film on Carmen's skin when she'd seen her body at the coroner's. Finn joined the dots. He looked at Soto.

"That's how you killed her," he said quietly. "You used AmeriCo to get the barrel into the detention center. You put Carmen in the barrel. You put her in the barrel with the snake."

Soto grinned. "I told her I was going to get her out. I told her to hide in the barrel. When I closed the lid, you could barely hear her screams."

The grin slipped from his face. "You're with that bitch lawyer, aren't you? The one I left a surprise for in her car."

Soto used his stick to corral the black mamba toward Finn. The snake flattened its neck, hissed, and lunged. "When she is finished with you, I'll introduce her to your wife," said Soto. "I'll put them in a barrel together, like I did with Carmen."

Finn was not a religious man in any conventional sense. He did not subscribe to a notion of evil. He did not think there existed some supernatural force that can get the better of us and make us do bad things. He did, however, feel on some gut level that the space he had ventured into, this warehouse, containing this barrel, this snake at his feet, and this man standing over him, was in some sense a forsaken place. He had known this intuitively when he had set out that day. He had left the house intending to kill a man, and that intention had led him out of the garden and into this dark wood. Finn thought, *This might be the last place I see.* He was fine with that. But he could not let Soto get to Mona. He had to survive, for her sake.

"I don't get it. Why torture Carmen?" he said. "Why not just a bullet?"

Soto's face wrinkled up. "The whore betrayed me. She had to pay."

Soto smashed the ground again with his hook, and the snake lunged again. It was swaying fast now, visibly upset, just inches from Finn's calf. Finn remembered a tip that Butterfield had given him: if confronted with an angry, striking snake, don't move. Well, thought Finn, he couldn't help but follow Butterfield's advice: his arms and legs were bound. But it occurred to him that the more relaxed he was, the less of a threat the snake would perceive him to be. If Finn exuded fear, he reasoned, the snake would sense it; if he felt anxious, the snake would know. Finn looked at the snake at his feet. The snake was angry, but it was facing Soto, not him. Soto was the one whacking the snake hook into the ground; Soto was the threat it was guarding against.

Finn closed his eyes. He resumed his breathing exercise, breathing deliberately through his nose and exhaling gently out of his mouth, not forcing anything, just focusing on his breath. Whenever the snake's hiss triggered a rush of adrenaline, Finn gently nudged his focus back to his breath. His entire body began to relax. The muscles around his eyes and jaw slackened. His neck unwound. His shoulders dropped. The muscles in his forearms loosened. Slowly, keeping his eyes closed and his focus on his breath, Finn put his palms together as though he were a penitent in prayer. He started sliding his right hand back. He did not open his eyes. He worked his right hand back, staying focused but relaxed. The goons hadn't tightened the zip ties as far as they could go. Finn detected a millimeter, maybe two, of give between the zip tie and his skin. He started wriggling the thumb of his right hand back.

Whenever Soto whacked the ground with his stick, trying to aggravate the snake into attacking Finn, Finn felt his muscles tense up, and he stopped his efforts and returned his focus to his breath. When his mind relaxed again, the tension slipped from his hands. Little by little, he wriggled his right thumb farther and farther back. The zip tie caught the hairs on his hand and ripped them out, but he didn't allow himself to hold on to the pain. After twenty breaths, Finn worked the thumb of his right hand out of the zip tie. He could hear Soto still moving around, still hitting the ground with his stick. He could hear the black mamba hissing. He kept his eyes closed. The mamba on the ground was free; that was its advantage over him. Finn had eyelids; that was his advantage over the snake, which, like all snakes, could not close its eyes. By removing his own sense of sight, Finn had sharpened his sense of hearing. By listening attentively, he had surmised what was going on in the room. He knew by the proximity of its hiss and the direction it was coming from that the snake was next to his right foot. He knew from the clank of the snake hook against the concrete floor that Soto was just to the left, trying to provoke the snake to bite him.

Finn could tell by the increased number of clanks that Soto was growing frustrated with the snake's refusal to bite Finn. Finn had a sense of where all the pieces were now, like a chess player playing blind who can see the whole board and not just the piece his opponent has just played. He remembered the savage nature show that Butterfield had put on for him, putting the green snake in the White Queen's cage, the way the snake had raised itself, had smelled the air with its tongue, had swayed gently for a long moment before striking with such speed that the kill had happened in a blur.

Finn swayed slightly in his chair, bringing his attention to all the muscles in his body. He counted out five, long deliberate breaths.

Then he struck.

In one motion, he opened his eyes, stepped with his bound feet on the snake hook to his left, slipped his hands from the zip tie and pushed a startled Soto as hard as he could, so that the murderer dropped his hook and fell on his butt. Finn felt a prick on his right leg but didn't pay it any attention. He stayed focused on Soto, who was scrambling away from Finn toward his gym bag. Finn picked up the snake hook, lunged forward, and whipped the hook down. The hook pierced the soft part of Soto's larynx right below his Adam's apple.

Soto opened his mouth wide and made a silent scream. He grasped at the handle of the snake hook now embedded in his throat. Blood pumped out of his neck, all over his shirt, all over the floor, and now it started gushing from his mouth, too, making a strange gurgling sound. He desperately tried to remove the hook from his throat, desperately wrestled Finn, but Finn held the hook firm. He looked in Soto's eyes, waiting for the light in them to go out. Finn could feel the strength draining from his adversary. He was almost done. Which was just as well, because Finn was starting to feel weak himself; a strange numbness was spreading over his lips and face. A moment later, Soto's hands slipped off the hook, and his head slumped back to the concrete floor. Finn let go of the hook. He turned and looked for the black mamba, but it was gone. He noticed that in the tumult, the White Queen's box had been upended, and she was gone, too. He looked down at his still-bound feet. He hauled himself over to the forklift's cabin, foraged around in its glove box, and found a box cutter. He used it to cut the zip tie around his ankles. The throbbing pain in his right calf was getting worse. Then he pulled up the hem of his jeans and saw the bite marks.

•••••

The burn in Finn's ankle traveled up his leg. His lips and tongue felt numb, and he had a metallic taste in his mouth, like after receiving a local anesthetic from a dentist. He thought of Mona recounting Butterfield's explanation of how venom works, of why the black mamba's venom was so especially toxic: it poisons not only the blood but the nervous system. That growing numbness he felt was his nerve cells dying. He needed antivenin, fast.

But first, he had to deal with the two goons outside. Finn noticed the gym bag with the money on the floor of the forklift. He unzipped it and found Soto's weapon: an FN Five-SeveN semiautomatic. He checked the magazine: fully loaded. The numbness in his right calf kept spreading.

He was sweating profusely yet felt a chill so pervasive it was making him shake. He knew he was running out of time. He walked over to Soto's body and pulled the bloodied snake hook from his neck. Then he went over to the forklift, hobbled around to the cab, and turned it on. He maneuvered the machine to face the door where the two goons had exited the warehouse. He raised the forks with the barrel on it. He wedged the snake hook between the accelerator and the seat. The forklift sped toward the door. Finn limped after it.

The forklift smashed through the door, knocking out the drywall around it. It crushed through the reception desk Finn knew was on the other side and kept careening toward the smoked-glass front, which it promptly shattered. The barrel on its forks fell off and rolled. Finn hobbled as quickly as he could in the forklift's trail of destruction. To the goons, he must've appeared like a figure out of hell, his silhouette emerging from the cloud of dust kicked up by the forklift crashing through the wall. The dust triggered a fire alarm, while at that exact moment the city of Anaheim released into the sky the first of dozens of volleys of its Fourth of July fireworks, adding to the bewildering cacophony. Finn had Soto's semiautomatic held out in front of him in a two-handed grip. He spotted flashlight goon to his left. Finn fired off two shots. Flashlight guy crumpled. Finn swung his arms, scanning for wand guy. He found him over to the right, his gun drawn and pointed at Finn. Both men fired. Wand guy missed. Finn didn't. Wand guy's head snapped back, and his body flopped to the ground.

Finn had the cold sweats now. The gun suddenly felt heavy in his hands, and he dropped it. He walked over to where the reception desk had been, found the desk phone on the ground, and dialed 911.

"911. What's your emergency?"

"I've been bitten by a black mamba. I need antivenin." Finn felt woozy. He realized his speech was becoming slurred. He needed to speak up against the crackling of the fireworks.

"Could you repeat that, sir?"

Finn's head whirled.

"Snake bit me. Call Butterfield. Antivenin."

Somewhere in the fog, Finn understood that he wasn't making sense. But he was still coherent enough to know that the most important detail was his location. He took a deep breath and made an effort to enunciate clearly.

"Ambulance. AmeriCo. Warehouse. Chapman. Avenue. Anaheim." He heard rapid typing on a keyboard in the background. He felt his legs giving way.

"Sir? Are you still there?"

Finn slumped to the ground.

"Yes."

"Sir, you say it was a black mamba that bit you?"

"Yes."

"Is the snake still in the vicinity, sir?"

Finn scanned the room. And though his vision was beginning to blur, he saw, through the hole in the wall that he'd just made with the forklift, in the pool of blood besides Soto's body, the White Queen, her jaws opened wide, swallowing the black mamba.

"It's. Okay. The. Cobra. Ate. Her."

The last thing he heard before losing consciousness was the dispatcher's voice asking him to say that again.

THIRTY-SIX

THE next day, July 5, for the first time in her career, Mona was late for court. She was only five minutes late, but Judge Ross reacted as though she had just burned the flag.

"Have you no respect?"

"Your Honor, I apologize. My husband was involved in an accident in Los Angeles. He's in the hospital. I was speaking with him, trying to decide whether I should return or not."

"Well? What did you decide? Do you want your associate to take your place? Where is he?"

"No, Your Honor. Thank you, Your Honor. My associate is fetching some documents relevant to today's proceedings. He should be here soon."

"Very well. Then let's proceed."

"Yes, Your Honor. Your Honor, if it please the court, the plaintiff calls Michael Marvin to the stand."

By the look on Ross's face, it did not seem to please the court. However, he gave a gruff nod.

Mona waited while Michael Marvin, who was wearing a navy suit with a flag pin on the lapel, white shirt, and red tie, was sworn in. She stood leaning on her crutches, a laser pointer in her right hand, looking down at the notes she had hastily scribbled the previous night. Once the sheriff had finished swearing in Marvin, she looked up, still leaning on the table.

"Mr. Marvin, what is your role at the Border Security Corporation of America?"

"I am the chief executive officer."

"You're the boss."

"That's right."

"And how long have you been the boss?"

"Since 2016."

"And before that, you were employed by the BSCA in another capacity, is that right?"

"Yes. I was head of new business."

"In that role, you were responsible for the rapid expansion of the BSCA's operations, correct?"

"We did develop significant new business, that's true."

"And that was a significant factor in the board's decision to appoint you to the top job?"

"So I understand."

"Mr. Marvin, would it be fair to say that as CEO, you are ultimately responsible for the actions and undertakings of the Border Security Corporation of America?"

Marvin looked at the jury and said, "I am the captain of the ship, yes. But the BSCA is a huge ship. We employ more than a thousand people at thirteen institutions across the country, including forty-four people right here in Paradise. I can't know what each and every one of them is doing at any given time."

"Sir, perhaps I should rephrase my question. What I meant was, are you not *legally* ultimately responsible for everything that the Border Security Corporation of America does as it pursues its business?"

"Within the scope set down by the law, I am responsible, yes. Although I can't claim responsibility for rattlesnakes."

Laughter from the gallery.

"Thank you, Mr. Marvin. I'm glad you brought up the scope of the law. It's certainly pertinent to this case."

Mona paused and glanced at her notes. She didn't need to read them, but she wanted to mark a pause before she opened her next point. She also needed to draw it out. She was waiting for Joaquin to bring her the missing key. Mona fetched a chart from her papers and put it on the projector. She took her time doing it.

"Mr. Marvin, can you please explain this graph to the court?"

"Sure. It shows the growth in the company's share price over the past twelve quarters."

"Twelve quarters means three years, right?"

"Correct."

"Which is roughly how long you've been in charge, correct?"

"Yes."

"Mr. Marvin, can you tell us what the numbers on the axes mean?"

"Sure. The vertical is the value of the company's shares. The horizontal is time."

"Thank you, sir. So looking at this chart, which you no doubt recognize from your annual report, the BSCA has tripled in value since you became its chief executive."

"Yes, it has," said Marvin. He wore a puzzled look. Mona figured he had been expecting her to hurl grenades at him. Instead, she was demonstrating how much value he had added to the company since taking charge. She turned around and pretended to look something up in her notes and surreptitiously searched the public gallery. She saw Marius Littlemore entering. He gave her a little nod. Mona smiled and signaled for the next slide to go up.

"Mr. Marvin, could you please explain *this* slide to us?"

"This one shows profitability. The horizontal axis is

time. The vertical axis shows how much net profit we made during that time." Marvin sounded bored.

"And this point here"—Mona used her laser pointer to indicate a bar that towered over its predecessor in the middle of the chart—"is June 2016, is that correct?"

"That's what it says."

"Mr. Marvin, what happened in June 2016 that sent your profits skyrocketing like that?"

"We opened two new detention centers."

"Which ones?"

"One in Texas. And one here in Paradise."

"And straightaway, your profits doubled."

"Yes."

Mona let her gaze linger.

"Business conditions are favorable, Mr. Marvin," she said.

"I beg your pardon?"

"That's what you wrote in your message to investors in your annual report. To quote you directly, 'Favorable business conditions and recent policy decisions being made in Washington continue to validate our investments in new facilities along the southern border. Our new migrant-detention centers at Paradise, California, and Dawes, Texas, have already exceeded our revenue projections.'"

Marvin was quiet.

Judge Ross said, "Is there a question, Counsel?"

"Yes, Your Honor. Mr. Marvin, to what do you attribute the jump in profit?"

"You just said it—favorable business conditions and current policy decisions."

"I beg your pardon, sir. What I should have said was, can you be more specific about what you mean by favorable business conditions?"

"A growing market. Increased efficiencies."

"By a growing market, you mean more migrants to detain?"

"Yes."

"Mr. Marvin, why do you think there are more migrants to detain?"

Marvin gave an irritated shrug. "Washington sets the policy, not us."

"That's true. But isn't it also true that your business model *depends* on an ever-increasing number of migrants to detain? For instance, the capital cost of building Paradise Detention Center meant that you needed a return immediately."

Mona paused, then carried on, "Mr. Marvin, the Border Security Corporation of America is now an entity known as a real estate investment trust. Is that correct?"

"Yes, that's correct."

"Is it true that the first thing you did, when you became chief executive, was to turn the company from a regular corporation into a REIT?"

"It happened on my watch, yes."

"Can you tell us why you made that change?"

Marvin gave Mona a condescending look. "It's complicated."

Mona glanced at the jury.

"You mean you don't think we'll understand?"

"I mean it will take some time."

Judge Ross intervened. "Where is this going, Ms. Jimenez?"

"Your Honor, I am trying to establish for the court the context surrounding the negligence that led to the death of my client. We are arguing for punitive damages, and therefore it's vital to show that the negligence at Paradise Detention Center is part of a wider corporate malfeasance. I wish to illustrate for the court the context of profit-seeking and cost-cutting that led to the negligence that caused my client's death."

Judge Ross looked unhappy. "Get on with it, Ms. Jimenez."

"Yes, Your Honor. Mr. Marvin, what are the benefits of a real estate investment trust over other types of corporate structures?"

"A REIT creates stability and security for investors."

"Isn't it also true that to qualify as a REIT, you need to pay 90 percent of your income back to investors?"

"Yes."

"Which means you pay tax on only 10 percent of your income?"

"Yes."

"So it means you pay the minimum amount of tax."

"I wouldn't be doing my job if we weren't. All companies in the world carry out tax-minimization strategies."

"I suspect that's true, Mr. Marvin. Let's continue. Can you please explain this slide to the court?" Mona put up another table.

"That's our balance sheet. From our annual report."

"Thank you, Mr. Marvin. I note that on the top line it says that in 2017, the BSCA had revenues of $1.6 billion."

"That's correct."

"Farther down are your operating expenses. I note that for 2017, the BSCA had operating expenses of around $1.1 billion."

"Correct."

"That's compared to operating expenses of around $1.2 billion in 2016, and $1.3 in 2015."

"Yes."

"Can you tell the court what the company's operating costs were in the last year?"

"Around $900 million."

"So operating costs have come down by almost $300 million since you became chief executive."

"It's my job to run the company efficiently. We've been running efficiency programs."

"I'm glad you brought those up, sir. I'll come back to them in a moment. But for now, can you tell the court how much money you earned from the federal government last year?"

"I can't remember the exact figure, but I think it was around a billion dollars."

"Allow me to help you, sir. According to your annual report, the federal government paid the BSCA $1.19 billion last year."

Marvin nodded. "That sounds about right. It's in the report, so it's public knowledge."

"Sir, can you see this line here?" Mona used her light pointer to point to a line on a table that read *Facility Operations*.

"Yes."

"Can you read this phrase, please?"

"Sure. 'Compensated man-day.'"

"Sir, can you tell the court what a 'compensated man-day' is?"

Marvin glanced at Judge Ross. This time, Mona noticed a very slight but noticeable shake of the head from the judge. She was getting close. She turned to the jury. "A compensated man-day is the fee the private-prison industry charges the government per inmate per day. Does that sound about right, Mr. Marvin?"

"That's one way of looking at it."

"Is there another way?"

"It's a unit of measurement."

At that point, the door at the back of the court swung

open, and Joaquin came in. He crossed the bar, apologized vaguely to the judge, and handed Mona some papers.

"Mr. Marvin, are you familiar with the teachings of Saint Ignatius of Loyola?"

A puzzled look came over Marvin's face.

"I'm sorry, I'm being opaque. More specifically, do you know the quote, often attributed to him, 'Go forth and set the world on fire'?"

"I'm familiar with that quote, yes."

"Can you remember where you first encountered it?"

"At school."

"Where did you go to school, Mr. Marvin?"

Marvin sneered. "You know very well where I went to school."

"Yes, but the jury doesn't."

"I went to Saint Ignatius Loyola Academy."

"That's a private Catholic prep school in Yorba Linda, correct?"

"Correct."

"Now, Mr. Marvin, can you tell the court whether there is anyone in this room who attended Saint Ignatius Loyola with you?"

Mr. Marvin sneered again. But all he could manage was a weak answer. "What kind of question is that?"

He looked pleadingly at the judge. The judge stared at Mona. Mona held his gaze. Then she turned to Marvin and said, "I must remind you that you are under oath, sir, and are obliged to answer the question honestly and truthfully. Not to do so is a felony."

The courtroom was dead silent, waiting for an answer.

"No."

"You mean to tell me that you do not recognize any-one in this courtroom from the four years you spent at Saint Ignatius College in Yorba Linda?"

"That's what I said," said Marvin. He was visibly sweating.

Mona said, "If it please the court, I wish to introduce new evidence."

Scott jumped up.

"What new evidence?" said Judge Ross.

"A photo," said Mona. She asked Joaquin to give copies of the photo to the judge and Morrison Scott.

Then she put a copy on the projector for the jury to see. It was a photo of nine young men in singlets sitting in a rowing eight. The one Katrina Wakefield had shown her on the wall of the Great Hall at Saint Ignatius.

"Mr. Marvin, can you name the people in this photo?"

Marvin said nothing.

"I'll start," said Mona. "Second person from the right—that is, the first person holding an oar—that's you, isn't it, Mr. Marvin?"

No answer.

"You're in what they call *stroke position,* aren't you? The most important position, the one who sets the rhythm for the other seven rowers?"

Still no answer.

"And here, in position number five, is the late Mr. Edward Maws, the CEO of AmeriCo, the catering company that supplies Paradise Detention Center. Number five: that's commonly known as the *meat wagon* in rowing parlance, isn't it, Mr. Marvin? Number five does the heavy lifting?"

Marvin said nothing.

"And finally, here at the front—right in front of you, actually, we have the smallest and lightest member of the crew and the only member without an oar. We can't see his face, because he's facing forward. But *you* can. In fact, sitting where you are in stroke position, you're looking directly at him, aren't you? He's the coxswain, isn't he? The one who steers the boat?"

No answer.

"Mr. Marvin, do you recall the name of the person who sat a foot in front of you and steered your boat for four years at Saint Ignatius, between the years of 1988 and 1991?"

No answer.

Mona did not smile. "Let's zoom in. Do you see this birthmark on his neck, sir? This diamond-shaped birthmark?"

She waited.

"Mr. Marvin, I remind you that you are under oath. Can you please tell the court when was the last time you saw the man in the picture?"

"I don't recall."

Mona did not say anything.

She waited.

Marvin kept sweating. The judge kept shrinking into his seat. Mona waited some more. Then she turned around, looked at Marius Littlemore, and said, "The man in front of you in this picture, sir—the man who steered your boat for four years at prep school—is Phillip Ross. He's sitting right there."

She pointed at Judge Ross.

A long, stunned silence filled the courtroom. Then a shocked murmur.

Michael Marvin looked like a deer in headlights. The judge had his gavel in hand but seemed unsure what to do. Mona allowed herself a moment to turn around and look at the audience. She could see the reporters frantically scribbling. And she could see Littlemore tapping into his phone, even though no one was supposed to bring a cell phone into court. She doubted if, at this point, Judge Ross was going to eject the DA from the room. She turned to face him.

After a long moment, he said, "Well done, Ms. Jimenez."

"Thank you, Your Honor."

"You're right, Mr. Marvin and I were at school together. I did not recuse myself, and I should have."

"No, you didn't. Your Honor."

"I will declare this case a mistrial, and you can begin again with another judge. I hope that satisfies you, Ms. Jimenez."

"No, Your Honor. It doesn't."

The murmur that had been steadily building behind her now fell off a cliff.

Mona put the BSCA's annual report back on the projector.

"Let us return to the operating costs, Mr. Marvin. Can you please read this line here?"

She used her laser pointer to highlight the line where the BSCA had paid AmeriCo $5,837,700.

"It's a payment to one of our suppliers."

"What's it for?"

"Catering."

"What's it for, Mr. Marvin?"

"They're a catering company. A food supplier."

"Mr. Marvin, don't tell me it's for catering. What did you get for your $5.8 million?"

He fell silent.

"Allow me to jog your memory," said Mona.

She hobbled back to her table on her crutches and got two transparencies from Joaquin. Joaquin distributed paper copies to Morrison Scott and Judge Ross.

"Your Honor," said Mona, with some irony, "*if it please the court,* I wish to introduce further new evidence."

Scott didn't bother getting up to object. Mona put the first transparency on the projector.

"When the late Mr. Maws got divorced last year, he was obliged to disclose his financial situation. This chart represents the moneys that, according to documents filed in the Orange County court, AmeriCo paid out to an entity in the Cayman Islands called Loyola Holdings."

She pulled the transparency off and put on another. "*This* chart shows the number of migrants sentenced to at least three months' detention in Paradise Detention Center by Judge Ross over the last twenty-four months. Now, if you superimpose these two charts"—the charts on the screen merged—"you will see that there is a perfect month-by-month correspondence between the amount of money that AmeriCo paid to Loyola Holdings in the Cayman Islands and the number of migrants sentenced by Judge Ross to at least three months in the Paradise Detention Center."

Mona glanced at the jury. Every jaw had dropped. She knew it didn't matter in legal terms, since this trial would be declared a mistrial, and a new trial, with a new jury, would eventually decide the punitive damages against the BSCA. But still. It was gratifying.

"Over the past year, this court has sent 853 migrants to Paradise, where they have served a total of 233,508 days, for an average of just over nine months each. Which brings me back to the figure of $5,837,700."

She paused. "That's the amount, ladies and gentlemen, that the BSCA paid AmeriCo to feed its inmates last year. When you divide that number by 233,508, you get the oddly round number of $25 per person, per day."

She paused again. "Half of that—$12.50 per person, per day—was funneled through AmeriCo to an entity in the Cayman Islands called Loyola Holdings. In other words, for every day a migrant sentenced by Judge Ross spent in Paradise Detention Center, the beneficiary of Loyola Holdings received $12.50."

Mona looked at Judge Ross.

"I was on the phone to Edward Maws when he was

killed. I heard his last words. I thought he said, 'Lawyer is lost.' I couldn't make sense of it. But last night, I listened to it again, and I realized I had heard it wrong. Maws didn't say '*Lawyer is lost*.' He said, '*Loyola is Ross*.' He was telling me that it was *you*."

Judge Ross stood. "I've had enough of this nonsense, counsel. I declare this trial a mistrial. Ladies and the gentlemen of the jury, you are free to go home. I know that's where I'm going," he said.

There was a great deal of commotion behind her. Mona turned and saw Littlemore rushing for the door, yelling into his phone—arranging warrants, she expected.

Michael Marvin was still on the stand, looking like a lost schoolboy. "Can I go, too?" he said.

"Of course you can, Michael. It's over," said Judge Ross.

EPILOGUE

AFTER the trial, Mona didn't think she would ever go back to Paradise, but in April of the following year, on the anniversary of Carmen's death, she did. She had recently found the entire season of *Aprendí a Llorar* on a streaming channel and had binge-watched the whole thing again—all 160 episodes. After the one-hour finale, her cheeks still wet with tears, and basking in the warm glow brought on by strong feelings and Zinfandel, Mona remembered her mother's comment that only people who repressed their emotions refused to enjoy telenovelas. (In Mona's childhood home, "people who repressed their emotions" was code for Anglos.) The show really had every hammy hook: an aristocratic, virtuous young heroine; a brave and capable young man; a stereotyped villain; a riches-to-rags-to-riches plot; improbable twists; forbidden longings; clear moral boundaries. The heroine, Dolores Romero, was so much Carmen's doppelgänger that Mona wondered whether she had just watched eighty hours of television in order to see Carmen's story told again, except this time with a happy ending, one in which the effects of the poison are reversed, in which the young woman is healed, and her story ends not with her body in a box but with a wedding party in a garden, complete with mariachis.

Mona went to bed but struggled to find sleep, and when she did she slept lightly, and the next morning at 5:00, before the sun was up and Finn had returned from patrol, she left a note on the kitchen counter explaining where she was going, got into her new lava-red car, picked up a cup of coffee and bag of doughnuts, and headed inland.

Nine months had passed since the day in court when she had joined the dots connecting Judge Ross to Michael Marvin. Ross and Marvin had been arrested, charged, tried, found guilty, and sentenced. Separately, so had Keith Klein. They would all die in jail. Dr. Woods had lost his license to practice medicine.

On Maws's laptop, Anaheim PD had found video footage of him with an underage girl. The footage had been emailed to him. It had been filmed with a hidden camera in a brothel in Tijuana, according to the sender, who had threatened to send the video to his wife, his parents, and the police unless Maws cooperated. Anaheim PD had turned it over to the DA's office, who had turned it over to the FBI. The FBI had revealed that the Tijuana brothel belonged to the Caballeros de Cristos cartel. They also said that the Papas Santas chip company was a cartel front. The Caballeros had been using AmeriCo to traffic cocaine into the country inside tubes of potato chips.

Mona asked Littlemore if she could see the video. Within seconds, she recognized the girl: Carmen, age fifteen, looking younger. She asked the investigator to turn it off.

Finn had spent five days in the hospital, then had taken a month off to convalesce. When he returned to work, he was appointed station director.

After the case before Judge Ross was declared a mistrial, Mona filed her suit again. This time, it didn't make it to court. The Border Security Corporation of America settled, and Clara Vega's future was now secure. Mona had helped Maria Elena Vega set up a charity in Carmen's name.

Under intense political pressure, the Department of Homeland Security had revoked its contracts with the BSCA, forcing the company to shut down several detention centers, including the one in Paradise. Its share price tanked.

After four hours' drive, Mona pulled into the PDC parking lot. Tumbleweeds had collected along the fence. Someone had spray-painted swastikas on the wall by the entrance. The entrance had been boarded up, but someone—Mona assumed the same young men who had tagged the walls—had prized away the boards. She squeezed through. Sand had found its way inside, a thin layer scattered evenly over the floor. She passed through the silent metal detector. She walked down the corridor, sand crunching underfoot, until she reached the canteen. She stood for a moment behind the counter and listened for ghosts. Hearing none, she made her way out to the yard. The tent was gone. A breeze was blowing. Mona walked the length and breadth of the empty yard, carefully searching the dirt ahead of each step she took. She saw crumpled beer cans, cigarette butts, and spindly bushes; she saw small yellow flowers growing close to the ground.

ACKNOWLEDGMENTS

Thank you first and mostly to my editor at Forge Books, Kristin Sevick, for her patience, belief, and sharp eye.

Thank you to my agent, Farley Chase, for regularly checking for signs of life.

This novel proved a tricky knot to unravel. Thank you to my wife, Karen, for listening while I worked the kinks out, and for everything else along the way.